SHADOWMAGIC

For Finbar, of whom I am exceedingly proud.

Chapter One
Aunt Nieve

'How come you never told me I had an aunt?' That was the first thing I said. I know, my first question should have been, 'Are you alright, Dad?' He didn't look alright. The light was awful, but I could see blood on the side of his face. I'm amazed I didn't say, '*What* is that smell?' because it sure stank in there. I'm not talking about a whiffy locker room smell, but the kind of stench that can make it possible to see your breakfast a second time around. Or most obviously I guess I should have asked, 'Where are we?' or, 'Why are we chained to a wall?' But instead, the first question I asked when I regained consciousness was about genealogy.

'Well, Conor,' Dad croaked, not even looking at me, 'the first time you met her, she tried to kill you.'

She had, too.

I was sitting in the living room watching crappy morning television. I was dressed, shaved and ready to go. You had to be with my father. It wasn't unusual for me to run out of the house two minutes behind him and find that he had left without me.

'Are you ready?' he called from the bedroom – in almost Modern Greek. That was a good sign. It was a simple matter to gauge my father's moods – the older the language, the worse his frame of mind. Greek wasn't too bad. I shouted back, in the same language, 'Born ready!' I had learned a long time ago that I had to speak in *the language of the day*, or else he would ignore me completely.

He came out of his bedroom in a white shirt with a tie hanging around his neck. 'Could you do this for me?'

'Sure,' I said.

Tie tying was one of the very few things that Pop found impossible to do with just one hand. Most of the time I didn't think of Dad as having a handicap at all – I know a lot of two-handed men much less dexterous than him, and anyway, I was happy to do him a favour. I was just about to hit him up for a bit of cash, so that tonight I could take Sally to a nice restaurant, as opposed to the usual crummy pizza joint.

'What's with the tie?' I asked.

'The dean wants me to smarten up a bit. There is some *famous* ancient languages professor visiting who wants to talk about my theories of pronunciation. As if I don't have anything better to do than babysit some idiot.'

That question was a mistake on my part. He said that last sentence in Ancient Gaelic. That was the language he used when he was annoyed or really meant business – it was almost as if it was his mother tongue. I'm not talking about Gaelic, the language of the Irish, I'm talking about Ancient Gaelic, a language found only on crumbling parchments and in my house.

'Aw c'mon, Pop,' I said as chirpily as I could, 'maybe this professor is a beautiful *she* idiot, and I can finally have a mom.'

He gave me a dirty look, but not one of his more serious ones, and tucked the bottom of his tie into his shirt.

I plopped myself down on the sofa. I could hear Dad humming some prehistoric Celtic ditty as he brushed his teeth in the bathroom. A fight broke out on the television show I was half-heartedly watching: two women were pulling each other's hair and the studio audience was chanting the presenter's name.

'Turn that damn television off,' he shouted, 'or I'll put a crossbow bolt through it!'

I quickly switched off the TV – coming from Dad this was not an idle threat. He owned a crossbow – as well as a quarterstaff, a mace and all sorts of archaic weaponry. If it was old, he had it. Hell, he even made me practise sword fighting with him every week before he gave me my spending money.

This gives you an idea of what life was like with my father – the mad, one-handed, ancient languages professor Olson O'Neil. People said that he lived in the past, but it was worse than that – it was like he was *from* the past. It was cool when I was a kid, but now that I was older, I increasingly thought it was weird – sad, even.

That Dad embarrassed me from time to time wasn't really the problem. Now that I was starting to get a few whiskers on my chin, what really got me down was that he seemed disappointed in me all of the time and I couldn't figure out why. I was doing well at high school. In a week I would graduate, OK, not at the top of my class, but pretty up there. I had never really been in trouble. My girlfriend didn't have pink hair and studs through her nose, or eyebrows, or even her bellybutton. Dad liked Sally. It seemed as if he wanted me to be something – but he wouldn't, or couldn't, tell me what.

A knock came on the front door that was so loud, it made me jump to my feet. Now, weird is what my life is these days, but here is where all the weirdness began.

We live in a converted barn outside of town with a regular-sized front door that is cut into two huge barn doors. When my father answers a knock, he always peers through a tiny hatch to check who's out there. I, on the other hand, like to undo the bolts and throw open the two big doors. It shocks visitors and it has the added effect of annoying Dad. I don't do that any more.

I dramatically swung open the two doors and found myself face to face with two of the biggest, sweatiest horses I had ever seen. Riding them was a man in full King Arthur-type armour and a woman in a hooded cloak. With hindsight I wish I had said something clever like, 'The stables are around the back,' but to be honest, I was too gobsmacked to speak.

When the woman pulled back her hood, she took my breath away. She was astonishingly beautiful, with a wild mane of amber hair. She seemed to be about five or ten years older than me – twenty-five, twenty-seven maybe, except something about her made her seem older than that.

'Is this the home of Oisin?' she asked.

'There is an Olson here, Olson O'Neil,' I stammered.

She considered this for a second and took a step into the room – or, I should say, her horse did. I had to back away to stop from being trampled.

'Who are you?' I demanded.

She looked around the room and her eyes stopped on an oak fighting stick that was mounted on the wall. A look of satisfaction crossed her face. 'I am his sister,' she said.

I started to say, 'Yeah, right,' and then two things struck me. One was that she was speaking in Ancient Gaelic – I was so stunned by the appearance of those two that I hadn't noticed it before. The second was her eyes – she had Dad's eyes, and nobody had dark peepers like my father.

'Dad!' I called out. 'There's a woman out here who says she's your sister.'

That is when all hell broke loose. Dad came charging out of the bathroom screaming at the top of his lungs, with toothpaste foaming out of his mouth like a rabid animal. He grabbed the war axe off the mantel, which I always assumed was there just for decoration, and hurled it at his sister. She pulled her head back just in time to avoid getting a quick nose job, but her companion wasn't so lucky. The flat side of the axe hit him square on the shoulder and knocked him from his saddle. The rider desperately tried to stay on his mount. The horse made a horrible sound as he pulled a handful of hair out of its mane, but it was no good. He hit the ground with a crash of metal and then, as if being attacked in my living room by equestrians wasn't surprise enough – he disappeared – he just vanished! One second I was watching the Tin Man falling through the air, arms and legs flailing in all directions, and the next second he was gone – poof! In the space where he should have been, was a pile of rusted metal in a swirl of dust.

Dad shouted, 'Conor, watch out!' I looked up just in time to see a spear leaving my aunt's hand – and it was heading directly for my chest. Then everything seemed to go into slow motion. I remember looking into my aunt's eyes and seeing what almost looked like pain in them, and I remember turning to my father and seeing the utter defeat on his face. But what I remember the most was the amazing tingling sensation that I felt all over my body. An amber glow seemed to cloud my vision, then I noticed the glow cover me from head to toe and then encircle the spear, just as it made contact with my chest. The spear hit me, I fell over from the force of it, but it didn't hurt. For a second I thought, *That's what it must be like when you receive a mortal wound – no pain.* Then I saw the spear lying next to me. I felt my chest and I was fine.

Dad sat me up. 'Are you OK?' he asked.

I wish I had a picture of my face at that point – I could feel the stupid grin I had pasted on it. A horn blew – Dad and I looked up in time to see my would-be assassin galloping away from the door.

'Can you stand?' Dad asked.

I remember answering him by saying, 'That was very strange.' I was kind of out of it.

'Conor,' he said, helping me to my feet, 'we have to get out of here.'

But it was too late. Two more riders, this time in black armour and on black horses, burst into the room. Tables and chairs went flying in all directions. Dad grabbed my hand and we tried to run out the back, but before we could take more than a couple of steps I saw, and heard, a black leather whip wrap around my father's neck. I tried to shout but my voice was strangled by the searing pain of another whip wrapping around my own throat.

The next thing I remembered, I was chained to a dungeon wall talking to my father about the family tree.

'What's her name?'

'Nieve,' Dad said, without looking at me.

I was about to ask, 'Why does she want to kill us?' when I felt something crawl across my ankle. It was a rat – no, I take that back – it was the mother of all rats. I'd seen smaller dogs. I screamed and tried to kick it away. It moved just out of reach and stared at me like it owned the place. Just what I needed, a super-rat with an attitude.

'Where the hell are we?' I yelled.

'We are in The Land,' Dad said in a faraway voice.

'The Land? What land?'

'The Land, Conor – Tir na Nog.'

'Tir na Nog? What,' I said sarcastically, 'the place full of Pixies and Leprechauns?'

'There are no Pixies here, but yes.'

'Dad. Quit messing around. What is going on?'

He turned and looked me straight in the eyes, and then with his *I'm only going to tell you this once* voice he said, 'We are in The Land. The place that the ancient Celts called Tir na Nog – The Land of Eternal Youth. I was born here.'

I began to get angry. I was in pain, we were definitely in trouble, and Dad was treating me like a kid, making up some cock-and-bull story to keep me happy. I was just about to tell him what I thought of him, but then I thought about the guy who fell off his horse. 'Did you see that guy disappear?'

'He didn't disappear,' Dad said, and I could tell he was struggling to make this so I could understand. 'He just grew old – quickly.'

'Come again?'

'When someone from The Land steps foot in the Real World, they instantly become the age that they would be there. That soldier was probably a couple of thousand years old.'

'What!'

'He was an immortal. Everyone from The Land is an immortal.'

I looked deep into his eyes, waiting for the twinkle that lets me know he's messing with me. When it didn't come, I felt my chest tighten.

'My God, you're not screwing around, are you?'

He shook his head – a slow no.

'So what,' I said half jokingly, 'like, you're an immortal?'

'No,' he said, turning away, 'I gave that up when I came to the Real World.'

I shook my head to clear the cobwebs, which was a mistake, because I almost passed out with the pain. When my vision cleared, Dad was staring at me with a look of total sincerity.

'So you *used* to be an immortal?' I asked.

'Yes.'

At that point I should have come to the obvious conclusion that this was all just a dream, except for the fact that dreaming isn't something I had ever done. Famously, among my friends and classmates at least, I had never had a dream. I had an idea what they were like from TV shows and movies but it was not something I had ever experienced. People always said, 'Oh, you must dream, you just don't remember it,' but I don't think so. When I put my head down, I wake up in the same place and I don't go anywhere in-between. And anyway, I knew this was real – there was something in the air, other than the stench, that felt more real than anything I had ever known.

I was silent for a long while and then I asked, 'Do I have any other relatives I should know about?'

The answer came, not from my father, but from a shadowy figure standing in the doorway on the far side of the room.

'You have an uncle,' he said.

Chapter Two
Uncle Cialtie

The instant he emerged from the shadows, I knew he was my uncle alright. He looked like an old high-school photo of my father, before the grey hair and the extra twenty pounds. He had that *evil twin* appearance about him, like one of those crappy TV movies where the same actor plays the part of the nice *and* the wicked brother. He even had the black goatee and a sinister sneer.

Don't get the impression that this was a comical moment. Even chained against a wall, I tried to take an involuntary step back – this guy was scary. But the person who scared me the most at that moment wasn't my uncle, it was my father.

'Cialtie,' he said, with more malice than I had ever heard from anybody – let alone Dad.

'Brother Oisin,' Cialtie dripped, 'you look, what is that word? Oh yes – old.'

'Where is Finn?'

'You mean our father? I thought he was with you. Last time I saw him he was riding into the Real World looking for you. His horse didn't look very healthy though.'

'You murdered him.'

'Oh no,' Cialtie replied with false innocence, 'I wouldn't hurt Father. I merely stabbed the horse,' and then he smiled. It was my first experience of Uncle Cialtie's smile, and it made my stomach churn.

'I'll kill you,' Dad hissed.

'No, I think you will find that that is what I am going to do to you. But first I am going to kill your boy here, and you know the best part? After that I'll be considered a hero – a saviour even.'

'Why would killing me make him a saviour?' I said, finding my voice.

Cialtie addressed me directly, for the first time, instantly making me wish I hadn't asked the question. 'Hasn't Daddy told you anything?' Cialtie scolded. 'Tsk, tsk, Oisin, you really have neglected his education. Haven't you told him of the prophecy?'

'What prophecy?'

'I didn't think this would ever happen,' Dad said without looking at me. 'We were never supposed to come back.'

'What prophecy?'

'You are *the son of the one-handed prince*,' quoted Cialtie, 'a very dangerous young man. It's true, it was foreseen by a very gifted oracle.'

'Who,' my father said, 'you murdered.'

'Water under the bridge, Oisin. You really must learn to let bygones be bygones. You see, your daddy here carelessly lost his hand – which I still have upstairs, you know, it's one of my favourite possessions – so that meant that having a baby was a no-no, but as always Oisin thought he knew best and it looks like it's going to take his big brother to sort things out.'

'You are using my hand,' Dad hissed, 'to keep the throne.'

'Oh yes,' replied Cialtie, 'I find it works just as well in the Chamber of Runes without the rest of you. Better, in fact – because your mouth isn't attached to it. That Shadowwitch you used to run around with did a really good job of preserving it.'

I could see the blood vessels in Dad's temple stand out as he strained against his chains. My temples must have been throbbing too. I didn't have a clue what was going on. Some oracle predicted that I had to die? Cialtie was using Dad's hand? And what throne?

'I would love to stand here and reminisce all day,' said Cialtie, 'but I have a nephew to kill. Now, your father's runehand has come in so useful these last few years, I thought I might as well have yours too. The start of a collection, maybe?' He reached into his cloak and took out an ornate golden box. Inside was an imprint of a hand.

'I'm going to cut off your hand,' Cialtie continued, 'preserve it with proper magic, not that Shadowmagic stuff she used on your dad's mitt, and then you bleed to death and die. Your dad gets to watch and everybody is happy.'

I used to think that anger was a bad thing, but now I realise that in times of extreme stress and fear, anger can be the emotion that focuses your mind and gets you through. Did I hate my uncle? You bet. And the idea of killing him was the only thing that kept me from whimpering like a damp puppy. I held on to that thought as he came at me.

Cialtie paused. 'You know, I just had a thought. Is it not ironic that the day you become an immortal is the day you die?'

'If I'm an immortal, how are you going to kill me?'

Cialtie laughed, a sickening laugh that deliberately went on too long. 'Oh my. I never thought I would see the day when I would meet a son of Duir who was so thick. Immortality, my boy, may save you from illness and getting old, but it won't save you from this.' He drew his sword and swung at my wrist.

Then it happened again. The world seemed to slow down and a golden – no – an *amber* glow encircled Cialtie's sword and me. I felt the pressure of the blade on my wrist but it didn't hurt, and more importantly, it didn't cut. Cialtie flew into a rage – he began hacking and stabbing at me. I didn't even try to dodge it – the amber glow seemed to protect me. Finally he threw the sword across the room in a rage.

'This is Shadowmagic,' he hissed. 'That witch's doing, I'll wager. Well, I have a sorceress of my own.' He turned to leave – then looked back. 'You have a reprieve, nephew. I suggest that you and Daddy say your goodbyes. Just don't take too long,' and then he was gone, leaving me shaking, half from fear and half from anger.

'I'm sorry, Conor,' Dad finally said.

'How come you never told me?'

Dad laughed. 'What was I supposed to say? "*Son, you are old enough now for me to tell you that I am the heir to the throne of a magical kingdom…*" You think I'm loony enough as it is. I can imagine what you would have said to that.'

'So, you're the heir to a throne?'

Dad thought for a second, and took a deep breath that looked like it hurt. 'My father – your grandfather – was the lord of this castle. His name was Finn and he held Duir – the Oak Rune. He was the king, if you like, of Tir na Nog.'

I was struggling to make sense of all of this. My head was spinning. 'You're a prince?'

'Yes.'

'The one-handed prince?'

He nodded.

'So why did Cialtie say I was dangerous?'

'Ona,' Dad said, 'made a prediction.'

'Who is this Ona?'

'She was my father's Runecaster.' When I looked puzzled he said, 'Like a fortune teller.'

'And what did she say exactly?' I could tell that the question pained him but I was angry. Some old bat throwing stones around was causing me a lot of trouble.

'She said, "*The son of the one-handed prince must die, lest he be the ruin of Tir na Nog.*"'

'That's ridiculous! You don't believe this crap, do you?'

Dad lowered his head, and when he spoke I could hardly hear him. 'Ona was never wrong.'

'So let me get this straight. You lose your hand in a gardening accident and then everybody wants me dead!' As soon as I said it I realised how ridiculous it sounded. 'You didn't lose your hand in a lawnmower, did you?'

'No.'

'Are you going to tell me about it?'

'That is a long story,' I heard a woman's voice say. It sounded as if it was coming from inside the wall to my right. 'And if you want to get out of here,' she said as she appeared right before my eyes, 'we will have to save it for later.'

You could have knocked me down with a feather. If I thought my aunt was stunning, this was the most beautiful woman I had ever seen. Dark, tall, with a straight black ponytail plaited to her waist and wearing – check this out – animal skins. She seemed to just step through the wall.

She worked fast. She placed what looked like honey in the locks that shackled our wrists and Dad's neck. Then she dropped to one knee, lowered her head, mumbled something and the irons fell away. I can't tell you how good it felt. If you have ever taken off a thirty-pound backpack after a twenty-mile hike, you have the beginnings of an idea. Dad and I stood up.

'Quickly!' she said, and walked straight through the wall.

Before Dad could follow I put my hand on his shoulder. 'Who's the babe in the skins?'

'That's no way to talk about your mother,' he said, and followed her through the wall.

Chapter Three
Mom

I stood there as if rooted to the spot. *I don't have a mother. My mother is dead. My father told me so.* Emotions swirled around me like a leafy breeze. I was five years old. I remembered the pain in my chest, the taste of my tears. I remembered the look on my father's face as I stared up to him from my bed.

'Is Mom in heaven?' I sobbed.

'I'm not sure I believe in heaven,' a younger version of Dad replied. 'The ancient Celts believed in a place called Tir na Nog, where people never grow old. I think that's where your mother is.' He held me until the tears slowed and my sobs were replaced by sleep. Was this the only time my father had ever told me the truth?

'Conor?'

I looked up and saw her standing there. 'Are you my mother?' I said in a voice I hadn't used in fifteen years.

'Yes,' she said, and I knew it was true. I looked into that feminine mirror of my own face, complete with the tears, and I could hardly stand it. I know it contravened all eighteen-year-old cool behaviour but I couldn't help myself. I threw my arms around her.

She held me tight and stroked the back of my head.

'Conor, oh my Conor,' she said.

I could have stayed in those arms for days, for months, for the rest of my life. She gently pushed me back by the shoulders, and in a motherly voice I so long had yearned for, said, 'Conor?' When I didn't reply I heard the other motherly voice, the one that says, *I'm your mother and you had better listen to me or else.* She shook me and said again, 'Conor!'

That got my attention.

'We don't have time for this. We must leave here.'

Still in a daze, I wiped my eyes and nodded.

Mom gestured to our right. 'This way.'

That was when I heard *his* voice at the door.

'You!' shouted Cialtie.

That snapped me right out of it. I looked to the door and saw my uncle standing there with some tall, spindly, pale woman. She was dressed in hanging black lace with dark, dark eyes, black lips and a skunk-like streak in the front of her jet-black hair.

I lost it – I flipped out. 'Leave me alone!' I screamed so forcefully that spit flew out of my mouth. Neither of them was prepared for a fight. They expected to find us chained to the wall. I loved the look on Cialtie's face as he reached for his sword and realised that he had thrown it across the room after he had failed to cut off my hand. It was lying on the floor to my left. We both looked at it at the same time. Cialtie went for the sword, but I went for Cialtie. Some people would think I was brave, but bravery had nothing to do with it. I was plain loco. All of the day's craziness, the pain, the revelations, the emotions – I had just had enough! I hit Cialtie with a picture-perfect American football tackle. My shoulder caught him square in the solar plexus and smashed him into the wall. I actually heard all of the air fly out of his lungs and I knew he wasn't getting up in a hurry. Out of the corner of my eye I saw the goth woman smash into the wall with a shower of golden light from something my mother did. I reached down and picked up the sword. It was so much lighter than it looked. The pommel fitted in my hand as if it was made for me. I started to raise it, fully intending to bring it down on my uncle's head, when two guards ran into the room. As they reached for their weapons my mother grabbed me by the collar and threw me at the wall.

Passing through a wall is a scary thing. I instinctively threw my hands in front of me but they went right through. When my face reached the stones every cell in my body said, *This is going to hurt!* – and then pop – I was on the other side. Technically speaking I hadn't gone through a wall, I had gone through an illusion of a wall. The real wall was in front of me with a big hole chiselled in it. I could see daylight through the opening and Dad beckoning me through. My mother appeared next to me and lobbed an amber ball behind her. I heard screams of, 'My eyes!' and then I crawled through. Dad was on the other side standing next to three enormous horses but I hardly noticed him. My eyes were filled with my first look at Tir na Nog – The Land.

Imagine spending all of your life in a world of black and white and finally seeing in colour… No, that's not right. Imagine never being able to smell and then walking into a bakery, or being sealed in a bubble and feeling a touch of a hand for the first time. Even that doesn't explain it. Try to imagine that you have another sense, one that you feel in your soul. A sense that activates every nerve in your body. Imagine a view that makes you feel like you could live forever – and you can. That's what I was looking at now.

Ahead of me I looked down onto a vista of magnificent oak trees. Trees that if you hugged, might just hug you back. Trees that you could call family without irony. Trees that if you were to chop one down, it would mark you as a murderer to the end of your days. To the left, rolling fields started as foothills and culminated in blue, snow-capped mountains that seemed to touch the sky. To my right the trees changed to beech, but not the thin spindly trees I was used to, but spectacular white-barked beeches with the girth and height of California redwoods. When I finally tore my eyes away, I saw that my father too was lost in that panorama, and his eyes were as wet as mine.

'Come on, boys,' my mother said as she came through the wall, 'tearful reunions and sightseeing will have to wait for later.'

'What about Cialtie?' I asked.

'He didn't seem to be breathing all that well,' she said with a smile. A smile of approval from my mother – I can't tell you how good that felt.

'Nice sword,' Dad said.

'Yeah, my Uncle Cialtie gave it to me.'

Dad smiled. 'I always liked that sword.'

'You recognise it?'

'I should,' he said, as he swung himself up onto a horse. 'It used to be mine.'

'Come, Conor,' my mother said as she jumped into a saddle, 'he will be back with reinforcements in a minute. Mount up.'

'I can't ride that thing!'

'Surely you know how to ride,' she said.

'Nope.'

She gave my father a stern look. 'You didn't teach him to ride? You, of all people, didn't teach your own son to ride?'

'I taught him to speak the tongue,' he explained, 'and I taught him swordplay.'

'But not ride,' she said, in a tone that made me realise she was not a woman to be trifled with. 'Typical.' She kicked her steed and galloped directly at me. Next thing I knew she grabbed me by the collar and hoisted me into the saddle in front of her.

'Hold on tight and be careful with that sword.'

She took two amber balls out of her pouch and hurled them over the top of the wall above us. 'Cover your eyes!' she said. Even at this distance and with my forearm over my eyes, I saw the flash and could imagine how painful it must have been up close. To the sound of more screams, we galloped off towards the beech forest.

Considering that this was my first getaway, I thought it went pretty smoothly. I got spooked by a couple of arrows that zinged past us, but by and large we just rode away. I sat in front of my mother as we galloped and imagined I was an infant and she was behind me in my pushchair.

'What is your name?' I asked.

'Deirdre,' she whispered.

We entered the beech forest. Every time I spoke she shushed me, like I was speaking in a library, but when the trees thinned out, Mom answered a couple of my questions. She told me that she had been planning this jailbreak for a long time. She and some people she called the Fili had been secretly tunnelling through that wall at night for weeks. Each morning she would cast some kind of magic to conceal it. I asked her how she could have known that we were going to be there. In a conspiratorial tone of voice, she told me that she cast Shadowrunes. When I asked her why we were whispering she answered, 'Because beech trees are very indiscreet.'

Other than that we rode in silence for about an hour. The beeches gave way to flowering ash trees. Fine yellow flowers covered the ground and marked our hoof prints like snow.

Dad pulled up beside us. He looked very tired. 'Castle Nuin is near. Can we get sanctuary there?'

'I'm afraid when the lords find out about Conor,' Mom said, 'we won't have friends anywhere.'

Dad nodded in resignation.

'We don't have much further to ride. I have a boat up ahead. If we can make it to the Fililands we will be safe.'

We travelled for another fifteen minutes or so until we came to a river. Dad dismounted and splashed his face with the water. 'River Lugar,' he sighed, 'I thought I would never see you again.' He looked up at my mother. 'Nor did I think I would ever see you again, Deirdre.'

'Come, Oisin.' Her voice cracked a little as she spoke. 'We don't have time for this. The boat is just a little way downstream.'

The boat was a canvas-stretched canoe. Dad called it a carrack. It was hidden under some ash branches. Mom returned the branches to underneath a nearby tree, then placed her hand on the trunk and said, 'Thank you.' Maybe it was a trick of the light but I could have sworn the tree bowed to her – just a little.

The boat was lined with straw mats and was big enough for Dad and me to lie down next to each other. Mom sat in the back and told us to rest. We had drifted downstream for maybe thirty seconds before I was out cold.

Let me tell you, the dreams in Tir na Nog are worth the price of admission. Even though I had nothing to compare it with, I can't imagine that people in the Real World have dreams anything like I had in that boat.

I dreamt my father was teaching a lecture at the front of a classroom and I raised my hand in answer to a question. He drew a sword and sliced it off! My hand landed on my desk where it seemed to be encased in amber glass, like a huge paperweight. When I looked back, my father was now my uncle and he was laughing at me, saying, 'No glow now.'

The classroom became a room in a high tower; my mother and my aunt were clenched in a fight to the death. Mom's pouch was open and amber balls were falling to the floor in slow motion. Each time one hit the ground there was a blinding flash, and after each flash the scene in front of me changed. One moment the two women were fighting, the next, they were embracing, like two sisters sharing a secret. Fighting – embracing – fighting – embracing – the scene kept changing until the flashes came so frequently that I could see nothing but bright light.

The last image I saw before I awoke was Sally. She was waiting for me outside the cinema. She waited so long that her legs became tree roots and burrowed into the ground. Her arms turned to boughs and sprouted leaves. At the last second before she turned entirely into a tree, she saw me. She tried to say, 'Where are you?' but the wood engulfed her in mid-sentence.

I awoke from my first dream with such a jolt that I instantly stood up, which was a mistake. I was still in the boat. Even though it was beached, it tipped over. I fell smack down in the shoreline as the boat flipped over painfully on the back of my legs. I quickly struggled out from under it and desperately searched for Sally (or the tree that had become Sally) before I came to my senses. I collapsed on the ground and rubbed the back of my calves. *So that's what a dream is like.* I couldn't decide if I wanted to close my eyes and continue it, or never fall asleep again.

A tug on my collar made me realise that something was hanging around my neck. Attached to the end of a leather strap was a beautiful gold ornament. It was shaped like a tiny tornado with leaves spinning in it. As I marvelled at the intricacies of my new jewellery, the smell of food and a campfire hit me. My nose went up like a batter who had just hit a fly ball. It was a smell I was powerless not to follow.

At least this day was starting better than the previous one. Yesterday I awoke to the nightmare of finding myself chained to a wall by a lunatic uncle who was determined to give me a new nickname – *Lefty*. Today I walked into the dream-come-true of my father and my mother sitting around a campfire. They were holding hands (well, hand) and deep in conversation when I came around a huge weeping willow. They broke off when they saw me.

'Good morning,' my father said.

'Good morning,' I replied, not really looking at him. My eyes were glued to my mother. At a glance I would have thought she was my age until I looked into her eyes. I was starting to learn that here, in Tir na Nog, it wasn't grey hair or a wrinkled face that betrayed someone's age, like in the Real World – it was the eyes.

'Good morning,' I said.

She stood up. It was an awkward moment, like we were meeting for the first time. She was nervous.

'Good morning, Conor.'

I wrapped my arms around her. I had a lifetime of mothering to make up for. Her return hug told me she felt the same.

'I could get very used to this,' I said, trying unsuccessfully to stop the dam from breaking behind my eyes.

'And I too.' She wept.

Dad left us for a respectable amount of time before he interrupted. 'Cup of tea, Conor?'

I wiped my eyes and saw Dad grinning from ear to ear, holding a steaming cup in his hand. 'Thanks,' I said as I took a seat next to him. 'I think I just had a dream.'

'Yeah, me too. Intense, isn't it?' he said.

'Are all dreams like that?'

'I don't know. Like you, I never had a dream in the Real World. This being your first one, it must have… What's that phrase you use? *Freaked you out.*'

'Freaked you out?' Mom said.

'You'll get used to it,' Dad replied.

I have had a lot of breakfasts in my day, but let me tell you, if all breakfasts were like this, I would never sleep late again. The tea was made from willow bark. It didn't taste good as much as it felt good. Mom said that it would ease the strains and bruises of the previous day. It wasn't until the willow tea started to do its work that I realised just how much pain I had been in: my neck from the whip, my arms and wrists from being clapped in chains, my back from the horse ride and my head from – just plain shock. Blessed relief came as each part of my body stopped hurting, like the peace you get when a neighbour finally stops drilling on the adjacent wall.

'Found this around my neck,' I said.

Dad reached inside his shirt and produced an identical necklace. 'Me too. It's one of your mother's specialities. It's a *rothlú* amulet.'

'Thank you,' I said, 'it's beautiful.'

'It's not for show,' she replied, 'it's for protection.'

'I don't think I need any protection around here. Every time I get attacked, I seem to be surrounded by some gold force field.'

'You have been lucky,' she said. 'I placed that spell on you when you were born, but it only protects you from attacks from your relatives.'

'Like a spear from Aunt Nieve,' I said, 'or Uncle Cialtie's sword.'

'If Cialtie had gotten someone else to cut your hand off…' she said.

'Then Dad and I would be bookends.'

'Yes. Also,' she said, 'it only works for one battle with each relative.'

'So next time Aunt Nieve decides to make a Conor kebab – I'm on my own?'

'What's a kebab?' Mom asked.

'That's right,' Dad said, 'that's what the *rothlú* amulet is for.'

'What's it do?'

'It's only to be used in an emergency,' Mom said. 'All you have to do is place your hand over the amulet and say "*Rothlú*". Then you're somewhere else.'

'Like on the edge of a cliff,' Dad said, 'or a snake pit.'

'There are no snakes in The Land,' Mom retorted. 'Oisin here is not a fan of this spell.'

'It's dangerous, Conor, you can end up anywhere and it hurts like hell. Did she mention that?'

Mom nodded reluctantly. 'But it may save your life. Make sure you do not use it unless you really need it.'

'Is this that Shadowmagic I've been hearing about?'

They both seemed to jump a little bit when I mentioned Shadowmagic, like I'd blurted out the plans of a surprise party in front of the birthday girl.

'No,' Mom said. 'This uses gold. It's Truemagic.'

My fifty next questions were stopped dead by the next course. I had never had roast rabbit before but I can tell you right now, I'm never going to be able to watch a Bugs Bunny cartoon again without salivating. Breakfast finished with an apple each. I thought it was a bit of an anticlimax but Dad took his apple like it was a gift from God. He held it in his hand like a priest holding a chalice, and when he bit it, a moan escaped from his throat that was almost embarrassing. I looked at my apple anew. It looked ordinary enough but when I bit it – I'll be damned if the same moan didn't involuntarily pour out of me. What a piece of fruit! It hit you everywhere and all at once. This was real food, not the fake stuff that I had been wasting my time eating all my life. This is all I will ever need – this is the stuff that makes you live forever. This was forbidden fruit!

'Wow,' I garbled with my mouth full, 'I feel like Popeye after his first can of spinach.'

Dad thought that was funny. Mom looked confused.

'Come,' Mom said, 'we cannot stay here any longer – I would like to reach the Fililands before tomorrow night.'

Dad packed up the mugs and the water skin. Mom placed the bones and the apple cores on the burning wood and then placed her hands *in* the flames. The fire died down and then went out. The charred wood and earth seemed to melt into the ground until only a dark circle remained.

As he left, my father placed his hand on the trunk of the willow we were under and said, 'Thank you.' My mother did the same.

When I started to walk to the boat, my mother said, 'Are you not going to thank the tree for his shelter and wood?'

Feeling a bit stupid, I went up to the tree and placed my hands on its bark and said, 'Thank you.'

I swear the tree said, '*You are welcome.*' Not with words – it felt like it spoke directly into my head. I will never make fun of a tree-hugger again.

I got back to the boat to see Dad rooting through the supplies. He found a belt with a sword in a leather scabbard. Without any of the clumsiness that you would expect from a one-handed man, he withdrew the sword from its case and replaced it with the one I had taken from Cialtie.

'You're taking your sword back?'

'Actually, I think you should have it,' he said.

He handed me the belt and I buckled it on. He reached for the hilt and withdrew the sword, holding the perfectly mirrored blade between us. It made for a strange optical illusion. I saw one half of my own face reflected in the blade, while the other half of the face I saw was my father's weathered countenance.

'This is a weapon of old,' he said with gravity, 'it belonged to your grandfather Finn of Duir. It is the Sword of Duir. It was given to me and stolen by my brother. He was foolish to lose it.' He turned the sword horizontal, breaking the half-father, half-son illusion I had been staring into. 'I want you to have it.'

'Are you sure?' I said as I took the blade.

'Yes, I'm sure. To be honest, I would be glad not to have it hanging around my waist – reminding me.'

'Reminding you of what?'

'That's the sword that chopped my hand off.'

Chapter Four
The Yewlands

I was so stunned I couldn't speak. Not until we were well under way and I had gotten the knack of paddling did I blurt out, 'You lost your hand in a sword fight?'

'I find it hard to believe,' Mother said, 'that you never told your son how you lost your hand.'

'Dad told me that he lost it in a lawnmower.'

'What is a lawnmower?' she asked.

'It's a machine that they use in the Real World to keep the grass short,' Dad said.

'What is wrong with sheep?'

Dad and I smiled.

'OK, Pop, tell how you lost your hand – the truth, this time.'

'I refuse to let you tell that story while we are in a boat,' Mom said, 'and we are approaching Ioho – we should not be talking in the Yewlands.'

'Why not?' I asked.

'Because it disturbs the trees and you do not want to disturb a yew tree.'

Under normal circumstances, I would have thought about calling a shrink and booking her into a rubber room, but I had just had a little chat with a tree myself. 'What could a yew tree do? Drop some leaves on us?'

She gave me a look that made me feel like a toddler who had just been caught with his hand in a cookie jar. It was going to take a while to get used to this mother and son stuff.

'Yew trees are old. The oldest trees in Tir na Nog. We of The Land think we are immortal, but to the yew we are but a spark. To answer your question, if you wake a yew, it will judge your worth. If it finds you lacking – you will die.'

'What will it do, step on me?' I said, and got that same icy stare as before.

'It will offer you its berries, which are poisonous,' she said, in a tone that warned me that her patience was thinning, 'and you will be powerless to resist.'

'I find that hard to believe.'

'Please, Conor,' she said, 'do not put it to the test today.'

I didn't have to ask if we were in the Yewlands, I knew it when we got there. Heck, I knew it *before* we got there. We rounded a bend in the river and ahead I saw two huge boulders on opposite sides of the bank. On top of them were the most awesome trees I had seen yet. They weren't as big as the oaks, but these were definitely the elders – the great-great-grandfathers of all of the trees and probably everything else in creation. The roots of the yews engulfed the rocks like arthritic hands clutching a ball. It seemed as if these two trees had just slithered up onto their perches to observe our approach. It made the hairs stand up on the back of my neck. Past the guard trees we entered a thick forest that stretched as far as the eye could see. A dense canopy turned the world into a dark green twilight, and there was no light at the end of *this* tunnel.

28

The first corpse was just inside the forest. Within ten minutes I must have seen fifteen of them. On both sides of the bank, human remains in various states of decay adorned the base of one tree or another. Some of them were clean, bone-white – others were still in their clothes. Many of them had quivers with arrows on their back. All of them were looking up, open-mouthed, as if to say, 'No!' or maybe, 'Thy will be done.'

Mom's warning about not speaking in the Yewlands proved to be unnecessary. I wasn't going to say a word. Never have I felt so humbled and insignificant as I did in the presence of those sleeping giants. I didn't want them to know I was there, and I definitely didn't want them to judge me. If they bid me to eat their berries, or throw myself off a cliff for that matter, I would do as they commanded, just to make them happy. Like a dog to a master – or a man to a god.

We spent most of that day silent, in an emerald dusk. It was slow going: each paddle was done with care so as to not make any splashing sounds. The frequency of the corpses diminished, but still from time to time a skyward-facing skull, encased in moss, would be just visible. As we came around a bend my mother's breath quickened. Ahead was a moss-covered altar surrounded by a semicircle of what must be the oldest of these primordial trees. The bases of the trees were littered with women's corpses. Each tree was surrounded with five or six sets of bones, some bleached white, some in white robes, a couple still with long, flowing hair, and all were in the same position. They were embracing a tree trunk, as if for dear life – which I suppose they were. I noticed that my mother didn't look.

When, in the distance, I saw a clear white light at the end of the forest, I let out a tiny yelp of joy that I instantly regretted. My parents shot me a disapproving look. Luckily the trees took no notice.

The fresh air and sunshine made me feel like I had been rescued from a premature grave. I waited until the Yewlands were out of sight before I dared to speak.

'Well, that was fun,' I said, trying to sound cooler than I felt. 'Who were all those dead people?'

'Archers mostly,' Dad replied.

'Why archers?'

'The best bows are made from yew; if you want to be a master archer, you have to ask a yew tree for wood.'

'And those were the guys that didn't make the grade?'

He nodded.

'Have you ever been judged by a yew?'

'Not me, I was never much of an archer. Good thing too – one-handed archers are traditionally not very good.'

'I have,' my mother said, in a faraway voice that sent a shiver down my spine. 'I have been judged by a yew. Next to giving up my son, it was the hardest thing I have ever done.'

I thought that maybe she wasn't going to say anything more – her face told me it was a memory that was painful to remember. I waited – she took a deep breath and went on. 'The place you saw with the altar is called the Sorceress' Glade. Like archers with their bows, a true sorceress must translate a spell onto a yew branch.'

'What, like a magic wand?'

'If you like.'

'And you were judged?'

In reply she reached into her pouch and produced a plain-looking stick, carved with linear symbols.

'What does it do?'

'It gives me power over the thorns,' she said.

'Huh?'

30

'You will understand when we reach the Fililands.'

We were floating by fragrant fields of heather, inhabited by sheep, rabbits and deer. I even saw a black bear fishing on a bank. It was like a 3-D Disney film. I almost expected the bear to wave.

'How did you become a sorceress?'

'Her father,' Dad said, 'wanted to make a superwoman.'

'My father wanted his daughter to be educated,' Mom corrected. 'He hired twelve tutors to teach me in the arts, philosophies, combat and magic. I loved all my tutors, almost as much as I loved my father for providing them for me. Of all my studies, it was at magic that I excelled. Against my father's wishes, I made the pilgrimage to the Sorceress' Glade with my tutor, my mentor, my friend.' Mom fell silent and sadness invaded her face.

'It was Nieve,' Dad said.

'Nieve? My Aunt Nieve? The one who tried to pierce my sternum with a javelin?'

'I am sure she took no joy from that task,' Mom said. 'Nieve has a very strong sense of duty.'

'Could you give her a call and maybe we could sit down and talk about this?'

'Nieve and I have not spoken to one another for a long time,' she said.

'Because of me?'

'No, before that, when I left her guidance to study Shadowmagic.'

Shadowmagic – there was that word again. Every time someone mentioned it, they sounded like they were selling a stolen watch in an alley.

'What is the deal with this Shadowmagic stuff?'

'Magic is never without cost,' she said. 'Like wood is to a fire, gold is to magic. Gold is the power that is made by the earth. In order to cast a spell you need to spend gold. The greater the spell, the more gold you need. That is what they call here in The Land, *Truemagic*. Gold is not the only power in the world, it is just the easiest to find and use. There is power in the air and the water, that is too difficult to control, and then there is another power – the power of nature that can be found in the trees. Harnessing this power is the force behind Shadowmagic. It is not as powerful, but it can do things that Truemagic cannot.'

'So what does Nieve have against it?'

'Shadowmagic is illegal,' Father said.

'Why?'

'Ages ago,' Mom explained, 'in the early reign of Finn, there was a Fili sorceress named Maeve. Maeve detected power in amber stones and devised a way to use amber to power magic. Since amber is only petrified tree sap, she started to use fresh sap, the blood of trees, to power her magic. She became very powerful and that power drove her mad. She decimated an entire forest and used its energy to raise a huge army. Maeve and her army laid siege to Castle Duir. No one knows what happened – it is believed that in the midst of the battle, Maeve cast a mammoth spell that catastrophically failed. Maeve and all of the Fili army were killed. Afterwards, Finn outlawed Shadowmagic and decreed that Maeve's name should never be uttered again. The Fili were so decimated it was thought they were extinct.'

'You found them, I take it?'

'Yes. Maeve's daughter Fand lives.'

'And she taught you Shadowmagic?'

'She was reluctant at first. She was deeply ashamed of her mother, of the wars and death and the forest she destroyed, but deep down she knew that it was her mother that was wrong, not her magic. Together, we found and read Maeve's notes to try and find out what happened. It was the killing of trees that corrupted her soul. We found trees that *agreed* to allow us to tap them for sap, and we swore never to kill a tree. We revived the art of Shadowmagic and found that it was good. Just as valid as Truemagic. After all, the yew wand is an integral part of Truemagic but at its heart, it is actually Shadowmagic.'

'Did you ever try to convince Nieve?'

'Oh yes. When I returned from the Fililands I told her about it. She was shocked and appalled that I would do such a thing. As I mentioned before she has a strong sense of duty, but she agreed to discuss it again.'

'And what happened?'

'We never had that talk.'

'Why not?'

'I was banished,' Mom said.

'Banished?'

'Yup,' Dad said, 'your mother here is an outlaw. A regular Ma Barker.'

'Who banished you?'

'Finn,' she said.

'Finn, my grandfather? Why?'

'Your mother performed a very public display of Shadowmagic in front of almost every Runelord in The Land. My father had no choice.'

'He should have had me executed,' she said.

'What happened?'

'That is part of the tale of how your father lost his hand. Not only is it a long-overdue story – it is a long one as well. I know a shelter up ahead. We can camp for the night and you can hear the tale properly over food and a fire.'

Food and fire, now that was a good idea. After paddling all day and the stress of the Yewlands, I was overdue for a break.

The meadows of heather gave way to fields of tremendously tall holly trees. We pulled the boat ashore and stashed it under a bush. (Mother of course asked the holly for permission.) We walked a faint path until we saw a stone hut with a thatched roof.

'This is a lovely Gerard hut,' Mom said.

'Is Gerard home?'

'I shouldn't think so.' Dad laughed. 'Gerard is an old Runelord who likes to travel. He built a bunch of these huts so he wouldn't have to sleep out-of-doors.'

'Well,' I said, 'it looks cosy.'

'They usually are,' my father said, opening the door.

I had heard the sound of a crossbow firing before, but I had never heard the sound of an arrow piercing flesh. In the old cowboy movies, the sound of an arrow entering a body was always a clean *thwap* – in reality, the sound is a pop, followed by a hideous squelch. Dad spun completely around like a top and hit the ground hard on his back – a crossbow bolt was sticking out of his chest.

Chapter Five
Rothlú

When I saw the air gurgling out of the wound in my father's chest, I dropped to my knees and screamed, 'Dad!' This turned out to be a lucky choice – if I had remained standing the second arrow would have got me right between the eyes. As it was, it still gave my hair its first centre parting. Dad had opened the door to an ambush.

'Don't move,' I heard a woman's voice order.

I looked up expecting a second attack, but instead I saw a deadly scene frozen in time. Aunt Nieve was standing in the doorway, and behind her were two soldiers with empty crossbows. My mother and my aunt were face to face, eyes locked – Mom was holding an amber ball while Nieve was holding a gold sphere made of wire.

'Make one move towards him and we all die,' Mom said.

'If the boy dies then my duty is done,' Nieve replied. 'If we die with him – so be it.'

'If I set off this Shadowcharm then all will die *except* the boy,' Mom said. 'You have seen the protection I have given him already. Your *duty* will fail and you will be dead.'

They stared at each other for a time.

'You should be with me in this,' hissed Nieve.

'You want me to stab my own son in the *neck*?' My mother said *neck* with such vehemence that it made me jump. 'We all realise that if Conor wasn't around we would all be safe.' She spoke in such a strange voice that it made me think she wasn't talking to Nieve – she was talking to *me*. 'You don't expect me to risk his *neck* just to make us *safe*.'

The amulet! She was talking about the *rothlú* amulet around my neck. I reached up, slowly wiped my lips and casually let my hand drop to the gold charm hanging around my neck. I wrapped my little finger around it.

'Do you really think you and Dad would be safe if I was gone?' I said to my mother.

'Listen to him,' Nieve said, 'the boy is beginning to understand.'

'I hope he does understand,' Mom said, talking to me, while never taking her eyes off Nieve. 'Yes, it would be safer for all if you were gone.'

I looked down at my father, who nodded to me with his eyes. I did understand. Mom wanted me to escape with the amulet and defuse this situation, so that maybe Dad could get some help.

'You know, Aunt Nieve,' I said, 'all of my life I wished I had an aunt that would send me an unexpected birthday present, like other kids. Instead I got one that tries to kill me every time we meet. Well, I want you to know that I am taking you off my Christmas card list. Oh, and by the way – *rothlú!*'

A *rothlú* spells kick in fast but I did have a split second to see Nieve's expression before all went black. It was so satisfying that it was almost worth the pain.

Pain! Did I mention pain? Man, did I hurt. I didn't hurt all over, like with a killer hangover – it was more like every little bit of me hurt. My lips hurt, my earlobes hurt, my toes hurt, my hair hurt and I don't even want to talk about my groin. It felt as if every tiny fragment of me was torn apart and then quickly reassembled. For all I know that's what actually happened.

I was lying on my side in a foetal position. I must have been unconscious all night because I could feel the hot sun on my eyelids, but there was no way I was going to open my eyes, let alone move – I knew it was going to hurt too much. I think I would have stayed like that for a day or twelve, if I hadn't been disturbed by a tug on my foot. Normally, a tug like that would have had me alert in a flash, but I was so out of it that I only managed to crack one eye open, a slit. The light sent a pain into my head that made me want to moan, but I was sure that moaning would have hurt too. When I finally could focus, I saw a disgusting leather sandal on the ground next to my face and a pair of hands fumbling with a shoelace as they tried to pull one of my Nikes off.

I heard a voice say, 'Not bad,' and then I felt a tug on my other foot. He was stealing my shoes. Some twerp was nicking my sneakers! Concussion or no concussion, I wasn't going to stand for this. You can whip me, shoot me, kidnap me or try to kill me, but there is no way I was going to let my Nikes go without a fight. I jumped to my feet, and in one swift movement drew my sword. I caught the thief completely off guard. First, he was utterly engrossed with my shoelaces and second, I think he presumed I was dead. I must have looked dead – I certainly felt it.

I found myself standing over him with my sword pointed at his chest. He was a young man in both face *and* in his eyes. His hair was the remarkable thing – it was jet-black with a pure white tuft in the front.

He was surprised to see me standing over him, and to be honest, so was I. Then the world began to spin – I had gotten up *way* too fast. I was going to faint.

As I swooned, I blurted out, 'Were you stealing my shoes?' Then I lost my balance. I stumbled forward, the tip of my blade inadvertently moving towards his chest. He understandably thought I was going to kill him. I tried to pull my sword away. I tried to keep my balance. I thought I was going to be sick. That's when I saw his sword. Even if I had been alert I don't think I could have parried it. With the quickest of flicks, he cocked his right wrist and a short blade travelled like lightning out of his sleeve. In one instantaneous motion he caught the pommel in his hand and stabbed me in the chest.

The amber glow engulfed the two of us the microsecond before his blade touched my chest. I realise now that life is made up not of days, or hours, or even seconds, but moments. One tiny moment follows another. One moment I saw the blade about to enter my heart – the next I was impossibly balanced on the tip of a razor-sharp sword, protected by my mother's wonderful amber force field.

I had just met another member of the family.

Chapter Six
Fergal

I stood there at a forty-degree angle with the shoe thief's blade holding me up, and I started to chuckle. I couldn't help it. I was losing it. I held my arms straight out at my sides and laughed. Not a *that's a funny joke* sort of a laugh but a crazy laugh, the kind of maniacal sound that comes out of Dr Frankenstein just before he screams, 'It's alive!'

Through the golden glow, I could see that my opponent was confused. He pushed at my chest a couple of times, trying to figure out why I wasn't perforated. Every jab just made me laugh louder. Finally, I rolled off the point of his sword and fell to the ground, in hysterics. He stood up fast, leaned over me and actually poked a couple of times. Each prod made the glow return and I howled, tears pouring from my eyes. I saw the thief take off my Nikes and carefully pick up his sandals. I could tell he was a bit freaked, ready to run.

I tried to compose myself. 'Wait,' I croaked, as I struggled to sit up. He started to back away. 'No, wait,' I repeated as I wiped my eyes on my sleeve, 'I won't hurt you – look.' I threw my sword away and held up my hands. 'Sit down for a second.'

He stopped, still wary. 'I'm not looking for any trouble,' he said. 'Honest to the gods, I thought you were dead. Well, not dead but I didn't think you were going to last long.'

'I believe you. Sit down.'

He sat a respectable distance away. I rubbed my eyes with my palms, trying to make them focus. The specific pain of before was becoming one giant all-over pain – an improvement but not much.

'I think we have gotten off on the wrong foot.'

He stood up and started to back away. 'I told you I was sorry for the shoe thing.'

'No, no, relax,' I said, palms forward. 'I mean, I don't think we should be fighting. I'm sorry I pulled a sword on you but I have had a really rough couple of days. Can we start over?' I stood up and extended my hand. 'My name is Conor.'

He looked me square in the eyes for a time and then slowly an amazing smile took over his whole face. It was so infectious that I couldn't help turning up the corners of my own mouth in reply. He cocked his wrist and his sword disappeared instantly up his sleeve. He stepped right up and shook my hand enthusiastically (which hurt) and said, 'They call me Fergal. Pleased to meet you, Conor.'

'The pleasure is all mine, Fergal.'

'So tell, Conor,' Fergal said like we were old mates, 'what the hell were you doing lying in a ditch?'

'That's a long story. You wouldn't have a couple of aspirin and a glass of water, before I start, would you?'

'Don't know what that first thing is but there is a lovely wee stream just over there if you're thirsty. Follow me.'

We put our shoes on, I picked up my sword and we climbed up out of the ravine. My legs howled in pain, as if I had just run a marathon with a sumo wrestler on my back. When we reached the top I saw that we were in the middle of rolling farmland. Fields of waving grain, periodically interrupted by the odd tree, stretched as far as the eye could see.

'Where are we?' I asked.

'The fields of Muhn. The Castle Muhn vineyards start not far – just over that rise.'

My vision was clearing. I looked in the direction of Fergal's finger and saw rolling hills in the distance. Fergal's definition of not far was quite different from my own.

'Oh, I get it,' Fergal said, way too loud for my liking, 'you were at a shindig at Castle Muhn last night – weren't you?'

I almost said, *I wish*, but then it occurred to me that everyone who knew who I was had tried to kill me. 'Maybe,' I said, thinking that lying might be a sensible idea.

'Well, that explains it.' Fergal laughed. 'You wouldn't be the first guy to be found hung over in a ditch after a party at Castle Muhn.' He slapped me on the back. It felt like I was hit with a sledgehammer.

The water made me wonder if I had been drinking sawdust all of my life. It was cool and crystal clear. It hit the back of my throat and made me feel like I would never be thirsty again. That's one of the best things about The Land, it forces you to appreciate the simple things in life: fresh water, fragrant air, magnificent views, and not being dead. All of my problems and pressing engagements in the Real World were fading in my mind, except for that nagging image of Sally, still waiting outside the movie theatre.

'I thought the big party was at moon bright,' Fergal said. 'Oh no! I haven't missed it, have I? I could have sworn it was tomorrow night.'

'No. You're alright. It was an unofficial thing last night,' I lied, 'tomorrow's the big night.'

'Phew. I would have been well upset if I'd missed it,' he said, slapping me on the back again. I had to figure out how to break him out of that habit. 'So what are you doing then, Conor me friend? Are you on your way home or are you coming back for a bit of the *hair of the dog?*'

What to do? I knew that I should keep a low profile, especially when the motto around here seemed to be – *to know Conor is to kill Conor*. But what could I do on my own? I had to find my mother and father again. But where were they and how could I find them without telling people who I was? And a party! Why not? After all I'd probably get murdered by an in-law before the week was out – so why not party? This Fergal seemed like a nice guy and he *was* family (which may or may not be a good thing). If I hung around with him maybe I could come up with a plan before someone figured out who I was.

'What the hell,' I said. 'One more night of partying can't kill me.'

'Well, maybe you should go easier tomorrow, you look awful rough.'

'Thanks for the advice,' I said, and together we set off for a party at Castle Muhn.

'That was a clever bit of magic you pulled back there,' Fergal said.

'Yes, I liked it at the time.'

'It's a snap spell, isn't it?'

'A snap spell?'

'Hey, sorry,' Fergal said, raising his hands. 'I shouldn't be prying into another man's magic.'

'No, it's OK,' I said, 'I just never heard of a snap spell.'

'A snap spell is one that happens by itself. You don't have to cast it or pay for it or anything – it just happens. Kings put them on their jewels and such to stop them from getting nicked. I never saw a proper one before – till now.'

'I guess it is a snap spell then.'

'Where'd you get it?'

What should I say to that? The problem with lying is that it gets you into trouble. I learned that painful lesson last year. I was dating a girl named Dottie when I met Sally. I told Dottie I was going out to dinner with my father when I was really taking Sally to the movies. The next day I saw Dottie and she said, 'What did you have for dinner, popcorn?' Man, was I busted.

The other problem with lying is you have to remember what you said, and since it seemed like I was going to be doing a lot of lying in the near future, I decided to tell the truth as much as I could.

Fergal noticed my hesitancy. 'Hey, mate, you don't have to tell me nothing. I talk too much and ask too many questions. Just tell me to shut up, that's what all my friends do.'

'No, it's alright. My protection spell was a gift from my mother.'

'Phew. Nice gift. Must have cost her weight in gold.'

'Don't know. Never asked.'

'Well, I'm glad she gave it to you. I never stabbed anybody before, it would have been a shame for you to be the first. There's something about you, I don't know what it is but it seems like we are old friends already, or should be. You know what I mean?' Then he slapped me on the back – again.

'I do,' I said, and meant it. We were definitely related. Fergal didn't know what this feeling was, but I did, my mother's spell confirmed it – we were kin. I slapped Fergal on the back, hard, so he would know what it felt like. It hurt my hand.

'That sword of yours appeared like it was magic,' I said.

'What, this little thing?' he clicked his wrist and the long knife popped into his hand with frightening speed. 'My Banshee blade.'

'You're a Banshee?' I blurted.

'No,' he said sarcastically. 'What gave it away? Was it the bit of white hair? Or was it the bit of white hair?'

'I think it must have been the bit of white hair.' I smiled and replied as casually as I could. Banshees have a tuft of white hair. I stored that piece of information away.

'So how do you get it to pop out so fast?'

'Ah well, that's the magic part. Here, let me show you.' He stopped and took off his shirt. His right arm was strapped with leather in three places. Entwined in the straps was a gold wire that seemed to be on some sort of pulley system. The wire was attached to the blade, so as to propel it in and out of his sleeve. 'The magic is in the gold wire,' he said. 'It cost me a packet. When I need the blade, I do this motion and this half of the wire straightens and expands – poof – instant sword. The spell doesn't use much gold. The wire's supposed to work for years.'

'Cool.'

'No, it doesn't get hot or anything.'

'I mean, nice.'

'Oh, I could set you up with a guy to make you one if you like. It isn't cheap though.'

'I am afraid I'm a bit broke at the moment.'

'Me too. You and I have got so much in common,' he said with another slap.

As we followed the stream Fergal waxed on about the intricacies of Banshee blade manufacture but I didn't take much in. His voice was increasingly drowned out by the bass drum solo that began playing in my head. After I don't know how long (by which time the pounding in my head had graduated into a full-blown marching band), Fergal turned to me and said, 'You haven't been listening to a word I've said, have you?'

'Huh? Oh, sure I have.'

Fergal looked me in the eyes and I had a scary moment when I thought he was going to quiz me. Then he broke into an ear-to-ear smile and said, 'I like you, Conor, it usually takes friends ages to learn to ignore my babbling – you figured it out right away.' He went to slap me on the back but then stopped when he saw me flinch. 'You know, you look awful rough. We're in no hurry; how 'bout we make camp here?'

We found the remnants of an old campfire under a tall, broadleaved tree that had roots creeping into the stream. Fergal said it should be OK to camp under an alder this far away from the Fearnlands. I wanted to ask him what that meant but I had a feeling asking too many questions would arouse suspicion, and anyway I was too tired. Fergal took some kindling out of his bag and piled it within the ring of stones.

'You wouldn't have a decent fire-coin, would you? Mine's practically silver.'

'No. I've lost everything except my sword,' I said, which was pretty much the truth.

Fergal produced a half-dollar-sized disc out of his pocket and placed it beneath the little bits of wood.

'I think this thing has one more fire in it.'

He mumbled under his breath, there was a faint glow and then smoke appeared under the wood. He blew it into a small flame. 'Keep an eye on this and I'll beg for some wood.'

Fergal climbed the alder as I lay on my side and blew on the tiny flame. Just this was enough to make me feel light-headed. I was still in pretty bad shape after that damn *rothlú* thing. Whether I fell asleep or passed out I don't know, but the next thing I remember, Fergal was shaking me awake and handing me a stick with a fish on it that he had just cooked on a roaring fire.

'Is there anything else I can do for you, Prince Conor?' For a second I thought he had figured out who I was. I sat bolt upright expecting his

Banshee blade to fly out of his sleeve, but then he smiled and said, 'You're a fat lot of good around here. Next time I'm nursing a hangover, you wait on me.'

'Deal,' I said with a nervous laugh, and took the fish. 'Thanks.'

We ate in silence. I'm not a big fan of food that can stare at me but I was too hungry to complain. I apologised to the trout's face and wolfed the rest of it down.

After dinner Fergal put a couple of logs on the fire and said that even though he would love to talk all night, he was beat. He touched the alder, put his pack under his head and closed his eyes. My short nap had done little to ease my overall body pain. I put my head on the ground and moaned. Just before I went out, I thought I saw some strange movement in the branches above. I sat up and had a good look but then decided I was just spooking myself.

I dreamt I was back in the Real World in a super-posh shoe store where I didn't even have to put the shoes on myself. Sales clerks actually knelt down and placed all kinds of really cool footwear directly on my feet.

Dawn, as it always does, came too early. I find that going to sleep under the stars is lovely but waking up outside is a drag. It leaves me itchy, damp and with terminal bed hair. It wasn't until I stood that I realised my shoes were missing. Well, that explained the theme of my dream. I walked over to the still-sleeping Fergal and lightly kicked him with my bare foot. He shot straight up.

'What?' he sputtered.

'Ha ha, Fergal, very funny. What did you do with my shoes?'

'What are you talking about?' he said, getting his bearings.

'My shoes, I don't know how you did it without waking me up but I want my shoes back.'

'I don't have your shoes,' he said, confused.

'Quit mucking around, Fergal, I had them on when I went to sleep.'

'I'm telling you I don't have your... uh-oh.' Fergal jerked his hand a couple of times and then pulled his tunic over his head. 'Damn it,' he said, 'damn it, damn it, damn it!'

'What? What is it?'

'My Banshee blade is gone – and the wire too.'

'What do you mean gone?'

'Robbed, we were robbed last night.'

Oh, just great, I thought, *now I'm going to have to walk in this godforsaken land barefoot.* Then I had a terrible thought. Slowly I reached down to my waist and felt for my scabbard – the Sword of Duir was gone.

Chapter Seven
Brownies

'They took my sword. Oh my God, my father is going to kill me.'

Fergal went over to the alder and placed his hand on the bark, then kicked it. A rain of branches showered down that made us run out from under its cover.

'Fergal, what the hell is going on?'

'We got rumbled by the alder last night.'

'Are you telling me the tree mugged us?'

'Don't be stupid.'

'Then who could take my shoes and your wire from under your shirt without waking us up?'

'Brownies, damn them.'

'Whos-ies?'

'Brownies – who else?'

'You mean like girl scouts?'

'Why do you think they were girls?' Fergal said, confused.

'Never mind. I have to get that sword back. It is very important.'

'Well, that's not going to be easy. Brownies weigh nothing and are famously difficult to track.'

We looked around at the dew-covered grass and then at each other. We were both wearing the same ear-to-ear grin. You see, Brownies are usually difficult to track – except when one of them is wearing Nikes.

Whoever stole my shoes must have had tiny feet because he dragged them along the ground, trying to keep my size elevens from falling off. The tracks led into the stream but were easy to pick up on the other side. Fergal dashed under the tree and grabbed a couple of branches that we could use as weapons. He shouted a sarcastic, 'Thanks,' as the alder tried to rain more wood down on him.

We followed the trail across some wide, open fields that led to rolling hills. The trees were thin and the ground pretty spongy but periodically my bare feet made contact with a rock or a twig that made me yelp. I wasn't sure how long I would be able to keep up this pace, but saying that, I felt a lot better than I did yesterday.

Every time I wanted to ask Fergal if we could rest, I remembered the Sword of Duir – I had to get it back. I had a vision of meeting up with Dad and him saying, 'Let me get this straight, I give you a sword that has been in our family for *thousands* of years and you lose it – in a day!' I really wanted to avoid that conversation. After about an hour of jogging we rounded a small hill. I lost the trail but Fergal laid his head on the ground and pointed to a small cliff face about a quarter-mile to our right.

'If we are lucky, they are camping in those rocks,' Fergal said.

'What makes you think they made camp?'

'Look, my Nanny Breithe always got mad at me when I talked badly about any race but the truth of it is, Brownies are cocky and stupid. They think they are so stealthy that they are untrackable, but look at these idiots. Not one of them bothered to look behind them to check if they were leaving a trail. My guess is that they were up all night watching us, so I'm hoping they are camping in those rocks.'

'And if you're wrong?'

'Then you're going to have to buy a new pair of those fancy shoes of yours. Where did you get them anyway?'

'Scranton,' I said without thinking.

'Scranton? Never heard of it.'

'Yeah.' I laughed. 'A lot of people say that.'

The way was a bit harder here and Fergal shushed me every time a pebble underfoot made me bark. When we reached the foot of the knoll Fergal and I took a minute to rub the small stems and leaves off the branches we were carrying so as to fashion them into staffs. They weren't the best weapons in the world but they would have to do.

Climbing the rocks would have been a cinch if I'd had anything on my feet, but barefoot it was flipping difficult. What was harder than the actual climbing was trying not to curse every time I stepped on some jagged edge. My poor tootsies were taking a beating. If I got through this without getting stabbed by my own sword, I was going to throttle whoever took my Nikes. Fergal reached the summit before me. He peeped over and instantly ducked down, placing his index finger over his lips and indicating that our light-fingered quarry was just over the rise. I pressed up next to him.

'There's only two of them,' he whispered. 'We need a plan.'

'Have you ever done this before?'

'Done what?'

'Attacked two armed men with sticks?'

'No, but I'm looking forward to it.' He smiled.

His smile was so infectious I said, 'OK, what's the plan?'

'One of us should circle around behind them, and when he is in position the other one makes a frontal attack from here. The one of us that comes from the rear should be able to take them out before the one who attacks from here gets sliced up too much.'

'As much as I don't fancy the idea of getting "sliced up too much", you have to go around the back – my feet are killing me.'

'OK, take a quick look and you'll see the gap in the back. I'll be coming from there.'

I was nervous until I stuck my nose over the ledge. They looked like a couple of teenage street urchins. They had black matted hair and wore tight dark green clothes stretched over bodies so skinny they would have made a supermodel look chunky. Between them was a campfire that had a dome of gold wire over it. The smoke rising from the fire seemed to disappear when it hit the wire. The two swords and Fergal's pack were lying behind them on the ground. When the larger guy got up to tend the fire I saw that the smaller one had my shoes on the ground between his legs. He had removed the laces from one of them and then to my horror I realised he was about to cut the tongue out of the sneaker. That's when I kind of forgot where I was. I stood up and yelled, 'Hey!' vaulted over the ledge and slid down to two very surprised Brownies.

'What is the matter with you?' I shouted.

The little guy just froze. The bigger one grabbed the Sword of Duir and pointed it at me. What confused him was that I just ignored him. I walked over to the little guy and grabbed the shoe – I was mad.

'What's the matter with you? If you are going to steal my Nikes the least you could do is give them a little respect. What the hell are you cutting them for?'

The bigger guy poked me in the back with my sword. I turned to him and said, 'I'll deal with you in a second.' I looked around – Fergal was nowhere to be seen.

I turned back to junior. 'I'm talking to you. Why the hell were you cutting up my sneakers?' He seemed too terrified to speak. I towered over him. 'Well?'

'My, my feet got sweaty in them,' he stammered.

'Oh, so after sweating in my shoes you decided to cut them up.' I think I would have slapped him if the big guy hadn't just then given me a good jab in the ribs that demanded my attention.

'If you take one more step towards my brother,' the bigger one said, 'I'm going to run you through.'

I turned. He had striking pale blue eyes that, unlike his brother, had no fear in them. He was holding my sword to my chest but I remained calm.

'That is my sword,' I pointed out, 'and in about three seconds I'm going to take it back.'

'And how are you going to do that?' His voice betrayed a tiny loss of confidence.

'I'm going to pick it off the ground after my friend Fergal clocks you in the head with a tree branch.'

He went down like a house of cards. I quickly turned to little brother, who was still frozen like a rabbit in headlights. I picked up my sword and pointed to the soles of my feet.

'Look at my tootsies! Do you see how dirty they are? I should make you lick them clean.'

I took a step towards him and he started to shake. I instantly felt sorry for him – this kid was way out of his league. I crouched down.

'Hey, little guy, relax, we're not going to hurt you.' I turned to Fergal. 'We're not going to hurt them – right?'

'Well, I'm not going to hurt anybody,' Fergal said as he began to tie up big brother, 'but you seem a bit worked up about your footwear.'

'Well, I like these shoes.'

'I've noticed.'

I turned back to the boy. 'OK, it's decided, no one is going to hurt you. What's your name?'

'My brother said I'm not supposed to tell you my name even if you torture me.'

'Wow, you guys are a real bunch of desperados. Mind if I call you Jesse?'

'I, I guess.'

Fergal finished hogtying the brother and came over.

'Fergal, meet Jesse.'

Fergal leaned over the boy. 'What kind of a name is Jesse?'

I tapped him on the shoulder and said, 'I made it up but I think he likes it – just go with it.'

'OK, hi, Jesse. What are you two doing so far from the Fearnlands?'

'My brother said there would be easy pickings out here but we haven't seen anybody for ages. I wanted to go home – only he made me keep going. He said Father would let him take his scrúdú early if we came back with quality acquisitions. I, I didn't mean to hurt your shoes, honest. What are you going to do to us?'

'Scrúdú?'

'It's the manhood test,' he said, then the poor kid turned ghastly white. 'Oh gods, I shouldn't have told you that.'

So that was it – a story as old as time, big brother with delusions of manhood, roped little bro into doing something incredibly stupid.

I picked up a canteen from the ground, walked over to big bro and poured some water on his head. He spluttered awake and tried to get up. When he realised he was hogtied he looked at Fergal and me. His bravado from earlier had vanished.

'Good morning, Frank,' I said.

'What is Frank?' he said.

'You are. Since your little brother over there has informed me that we won't know your real names until after we torture you, I decided to call you Frank and him Jesse until then.'

'My name is Demne and my brother is Codna.'

I turned to Jesse/Codna, who now had his mouth wide open in amazement. 'Well, Jesse, it looks like your brother isn't much for torture.'

I turned back to the big bro. 'You know, Demne, I like Frank better. You don't mind if I call you Frank, do you?'

'No, sir.'

'Good. OK, Frank, here's what we are going to do. First, we are going to take our *acquisitions* back. You don't have any problems with that, do you, Frank?'

'No, sir.'

'You know, I really am starting to like your attitude, Frank. Next I'm going to borrow your shoes and let you have the opportunity, like I had, to climb barefoot over those rocks.' I crouched down and took Frank's sandals off his feet, picked up Jesse's from the ground and threw them over the stone ridge as far as I could. 'We are going to leave you now, but before we do, you are going to promise me that the next time you have a harebrained idea, you are not going to drag your brother into it. Right?'

'Yes, sir.'

'Good. Fergal, do you have anything to add?'

Fergal had reattached his Banshee blade and was now examining the gold wire dome he had taken from its position over the fire. Smoke was now floating freely in the air. 'Now that you mention it, Conor, I was thinking of taking this interesting thing as payment for our troubles.'

Frank tried to stand when Fergal said this, and fell on his side. 'Please don't take our father's smokescreen. He'll kill us if we lose it.'

I grabbed Frank by the arm and pulled him back up into a sitting position. 'So let me guess, Dad doesn't know you took it?'

He shook his head – a pathetic no. I took the smokescreen from Fergal and placed it on Frank's head like a skullcap.

'Jesse, can I give you a little piece of information that will help you for the rest of your life?'

Jesse just stared at me and then slowly nodded yes.

'Your big brother is an idiot.'

He nodded to me again.

As we walked to the rim of the knoll Fergal said, 'I would really have liked that smokescreen.'

'Yeah,' I said, 'but I know what it's like to get in trouble with your dad and I didn't have the heart to do that to them.'

I gave them one last look before I climbed back down. Jesse was still sitting stock still.

I called to him. 'Jesse, you can untie your brother any time you want but if I were you I would make him suffer for a little while longer.'

He looked up to me and then gave me the tiniest of smiles and then waved.

'Behave, you two,' I shouted as I jumped down the rock face.

Our encounter with the outlaws had put us behind schedule for the party. Fergal set a jogging pace that made me wish I had tortured those two a little bit.

'So I said we need a plan,' Fergal said to me as he ran alongside, 'and you said "OK". Do you remember that?'

'I do.'

'And then we made a plan. Do you remember that too?'

I nodded, conserving my breath.

'Good, now here is the point I'm getting to. I don't know how they do things in Skwinton.'

'Scranton,' I corrected.

'OK, Scranton, but where I come from, after you make a plan you don't just up and jump over a wall screaming.'

'Well, it worked, didn't it?'

'Yes, Conor, but remember, some of us don't have a priceless snap spell to come to our rescue.'

I almost told him that my mom's protection spell didn't have anything to do with it, since it works solely on relatives and only once, but then I thought, *He doesn't need to know all that and I'm a bit out of breath anyway*, so all I said was, 'Yeah, sorry.'

'Do not worry about it,' he said, slapping me on the back, almost precipitating a full-speed jogging wreck – somehow I kept my footing.

Fergal seemed to think that running at this pace for a couple of hours was an OK thing to do. It wasn't easy but amazingly I kept up. Usually any sport more strenuous than bowling pushes me over the edge. Maybe those annoying callisthenics that Dad used to make me do before and after sword fighting lessons were paying off. After a while I started to enjoy it. I got a glimpse of the high that joggers say they get from running. I took in the magnificent scenery as my body set a cadence that echoed in my brain. I think I was about to slip into a perfect Zen-like state when Fergal slapped me on the back again and snapped me out of it.

'Hey, you hungry? There's an apple tree over there.'

Hungry? Now that I thought about it, I was starving! I saw the tree and ran straight towards it. The apples looked even better than the one that my mother had given me. I know I go on and on about the trees in The Land, but I can't emphasise enough how magnificent they are. Never in my life had I ever seen a fruit tree so bountiful. Directly above my head was an apple bigger than my fist. I stared at it for a moment and marvelled at how my face reflected in its mirror-like red skin. I bent my knees and jumped to grab it.

That's when the bus hit me.

Chapter Eight
Araf

OK, it wasn't a bus, but it sure felt like one. One moment I was in mid-jump with an apple in my hand, the next moment I was hit – hard in the shoulder and went flying ass over teacups through the air. Luckily I landed in a pile of thick barley that was pretty soft.

Fergal was at my side in a second. 'Are you mad?'

'Did you get the licence number of that truck?' I groaned.

'Are you OK?'

'Give me a second to check my bones to see which of them *aren't* broken.'

'For the gods' sake, haven't you ever picked an apple before? Wait here and I'll talk to her.'

'Talk to who?'

I sat up and found that I was a considerable distance from where I had been moments before. Fergal slowly approached the apple tree and placed his hands on the trunk. He mumbled a few things, pointed to me and then jogged back.

'She said she won't hit you again. She wants to talk to you. If I was you I'd start with an apology.'

The tree hit me? The tree hit me! Of course it did. If I had to thank a willow tree for its shade, I must certainly have had to ask permission before picking an apple. I just wished I could learn something in this place without it being so painful.

I stood up. I wasn't hurt as bad as I should have been. The blow was so unexpected that I didn't have time to tense up. Still, I had one hell of a dead arm. I walked warily towards the tree. I had spent a lifetime with trees. I always knew they were living things but I never really treated them like they were living in the same world as me. Again, The Land was forcing me to re-examine my perceptions. I placed my hand on the trunk.

A conversation with a tree is not like communicating with anyone or anything else. It's not a dialogue, it's more of a meeting of the minds. Even though I spoke out loud it was not necessary – words are not the medium of communication.

I didn't have to worry about convincing the apple tree that I was sorry, she knew as soon as I touched her and I knew I was forgiven – the sensation of it washed over me. She was happy I was not seriously hurt – she had never hit anyone so hard before. I learned that it was not uncommon for her to give a child a little smack, just to teach a lesson, but she had never had a poacher as old as me and let loose a good one. She told me (felt me?) that Fergal and I could each have a couple of apples with her blessing. The only part of the conversation that was almost in words, was when I thanked her and said goodbye. I could have sworn she said, '*Good luck, little prince.*'

We sat under the apple tree's shade and ate and drank water from Fergal's canteen. Who'd have thought that an apple and some water could make such a superb meal? It was so satisfying I felt as though I could live on these two things alone. I have since found out that many people in The Land do just that.

'You still look pretty wrecked, Conor. The castle's only an hour or so away and we don't want to be too early. Why don't you have a snooze? I promise I won't steal your shoes.'

'I won't argue with that,' I said as I put my head on the soft grass. Before I dozed off I raised my hand behind me and touched the apple tree. I asked her if she minded me resting here a little bit. She told me she would look after me as I slept. Next thing I knew, I was dreaming again.

I dreamt I was a child, maybe five years old. I was walking between my parents, holding their hands as we passed under huge yew trees. These yews were not menacing like the ones on the river. The trees moved out of our way and bowed to us as we passed. An arrow sailed through the air and hit my father in the shoulder. I was upset but my father told me not to be silly and pulled the arrow from his flesh, like he was dusting dandruff off his suit. Mom rubbed the wound and it healed.

We sat together under a tree. Mom pointed and I looked up. I saw that the yew we were sitting under was now an apple tree. I turned to ask my mother if I could have an apple but she and my father were gone. Next, the apple tree raised itself up on huge roots, pushing itself free from the ground and kicked me! I rolled like a ball into the base of another tree and that one kicked me as well. Soon all of the trees had gathered around me having a kick-about, with me as the ball! The funny thing was I liked it. They weren't hurting me, it was fun. After a while I got bored with the game and I laid down under a tree. The tree kept kicking me but I refused to move.

I awoke with a tree root sticking in my back. I am sure it wasn't there when I fell asleep. Fergal was snoring away to my left. I toyed with the idea of stealing his shoes as a joke, but I wasn't sure he wouldn't stab me first and get the joke second. I sat up and rubbed my eyes. That's when I saw him approach.

He was close enough that I could see that he was short, but not slight. He was built like a brick outhouse – not fat, just a solid body with a head sitting directly on the shoulders. I got the impression that if I ran at him with all of my might I would just bounce off. Maybe that's where they got the word *bouncer* from – 'cause that's exactly what he looked like. If you got rid of the leather toga he was wearing and put him in a tuxedo, you could imagine him standing in the doorway of any night club. He was walking directly towards us.

I stood and said, 'Hi.'

He didn't even notice me. In his hand he held a thick wooden stick with a gnarled top and seemed to be heading for Fergal. 'Ah, excuse me,' I said, trying to be polite, 'can I help?'

He walked straight at Fergal and raised his stick. I drew my sword and covered the ground between us. That got his attention at least.

'If you are looking for your neck, I can assure you we don't have it.'

I looked him in the eye but he gave me nothing back. I couldn't read the face at all. I kicked Fergal and said, 'We've got company.'

Fergal opened his eyes to see the Incredible Hulk Junior and myself standing over him with weapons drawn.

He looked at Hulk, then at me. 'For the love of the gods, Conor, haven't you ever met anybody without drawing a sword?'

'A friend of yours?'

Fergal nodded and I lowered my weapon. 'Conor, meet Araf – Araf, meet Conor.'

'Sorry,' I said, offering my hand, 'I've had a rough couple of days.'

'That's what he said when he pulled a sword on me,' Fergal said.

'That's not fair – this time I was defending you.'

Araf shook my hand and almost broke it.

'He was coming at you with a club.'

'It's a *banta* stick,' Fergal said, 'and Araf always wakes me with it.'

'Why?'

'Because once, *and only once*,' Fergal said defensively, glaring at Araf, 'I attacked him with my Banshee blade when he woke me up. I was having a bad dream – and it was a long time ago. Ever since then he always wakes me with a stick.'

'Sounds sensible,' I said, thinking that I was lucky not to steal Fergal's shoes while he slept.

Araf nodded at me in agreement. It was the first true communication between us.

'Come on,' Fergal said, picking himself off the ground, 'we've got a party to go to.'

'Are you coming to the party, Araf?' I asked.

'Are you kidding?' Fergal replied for him. 'Araf here is a party beast!'

As we walked to the party I got Araf's life story – not from Araf, I might add, but from Fergal. I was starting to wonder if Araf could speak at all. Araf and Fergal had grown up together in a place called Castle Ur in the Heatherlands. It was obvious they weren't blood relatives. One look at the two of them told you that they came from different gene pools – hell, different gene oceans. It turned out that both had been raised by the same nanny, who was now dead. When I asked Fergal about his parents he seemed to sidestep the question.

And check this out – Araf is an Imp! I came very close to bursting out laughing and saying, 'Isn't he a bit big for an Imp?' but I kept my mouth shut. The Land was going to throw quite a few surprises at me. If I wanted to look like a native, I would have to take stuff like this in my stride. I couldn't help thinking what a funky couple of days I was having. How many people can say they've been in a sword fight with a Banshee and an Imp and then went off to a party with them?

The landscape changed the closer we got to Castle Muhn. The fields of grain changed into towering vineyards. Ancient trellises of black hawthorn were draped with vines producing grapes in bunches so large I was amazed that they could stay on the vine. Bees the size of hummingbirds roared through the white and pink blossoms. Castle Muhn was not like the imposing fortress of Castle Duir. It was huge – it must have taken up over an acre, with low walls, and I noticed a conspicuous lack of sentries. Actually, with the vineyards around it, it looked more like a sprawling French chateau.

We walked in silence for a while, which I was starting to realise was unusual for Fergal. Things had been so crazy, this was the first moment I had time to collect my thoughts. Jeez, I hoped Dad was alright. He looked bad when I left him but he was definitely alive. I felt guilty going to a party, but something in my mother's voice back there made me think Dad would be OK. And then there was my dream. Was that a vision or just wish-fulfilment? Well, as much as I would like to be able to help him, there was nothing I could do about it. Still, that didn't stop me from worrying.

I decided to look at the big picture. Right. My father is a prince or maybe a king. My mother is an outlaw sorceress, and everyone in this place (that shouldn't even exist) wants to kill me. OK, let's forget the big picture – that was just freaking me out. I needed a plan for the here and now. What should I do? I should get out of here, that's what I should do. I needed to get out of The Land. If the prophecy was right, and everyone around here seemed to take it seriously – deadly seriously – then my parents' plan was a good one. Let me live a long and happy life in the Real World and when I reach a ripe old age, I pass away in my bed. The son of the one-handed prince will die, and Tir na Nog will be saved. Good plan – I liked it. But how do I get back to the Real World? There had to be a way, after all my father and I had done it. The answer was Mom. She was the one that sent us in the first place. If I could find my mother, I could get out of here. OK, I had a plan – find my mother. Where? How? She said she was going to the Fililands, so now all I had to do was find out how to get there. I chuckled to myself – the fact of the matter was that I was lost and scared and the only plan I could come up was – *I want my mommy!* – real mature.

The approach to the outer wall of the castle was strange – eerie, in fact. The gate was wide open but there were no guards, no anybody. I could just about hear music coming from within but there was no one outside or inside the doorway as far as I could tell.

'I'm not an expert on castles,' I said, 'but aren't you supposed to, like, guard them?'

'Gerard doesn't need guards, he's got a mountain of gold,' Fergal said. 'This place is crawling with snap spells. I'm sure if you were up to no good, you wouldn't get in here.'

'Gerard?' I said. 'Is this the same guy who built the huts?'

'Of course.'

We were actually inside the castle and still there was nobody around. There was definitely something going on. I could hear music but there was no sign of a party. I was startled when huge wooden doors at the end of the hallway opened and half a dozen servants with trays of dirty mugs and plates hurried past us without even a second glance. Music and the smell of food escaped from the room like a caged bird. The sound and the aroma were instantly intoxicating. I had been thinking that maybe going to such a public event was a bad idea, but after I got that nose- and earful – just try to keep me out.

Fergal reached the door first and then jumped when he heard a voice saying, 'Name?'

To the right of the door was an alcove with a split door, the top half open. Behind the door was an old guy – and I mean an ancient old guy. Physically he didn't look that old, but I could see the years in his eyes. It's amazing how quickly I had gotten used to examining people's eyes. This guy's peepers had been around for a long, long time.

'Name?' he repeated.

'Fergal of Castle Ur.'

'Castle Ur?' the old man questioned. 'You don't look like an Imp to me.'

'He is with me,' Araf said, in a beautiful bass voice.

'My God!' I said. 'He can speak.'

'Ah, Master Araf,' the old guy said, 'it is good to see you again.'

'This is my kinsman, Fergal,' Araf said. 'He is indeed of Castle Ur, and this is Conor of…'

They all three looked to me for an answer – what could I say? 'I am Conor of – the Fililands.'

They all looked at me like I was from another planet (which I guess I was) and then burst into laughter.

'The Fililands!' the old man repeated. 'That's a good one. Try not to eat any babies tonight, will you?'

Fergal and Araf laughed at this. So I did too.

'I promise,' I said.

'Any friends of Master Araf are welcome in Castle Muhn,' said the old man. 'I'll take your weapons now, if you please. That would include the one up your sleeve, Master… Fergal, was it?'

Fergal looked shocked but produced and unhooked his Banshee blade.

'I was hoping to get into a banta match.' Araf spoke again. 'Can I not keep my stick?'

The doorkeeper held out his hand and Araf handed him his banta stick. The old man inspected it and placed it with a bunch of others behind the door. 'There will be sticks provided if you wish to compete. And our sticks,' the old man said with a wry smile, 'have the added advantage of not being hollowed out and filled with lead.'

Araf nodded like a guilty schoolboy.

Fergal and I both handed over our weapons. He filed Fergal's blade away, but looked at mine for quite some time.

'This is an exquisite sword,' the old man said, as he placed it alone in a narrow cupboard. 'Does it have a name?'

'Does what have a name?' I asked.

'Your sword – a weapon as superb as this should have a name.'

'Oh, of course – I – I call it,' I announced, '*the Lawnmower*!"

Chapter Nine

Essa

Since my first experience of a castle was inside a sewer-scented dungeon, I was expecting the other side of the door to be filled with disgusting barbarians in bearskins. I imagined them chomping on huge legs of animal flesh as they slapped the backsides of passing serving wenches, their greasy chins glistening in dim torchlight. How wrong can a boy be?

This place was spectacularly elegant. We were no longer strictly in the castle but in the Great Vineyard, a football-pitch-sized courtyard adorned with fountains and huge black and white marble statues. The statues were like oversized chess pieces strewn about in a haphazard manner – some upright, others on their side. It was as if the gods had just dumped out a giant chess set before they set up for a game. Roofing the courtyard was a black trellis that supported grapevines with fruit as big as plums. What was left of the day's light filtered through the leaves, giving the room a majestic green hue.

Remembering the incident with the apple, the first thing I did was place my hand on a vine and ask nicely if I could have a grape. '*NO YOU MAY NOT!*' The answer came back so clear it made my head hurt. These were proud plants.

Fergal whacked me on the back, 'You weren't thinking about plucking a grape from the Great Vineyard, were you?'

'Who, me?' I lied. 'I wouldn't be that stupid.'

'Come on, let's try Gerard's new vintage.'

The party was in full swing. The music was infectious. It instantly lifted me into a party mood and made my walk resemble a little dance. It reminded me of Irish traditional music – but not quite. I was starting to think that there must have been some cultural exchange between my world and this one, because so much of The Land was *almost* familiar. The couple of hundred guests were standing around with mugs or sitting at wooden tables. I noticed that no two tables were of the same wood and each one would have made an antique dealer drool.

It seemed that all were welcome here. The guests' clothes ranged from farmers' rags to elegant flowing gowns, and everyone was mixing. I was expecting to get that *we don't like strangers around here* stare but everyone was smiling and nodding, especially to Araf. We got to the bar and Fergal ordered 'three of the new stuff'. While we were waiting for our wine, Fergal noticed he was standing next to someone he knew and slapped him on the back. He was a tall, lean man with very straight, shoulder-length blond hair. I could see by his expression that he liked being slapped on the back almost as much as I did.

'Esus! How the hell are ya?'

'Ah, Fergal, this must be your first celebration at Castle Muhn.'

'It is indeed.'

'And good evening, Master Araf,' the tall man said.

Araf bowed.

'Esus,' Fergal said, 'I would like you to meet Conor. Conor, Esus.'

'Good evening,' I said, bowing in the same manner as Araf.

The tall man bowed back, but only slightly.

'Esus,' Fergal explained, 'is the Elf that takes care of the trees around Castle Ur.'

'You're an Elf?' I blurted before I could stop myself.

'I have that distinction – yes.'

'Well,' I said, trying to recover my composure, 'some of my best friends are Elves.'

'Oh yes,' Esus said, 'who?'

What a stupid thing to say. What was I going to do now? This was the first person I had met in The Land that I hadn't tried to stab – I was starting to miss my old method of greeting people.

'Ah… Legolas. Do you know him?'

'No,' said Esus. 'What clan is he in?'

'I don't know,' I said. 'Hey, when I said best friends, I really meant acquaintances.'

The awkward moment was saved by the arrival of our wine. Fergal and even Araf got very excited.

'Ah, my first taste of the new vintage. To Gerard and his vines,' Fergal toasted, and we all clinked our mugs.

I'm not a real big fan of wine. Oh, I'll have the odd glass at a posh dinner, but by and large I'd rather have a beer any day of the week, but this was wine I would sell my soul for. It was the nectar of the gods. I had an image of Bacchus, the Roman wine god, waltzing in and throwing a barrel of this stuff over his shoulder.

I don't know why I was so surprised that this was the finest wine I had tasted, as everything I had tried in The Land had been the best thing I had ever seen or smelt or tasted – but surprised I was. 'Wow! This is awesome!' I shouted, so loud that everyone around the bar turned to look.

'It's alright,' Esus said, dropping his voice to a whispered, 'I think Gerard is skimping on the gold a bit this year – but so is everyone.'

'You mean there is better wine than this?' I said, between slurps.

That was a mistake. Esus went into a litany of vintages, giving detailed descriptions of each year's colour, flavour and bouquet. He was a wine bore. I spotted it instantly and didn't even try to keep up. While I pretended to listen to him, I contemplated meeting my first Elf. He didn't look like an Elf. Here I was in a room full of Elves, Imps, Banshees and God knows what else and everyone looked so – normal. To be honest I was a bit disappointed. In the back of my mind I wanted this party to be like the Cantina scene in *Star Wars*, but it seems that the difference between an Elf and a Banshee is like the difference between a Norwegian and an Italian. Sure, you could tell the difference, but underneath they were all pretty much the same.

The sun had almost set, and the light shining through the vine trellis was waning. Just as I thought, *We could use a little light in here*, as if on cue about twenty of the waiting staff entered the room each holding a small pyramid of glowing gold wire balls. A handsome and distinguished man, also holding five glowing wire balls, strode into the centre of the room. The golden glow from his hands was brighter than all of the others – it illuminated his purple velvet outfit and his silver beard, and twinkled in ancient but still-mischievous eyes. He looked like a king out of a pack of cards. The crowd parted and applauded as he made his way to a small dais in the centre of the room.

Fergal nudged my side. 'Look, it's Gerard.'

Gerard tried to raise his hand to quiet the crowd and almost dropped the balls he was holding. He laughed heartily at this, as did everyone. We all quietened down to hear.

'My good friends,' he boomed, and I instantly knew he meant it – he loved these people and they loved him. 'Welcome to Muhn. Every year I am amazed and humbled that so many of you would travel so far just to sample my newest vintage.'

Someone shouted, 'Wouldn't miss it for the world!' and the assemblage replied with a, 'Hear, hear!'

'Thank you,' Gerard continued. 'I am especially heartened that so many of you have come for this harvest. I know how difficult a time you have had this year.'

The crowd mumbled. I heard Esus whisper, 'That's a first.'

'What is?' I asked.

'Gerard never makes political statements like that.'

'But as you know,' Gerard continued, 'Castle Muhn is no place for talk like that – even by me. Anyone heard grumbling tonight will be tossed out of my highest window' – this brought laughter and cheers – 'for tonight is a celebration!'

At that, he threw the five glowing balls he was holding up into the air and began to juggle. All of the servants threw theirs, and all at once the air was full of cascading, glowing wire orbs. The jugglers then began to pass the balls among themselves. Guests everywhere were ducking as glowing missiles just missed their heads. Now I have done a bit of juggling in my day and I can tell you – these were no ordinary juggling balls. The jugglers weren't even breaking a sweat. They never dropped one or hit anybody and if you watched closely, you could see sometimes the balls waited until the juggler was ready before they fell back to earth.

Someone shouted, 'Hup,' and all of the jugglers threw their remaining balls high in the air, where they just kept on going! The balls intertwined themselves with the vine trellis and then glowed even brighter. They bathed the room in golden light. The applause, the hoots and hollering were deafening. The music kicked in and the party truly began.

Fergal slapped me on the back and said, 'We need some food!'

Food! Every time I heard that, I thought, *What a good idea*. We weaved our way through vines of people until we came upon what looked like a five-acre buffet table. I have never seen so much food. Who was it all for? It made me worry that the busload of three-headed

Giants and Trolls hadn't arrived yet. I found a plate and just piled it on. I took a little bit of everything – if the apples were anything to go by, this was going to be the best meal of my life. I stopped when the food on my plate started to resemble the Leaning Tower of Pisa. One more crumb and I would have had a spilled food disaster of horrific proportions.

I looked up to find that I had lost my friends. I searched around a bit but I couldn't see them. I couldn't risk weaving through the crowd looking for them with this overflowing plate, so I sat down alone in a nearby chair. My intention was to try to eat the top off my food mountain until it was transportable. The food was so good, my moaning drew stares. I chomped in ecstasy as I spied on the other guests. I was starting to figure stuff out. Banshees and Elves were mostly tall, with Banshees being dark while the Elves were fair. Imps were shorter and, as a rule, built like bowling pins, including the women. There were others that looked like they could have been TV presenters and still more that I couldn't put into any category I knew yet. I was also starting to gauge how old people were without seeing their eyes. A sense of seniority poured out of some like an aura. The way they talked and walked, or just held themselves, made it easy to separate the young ones from the elders.

A large dance started up. It looked like fun, but unbelievably complicated. It seemed as if the dance was designed for the room. Partners held hands and then danced around the statues in circles of eight, then sixteen, or more if a statue was on its side, and then as if they all had a secret radio in their ears, they made a huge undulating circle around the room before somehow finding their partners again. It was lucky they were immortals because it probably took a couple a hundred years to learn it.

The monument of food on my lap had vanished. My stomach was full and the wine had pleasantly gone to my head. I was just about to dance my way through the room and search for my newfound friends when I was overcome by an awful pang of guilt. I slumped in my chair and thought, *What right do I have to celebrate? My father is lying wounded somewhere, maybe even dead. I may never get back to my life in the Real World and even if I do it will be in tatters. I'll most likely flunk out of high school and Sally will never speak to me again.* All of a sudden I felt out of place and alone – just a little boy who had lost his mother. That's when I heard a woman's voice behind me.

'My father says that Castle Muhn does not have enough magic to solve all your problems – just enough to allow you to leave them outside the front door.'

I turned and almost fell in love. She was casually rolling one of those glowing juggling balls over her fingers and from hand to hand, making the light waltz around her face and sparkle in young, dark eyes. She wore a purple velvet dress and her curly black hair cascaded onto her bare shoulders. I know I should be ashamed of myself, but at that second, my parents, Sally, my life – all shot straight out of my head. I was filled with the vision before me.

'It seems by your face,' she said, 'that you have smuggled your problems in with you.'

'Not any more,' I said. 'They're gone, out-a-here.'

She smiled and my heart pounded.

'I couldn't help noticing the strange runes on your tunic.'

I looked down and laughed. I was amazed that no one had mentioned it before. I was wearing my New York Yankees sweatshirt.

'These are special runes where I come from, they mean I'm cool.'

She reached out and touched them. 'They don't feel cool.'

'My name is Conor.'

'I am pleased to meet you, Conor. I am Essa.'

We bowed to each other without losing eye contact.

75

'I am sure we have never met, Conor. What house are you from?'

'I came with Araf,' I said, sidestepping the question.

'Araf!' she screamed and jumped up and down. 'Is he here? Where?'

'I don't know, I've lost him.'

'Well, we must find him.'

She grabbed my hand and pulled me into the party. She was moving fast and I was being thrown into fellow guests and upsetting mugs, but there was no way I was going to let go of that hand. We found Fergal and Araf with a bunch of others sitting on a horizontal black pawn. Essa released my hand and launched herself at Araf, who caught her and returned the hug. It was the first time in my life I wished I was an Imp.

'Why didn't you tell me you were coming?' she said.

Araf shrugged.

'And you must be Fergal. Araf has told me so much about you.'

I couldn't help wondering when Araf did all this talking. A servant brought us fresh mugs of wine. Fergal looked as if he'd had plenty already. Essa whispered into the servant's ear.

'Your father throws a hell of a party,' Fergal slurred.

'He does, doesn't he? Here's to Dad!' Essa said, raising her mug in a toast.

'Your father is Gerard?' I asked.

'The one and only.'

'Well, I'll drink to that.'

The waiter returned, carrying two banta sticks that he handed to Essa. She took both sticks and threw one to Araf. The assembled crowd *oohed* at the challenge. Araf caught the stick but didn't look interested. Another servant arrived with headgear and protective clothing. Essa put on leather gloves, a heavy leather jacket that almost came down to her knees and a protective headpiece – a white helmet with a thin gold wire mesh covering the face.

Despite the heckling of the crowd, Araf refused to stand up. Fergal came up behind him and put a helmet on his head – but still he sat there.

'I, Essa of Muhn, challenge you, Araf of Ur, to single banta combat.'

She struck a stance similar to an *en garde* position in fencing – right foot forward with knees bent. She looked magnificent. In her right hand she held the banta in the middle. The weapon had a knot of wood at one end which she pointed directly at Araf. If this was a proper and formal challenge, Araf showed no sign of partaking. He just sat there.

A smile crossed Essa's face. She spun the banta in her hand like a baton twirler and in a flash covered the distance between her and Araf. She brought the smaller end of her stick down on his head and then bounced backwards, retaking her defensive stance – her stick across her chest with the left hand stretched forward for balance. I had never seen anything so graceful. She obviously knew what she was doing.

The audience loved it. The group erupted when the thud came from Araf's helmet. Someone shouted, 'One to Essa.'

Essa waited in her defensive pose but it was unnecessary. Araf wasn't playing. He sat there like an old dog ignoring a rambunctious puppy. This didn't seem to bother her. She launched herself into a spinning, swirling attack that hit Araf on the right shoulder. If it hurt, and it sure looked like it did, Araf didn't show it. The crowd, that was getting larger by the minute, howled with delight.

'Two to nought for Essa!' Fergal shouted.

'How high does the score go?'

'Essa challenged him to a formal match,' Fergal said. 'Each landed blow is one point and a knock-down is five. The first to eleven is the winner.'

Essa attacked again. This attack was a mirror image of the previous one. This time she landed her stick on Araf's left shoulder.

'Well, it looks like Araf is going to lose this one,' I said.

'I don't think so,' Fergal said.

John Lenahan

'Why not?'

'Because he never has.'

'Never has what?'

'He has never lost. Araf is the undefeated banta fighting champion of all of The Land.'

'Well, at the moment,' I said, 'Essa looks pretty good.'

Fergal smiled. 'Keep watching.'

Essa backed away and then launched into a new and bolder attack. She came at Araf and then leaped over his head! I once saw a deer on a country road jump over a tall fence – Essa had the same majestic poise. In mid-air she connected with two blows on the side of Araf's helmet and landed behind him with two more points under her belt. The crowd applauded. Araf didn't even turn around.

Essa walked around Araf and stood directly in front of him. She crouched down and looked into his eyes and smiled. There might have been a flicker of a smile from Araf in reply. With the big end of her stick she tapped Araf's faceplate. The wire mesh glowed for a second. There was obviously some magic protecting the face. The entire audience shouted, 'FIVE.' She tapped again. 'SIX,' again, 'SEVEN, EIGHT, NINE.'

On the blow that should have been 'TEN', Araf moved his head quickly to the left, Essa was thrown off balance and Araf poked his stick between her feet and tripped her. She went down fast. The audience booed but in good humour. Essa had been cocky – she had that coming. She rolled quickly to her feet. Araf slowly stood.

Now things were getting interesting. The crowd was buzzing. Essa backed away and the partygoers gave them room. A giant people-edged arena formed, with everyone watching. Essa backed into the middle of the room and retook her defensive posture. Araf walked towards her and stopped two stick-lengths away and bowed. Even though the score was nine-to-five, he was indicating that *now*, the duel had truly begun. Essa nodded in reply.

Araf took a stance. Not the graceful Tai Chi-like posture of Essa, but a flat-footed straight-on stance. He held his banta across his chest with both hands, like the staff fights in old Robin Hood movies. This was a battle between style and brawn.

Essa mounted a twirling attack to the head. Araf parried it and brought the bottom end of his stick up for a counter-attack. Essa spun and dodged it – just. The two of them were feeling each other out. Essa tried a lower attack but this failed. Araf's parry was so strong that she momentarily lost her balance, allowing Araf to get her with a counterblow to her side that made me wince.

'SIX,' came a cry from the crowd.

The combatants stared at each other for a minute and then Araf initiated his first offensive attack. For a big guy, he moved fast. There was no twirling or pirouettes, just a direct attack – wide, quick, sweeping blows from alternating sides. Essa had no difficulty with the speed but she didn't have the strength to block the blows without a step backwards. She gave ground with every parry and was running out of room. I expected her to start swinging around in a circle but she continued straight back, each block pushing her closer into a corner. Just when I thought it was all over for her, she bent her knees and dived, head first over Araf's head! With the poise of an Olympic high diver, she jumped Araf's banta stick and then planted her own stick on top of Araf's shoulder, pole-vaulting and somersaulting behind him.

The crowd went wild. 'TEN,' they screamed in unison.

Six to ten – if Essa could land one more blow, she would win. I heard someone yell, 'Who is the student and who is the master now?'

So that was it, Essa had studied under Araf. This was a student–teacher grudge match. The light-heartedness that marked the beginning of the duel was gone. Araf clumped into his stance – Essa flowed into hers. We waited to see who would initiate the next attack. The only sound was Essa's breathing.

Araf broke the calm. With an unexpected twirl of his banta stick he came at Essa with a series of angled-down swings that blurred into a continuous figure of eight. It looked as if Essa had just stepped in front of a taxiing airplane. I could see in her eyes that the master had not taught the student everything. Initially she didn't even try to parry. She backed away, attempting to decipher the rhythm of the attack. Before she ran out of space, she experimented with parries that succeeded in slowing down the attack – but only a bit. For a second time she tried her flipping pole-vaulting manoeuvre – she should never have attempted it twice. Araf dodged her stick, turned and made contact with her calf in mid-air. She landed on one foot, not enough to keep her balance. She hit the floor skidding. The only thing hurt was her pride. A five-point knockdown – she had lost.

Araf helped her to her feet, then stood in front of her and formally bowed – Essa hit him over the head with her stick. The crowd erupted in laughter. The fighters took off their masks and Essa planted a huge kiss on Araf's cheek. For the second time today I wished I was an Imp.

Essa hung on Araf's arm as they returned. Fergal added his slap to all of the others that Araf had received on his back as he travelled through the crowd.

'Thank you for upholding the honour of the House of Ur,' Fergal slurred. He was past tipsy and well nigh on to very drunk.

'That was very impressive,' I said to Essa.

'I would have been more impressive if I had won.'

'I was rooting for you.'

She smiled. It was very nice.

'You should have a fight, Conor,' Fergal said as he stumbled into me. 'You would kick ass around here with that snap spell you are wearing.'

'You are *wearing* a snap spell?' someone said behind me.

I turned to answer when out of the corner of my eye I saw Fergal grab Essa's banta stick.

'It's an amazing spell – watch this!' he said as he swung. I remember the look of surprise on everyone's faces as the stick hit my skull. Then everything went black.

The first thing I remember thinking as I came to was, *Is this my third concussion this week or my fourth?* In my whole life, I had never even been dizzy – now it seemed I couldn't go a day without being knocked cold. I was disappointed that you don't actually see stars and tweeting birds, like in cartoons, but I can assure you that you get great big bumps.

I felt a cold compress being applied to my forehead, and when I opened my eyes I saw that my nurse was Essa.

'I've died, haven't I?' I said.

'I don't think so.' She looked worried.

'No, I must be dead because you're an angel.' OK, it was a bit corny but I was quite proud of coming up with a line that good so soon after multiple concussions.

'I think you must be feeling better,' she said, and took the cold compress off my forehead.

I sat up. I had a pain in my head that I hadn't experienced since my last blow to the head – earlier that day I think. I winced.

'You wouldn't have any of that willow tea around, would you?'

'Here, drink this.' She handed me a tiny glass with no more than two thimblefuls of brown liquid.

'Is that all I get?'

'Believe me, that is all you need. It's my father's special tonic. It will make you feel better.'

I downed it in one. Had I been facing a mirror, I would have seen steam shooting out of my ears. I sat bolt upright in bed and croaked, 'WOW!'

Essa laughed. 'You'll be better now,' and stood to go.

I was instantly better but I didn't want to let her go. I grabbed the wet cloth and put it in her hand. 'Don't go, I think I'm going to faint,' I said, trying to look as ill as I could and lying back down on the bed.

'What makes me think that you are not being sincere?' She smiled.

'Oh, the pain!' I said and I pulled her hand, to make her place the cloth on my forehead. She lost her balance and pretty much fell on top of me. She laughed a little bit and didn't immediately get up. Her face was only inches away, her lips were so close I could feel her breath. I stared straight into her eyes, those magnificent dark eyes and then... her father came in.

Essa sat bolt upright. I think she moved even faster than she did during her banta fight with Araf. 'I think he is feeling better, Father.'

I sat up.

'That, I can see. Leave us, daughter, will you.'

Essa gave me a glance. She looked worried, and to be honest I didn't like Gerard's tone either.

Before she left Gerard said, 'May I borrow your pendant for a little while?'

This seemed to shock her. She removed a finger-sized crystal that was hanging from a plain gold chain around her neck and handed it to her father. She gave me one last apprehensive look and left.

Gerard took a step closer to the bed, drew a sword and pointed it an inch from my throat.

'Honest, sir,' I said, 'I didn't even kiss her.'

Chapter Ten
Gerard

'Do you recognise the sword at your throat?' Gerard asked. With extreme effort I released my attention from the point and glanced down the mirror-like blade to the pommel. 'It's mine.'

Gerard held Essa's necklace in his left hand. The crystal that hung from it was embedded with flecks of gold. 'This is an Owith glass,' he said, 'it will darken if you lie. If I were you, I would tell the truth. Did you steal this sword?'

Now that was a tricky question. I sort of stole it from Cialtie, but Dad said it was his. 'My father gave it to me.'

The crystal flickered but remained clear.

'Is Conor your real name?'

'No,' I said, just to see what would happen.

Essa's necklace instantly went dark. This truth crystal was the real thing. I felt the point of my blade at my throat.

'I suggest you try that again. Is Conor your real name?'

'Yes.'

'And who is your father?'

'I can't tell you that.'

'Why not?'

'Because you will kill me if I do.'

'Well then, Conor, you have a dilemma, because I'm going to kill you if you don't.'

'What do you have against me?'

'This blade, that you casually checked in at my door, is the Sword of Duir. Did you know that?'

'Yes,' I said. The crystal remained clear.

'The only way you could possess this blade, is if you stole it. I am a very tolerant man, but I cannot abide a thief.'

'I told you, my father gave it to me.'

'The crystal bears you out – so the thief must be your father.'

I felt my anger rise. 'My father is no thief – the sword was his to give.'

'Are you claming to be the son of Cialtie?'

'Cialtie?' I spat, and before I could stop myself, 'I am the son of Oisin of Duir.'

Gerard looked at the crystal and stepped back. 'Stand up,' he ordered.

I did as I was told. I wasn't as shaky on my feet as I should have been. That little drink had really done its stuff.

Gerard kept the sword pointed to my chest and looked at me as if anew. How could I have been so stupid? I just blurted out who I was and now he was going to do his duty and kill me.

'My gods! You *are* of Duir,' he roared. 'I don't know how I missed it before. Oisin's son – you are Oisin's son!' He raised the sword and came at me, fast.

There was nowhere to run, I was finished. I placed my hands in front of my chest and closed my eyes.

He wrapped his huge arms around me and gave me a hug that would have put an anaconda to shame. 'Oisin has a son!' He laughed – a hearty laugh that shook the room. He put both hands on my shoulders and looked at me from arm's length.

I opened one eye. 'Don't you want to kill me?'

'Why in The Land would I want to do that?'

'Everyone else around here does – the son of the one-handed prince thing.'

'Oh my, that *is* an old prophecy – one of Ona's, is it not?'

I nodded.

Gerard laughed. 'I can't tell you how many times some sorceress told me that my next harvest would fail or be the finest vintage – bah! I don't have much faith in soothsayers. The good ones (like Ona, may she rest in piece) don't lie – but that doesn't mean that what they say is the truth. Anyway, it takes an awful lot for me to kill someone, and I'm certainly not going to kill a young man as fine as you because of something an old witch said thousands of years ago. Oisin's son!' He hugged me again, this time lifting me off the ground.

'Tell me, Conor, where have you been hiding all of these years?'

I wondered for a second if I should make something up, but I just couldn't help trusting this man. I sat down on the bed and told Gerard the whole tale – it just poured out. Gerard pulled up a chair and I went through it all: my life in the Real World, the death threats, the revelations, the emotions, the journeys, the fights, the meetings – the concussions. I wasn't only telling Gerard, I was telling myself too. I had been living moment to moment, just trying to stay alive. Now that I had put it all together I realised it was a hell of a story. I ended by saying, 'So I have to find my mother. I think she is in a place called the Fililands, but Fergal says they don't exist. Can you help me?'

'Oisin and Deirdre have a son,' Gerard mused. 'This,' he said, breaking out of his reverie, 'is the finest news I have heard in a long, long time. Are you thirsty, Conor?'

'You wouldn't have a beer, would you?'

Gerard roared with laughter at this. 'In all of The Land I am the only man who could answer that question with a "yes".' He put his arm around me and waltzed me out of the room. We walked down a corridor that overlooked the courtyard. Through imperfect glass windows I could see another banta fight in progress. The party was still in full swing. At the top of an immense staircase Gerard bellowed, and several servants appeared.

'Bring ale and food to the library,' he ordered. 'After that, we are not to be disturbed.'

We continued and then turned down a corridor with numerous small alcoves cut into the walls. In each was a carved wooden statue. Some were model castles, some were miniature thrones, most were busts of men and women. All were of different wood. Gerard stopped at a bust of a handsome man with a full beard carved in red wood.

'This is your grandfather.'

'Finn?' I asked.

'No. This is your other grandfather, on your mother's side, Liam – the last lord of the House of Cull. He was a good man.' Sadness invaded Gerard's face and for a moment he looked old. 'He was my friend.'

We arrived at the library at the same time as our food and drink. I was expecting an impressive chamber with bookshelves towering to the sky, but instead I found a smallish, comfortable room with just a few books, a wine rack, a desk, some overstuffed chairs and a deerskin sofa.

'I'm not much of a reader,' Gerard said, guessing my thoughts. 'If you wanted to see a great library you should have seen your grandfather's. It was a huge affair with a courtyard in the centre where he grew the Tree of Knowledge.'

'The Tree of Knowledge?' I asked.

'Yes – I told you. He held the Rune of Cull.'

I must have looked confused.

'Oh gods, I forget you don't know about all of this. Right, Liam, your grandfather, was Lord of the Cull – the Hazellands. He sat in the Hazelwood Throne and was the custodian of the Hall of Knowledge. The best and the brightest from all The Land were welcome to study in his library, and before they left, they were allowed a hazelnut from the Tree of Knowledge. The fruit of the Tree of Knowledge ensured they would remember all that they had learned. It was a wonderful place.'

'You talk like it's no longer there.'

'It's not,' he said, the heaviness returning to his face, 'it's all ruin. The Land lost the Hall, and I lost a friend – and my only son.'

'Your son?'

'My son was studying at the Hall, in fact he was one of your mother's tutors.'

'What happened?'

'No one knows. Something, an army or a force, attacked Cull, and there was little defence. It was unthinkable that anyone would want to attack the Hall of Knowledge. Why would you defend against the unthinkable? Your mother and your Aunt Nieve were on some sort of sorceress' quest. They were the ones who found the Hall and the Tree destroyed, and all of the students and tutors dead.'

'I'm sorry.'

'As am I, but I have learned not to dwell on it. Although I will always remember, my mourning days are done. I do not want it to consume me like it almost consumed your mother.'

'My mother?'

'Yes, until I spoke to you today I had not heard of her since her banishment. You see, it is believed that the need for vengeance drove her to learn Shadowmagic. I think she thought it would allow her to discover who, or what, destroyed Cull. From what you say, it would seem she still does not know. Maybe like me, she has put the matter to rest. I hope so.'

I took a sip of my beer. It was dark, a bit sudsy and too warm but it was drinkable. 'Not bad,' I said.

'Thank you. I learned how to make ale in Ireland but I have never gotten it to catch on over here.'

'Ireland? You mean like the Ireland from my world?'

'Yes, long ago. I made a trip to the Real World the year before my Choosing. I travelled with my cousin, Cullen.'

'Cullen? Cu-cullen,' I said, using the Celtic prefix that literally means hound but is used to mean hero or king, 'the Irish warrior?'

Gerard laughed so hard at that he spat out his beer. 'A warrior!' he howled. 'Where did you hear that?'

'Irish mythology is full of stories of the great warrior King Cucullen, his great battles and how he slew entire armies single-handedly – but this was thousands of years ago.'

Gerard was still chuckling. 'Yes, I guess that would be about right. I went to the Real World with Cullen but I didn't return with him. He just loved those Irish women and they loved him. You see, Cullen was a wonderful storyteller and like all good storytellers, he never let the truth get in the way of a good tale. Those Irish folks back then just couldn't get enough of his stories and his music. Gods, when he played the flute it was like a spell, he could make you dance one moment and weep the next. I can imagine him telling a few tall tales about himself.'

'Did he never return?'

'Oh, he did, but he was never happy here. He was a fool, always wanting more than he had – a good man but a fool nonetheless. He used to take little holidays to the Real World on horseback – he never returned from the last one.'

'What happened to him?'

'Probably the same thing that happened to the poor guard that came to your home with Nieve.'

'You think Cucullen fell off his horse and got old quick?'

'There were rumours that he forgot and got off by himself. He never was the sharpest arrow in the quiver.'

'So if your foot touches the ground in the Real World and you become the age you would be in The Land, then how come my father didn't dust-it? I get the impression that he has a few hundred years under his belt.'

'That is a question for him and your mother – as are most of the other questions I can almost hear flicking through your mind. Before I send you to bed, Conor of Duir, I shall answer one more question – it is the first question you asked of me. You asked if I could help you find the Fililands. The answer is yes. Many people think the Fililands are a myth, a story to scare children, but they are real. Long ago the Fililands were sealed off by your grandfather, Finn, but since then a new frontier has opened. I think you may be able to enter the Fililands through the Reedlands.'

'The Reedlands?'

'The Reedlands came into being when your Uncle Cialtie chose the Reed Rune.'

'I thought I heard Cialtie say he held the Duir Rune?'

'He does now. But his first rune was the Reed Rune. After your father and then your grandfather went missing, he repeated the Choosing and chose the Duir Rune. People thought it was strange but he does hold the rune now.'

'What happened to the Reedlands?'

'Cialtie explored them, renounced them and left them to fallow. They lie just past the Hazellands and I suspect they border the Fililands. If I am right, the border will not be sealed there. You should be able to enter the Fililands from the Reedlands.'

'Can you take me there?'

'Me?' Gerard laughed. 'Good gods! The last thing you need is me giving you directions. No, I know someone who could get you there. Sleep tonight and tomorrow I shall see if I can persuade my guide to accompany you.'

'Thank you, Lord Gerard.'

'No, thank you, Conor.'

'For what?'

'For being the son of Cull and Duir. For a long time I have feared for the future of both of those houses – less now.' We stood and he put his arm around my shoulder as we walked to the door.

'Did you really like the beer?' he asked.

'To be honest, sir, I would like it a little lighter and colder – oh, and fizzier.'

He opened the door. A servant was waiting. Gerard instructed him to escort me to the tower and to give me a shot of pocheen to help me sleep. As Gerard closed the door I heard him mumbling to himself, 'Lighter and fizzier – hmm.'

The tower turned out to be a very comfortable room with a bed big enough for a football team. It wasn't until I saw the sheets that I realised how exhausted I was – I wasn't going to need the pocheen. I undressed and got under the covers, and the servant put a small glass of clear liquid on the bedside table. Sleep was seconds away when I remembered something that Cialtie had said to my father. He said the last time he saw Finn he was on horseback on the way to the Real World and that he had stabbed the horse! He killed him, he killed his own father. He killed my grandfather. Rage enveloped me, my blood boiled and my thoughts turned to revenge. Sleep was no longer an option. I sat up in bed and fantasised about the different ways I would kill Cialtie. My hand shook as I grabbed the glass and thoughtlessly knocked back the pocheen. Instantly, Cialtie didn't seem like such a bad guy after all. I laid back and put my hands behind my head. I thought, *Why make such a fuss out of everything?* I started to count my blessings. I was asleep before I got very far.

I awoke to a slap in my face – considering the dream I was having, I deserved it. But this slap in the face wasn't from Essa in dreamland, it was real. I opened my eyes to see a fully dressed Fergal passed out next to me in the bed. He had rolled over and backhanded me in the face. I threw his arm over to his side, only to have it come back and whack me a second time. I made a mental note never to sleep with Fergal again and got out of bed.

A servant was waiting in the hallway. He showed me to a bathroom kitted out with a steaming Olympic-sized sunken bathtub. Ah, life's simple pleasures. I had a feeling I had better enjoy it while I could – the trip to the Fililands didn't sound like it was going to be a Sunday afternoon stroll.

When I got out of the bath I noticed that my clothes had been replaced with linen underwear and a soft leather shirt and trousers. Well – when in Rome.

Breakfast was busy. Obviously many of the partygoers had stayed the night, or more probably hadn't gone to bed at all. I saw Araf sitting with Essa, and joined them.

'Good morning,' I said.

Araf nodded.

Essa said, 'Good morning, sir.'

'Sir? What happened to Conor? *Sir* is my dad.'

'Good morning – Conor, I have to go now,' she said and left.

I turned to Araf. 'What was that about?'

He shrugged.

If I hadn't just taken a bath I would have sniffed my armpits – she acted like I had just cleaned out the elephant stables.

'Have I done something to upset her?'

Araf shrugged again.

'You know, you're a real pleasure to chat with, Araf – and by the way my head is fine. Thank you for asking.'

This got a nod.

We ate in silence. I had a billion questions but I knew trying to strike up a conversation with Araf would be like trying to build the pyramids on my own. I was almost finished when a servant informed me that I was wanted in the armoury.

I followed him to a different wing of the castle until we arrived at a gymnasium-sized, glass-roofed room. Hanging on racks around the chamber was an impressive collection of weapons: swords, bows, crossbows and an entire wall of banta sticks. In the centre of the room stood the same old man who had taken our weapons from us when we first arrived at the party. He was holding my sword belt. He motioned me over.

'You are Conor?'

'Yes,' I said.

'This is your sword?'

'Yes.'

'Put it on.'

I fastened it around my waist.

'So, Conor of Duir – son of the one-handed Prince Oisin – BE AT GUARD!' He drew his sword and assumed an attacking stance.

I raised my hands. 'Hey, I'm not going to fight you.'

'Pity,' he said, 'I so dislike stabbing an unarmed man. Oh well – so be it.'

He drove the point of his sword directly at my heart.

Chapter Eleven
The Dahy

I jumped to the left, just in time to stop myself from being pierced.
'Hey! Let's talk about this.'

'I'm not here to talk,' the old guy said. 'If I were you, I would draw
my sword, or duck.'

He came at me with a high backhanded cut to the head. Not only did
I duck, I hit the floor and rolled to my left. I quickly got back on my
feet in a crouch.

'The roll was good,' my attacker informed me, 'but the position is not.'

I took a quick glance around me and saw what he meant. I had boxed
myself into a corner.

'Since you like to talk so much,' the old man said, 'I will tell you one
more thing. I am going to come at you with a forehand mid-cut. It will
be too low to duck and too high to jump. The only defence is to draw
and parry, or run and bleed.'

I only took a microsecond to realise he was right. He cocked his
sword way back and then came at me with both blade and body. I drew
my sword, deflected the attack with a low parry and retreated to the
middle of the room.

Our chatting phase was obviously over. He instantly attacked me with a series of sweeping and powerful cuts, alternating high and low. I blocked and back-pedalled. To be honest, I was terrified. For as long as I could remember my father trained me in sword fighting, and I had also won a few local fencing tournaments, but this was the real thing. The swords were steel and the points were sharp. One sloppy parry and I was dead! Then my father's words came back to me – '*In a real sword fight, son, all thoughts of winning and losing must be suppressed. Keep one eye on his eyes and the other on his blade. Be aware of your surroundings, block and counter until your opponent tires.*'

I used to laugh at him when he said stuff like that. 'When will I ever be in a real sword fight,' I'd say, 'and for that matter, when were you ever in a real fight?' *I take it all back now, Pop – if I live through this.*

I forced my father's advice into my head and the fight attained a rhythm. In fact it became familiar. This old guy's forearm attack was very similar to my father's favourite assault. My father would start a major attack with a flurry of forearm cuts, then change into a reverse grip, like he was holding an ice pick, then follow through with an elbow to the chin. He called the move a Dahy Special. Sure enough, that's exactly what this guy did! I knew from experience that the sword in this manoeuvre was less dangerous than the elbow. I parried the sword hard, forcing his arm to straighten, and then ducked the elbow. I sent the old guy off balance and then started a counter-attack of my own. I came at him with a series of low cuts. I like swinging up – it's unsettling for an opponent. It leaves my face exposed, but I'm pretty good at bobbing and weaving. The sword felt good in my hand, like an extension of my arm. The old guy parried the cuts with grace, but I could see that I had him working. He parried my last cut and countered with a high downward thrust that caught me by surprise. By the time I blocked it, I was down on one knee. We locked swords – pommel to pommel. I racked my brain for a means of escaping – I knew that as soon as our swords disengaged I was very vulnerable. The sweat was streaming into my eyes and my arm was starting to shake. I couldn't keep this up for much longer.

'That's enough!' came a shout from the door.

The old man pulled back and Gerard entered the room. I dropped my guard, sat on my feet, and breathed a huge sigh of relief.

'How is he?' Gerard said.

'Not too bad,' the old guy said, 'his left side is weak but his footwork is good. Nothing that cannot be fixed.'

'Wait a minute,' I said, 'this was a test?'

'It was indeed,' Gerard said. 'I wanted to make sure if I was going to risk my best guide, that you could at least take care of yourself. Dahy here is my master-at-arms.'

'Dahy! You taught my father.'

'Yes, I did. And may I say, my student taught you well, but not well enough.' He addressed Gerard. 'In two days I can get him to a minimum preparedness.'

'Conor, you are under Dahy's tutelage now, so work hard. You shall leave for the Fililands in three days' time,' Gerard said, and left us alone.

'Now, Conor,' Dahy said, with a gleam in his eye that I wasn't sure I liked, 'we begin.'

The next two days were the hardest of my life. Dahy drilled me like an SAS sergeant gone berserk. We worked on swordplay, archery and banta stick fighting. My biggest difficulty was my left hand. I had always fought with my non-sword hand empty but Dahy taught me a method of using the sword in my right hand and a banta stick in my left. It made my head spin and my muscles scream. Luckily I found a supply of willow tea that helped me make it through the days, and some pocheen to help me through the nights.

At mealtimes, I met a handful of people who had still not gone home from the party. Discussions of politics were outlawed in the castle, but when Gerard was out of earshot I learned that my Uncle Cialtie was universally hated. It seemed that Castle Duir sat on The Land's only gold mine. My grandfather Finn used to allocate a stipend of gold to each of the lords. The gold was used to fuel necessary magic. As of late, Cialtie had refused gold to most of the families and cut back considerably to the rest. The question was – what was he was doing with all of that gold? No one seemed to know.

I only saw Essa twice. Once I caught her watching Dahy and me from the viewing box above the armoury. I looked up and smiled. Dahy hit me painfully in the shoulder with a stick, and by the time I looked back, she was gone. The second time was at lunch on my second day of training. I spotted her sitting at a table and sat down next to her. She immediately stood up to leave. I grabbed her wrist so I could talk to her – big mistake. The next thing I knew, I was face down in my lunch with my arm twisted painfully up my back and her forearm pushing my head into a bowl of salad.

'Don't ever grab me again,' she hissed in my ear.

'What is your major malfunction?' I spluttered.

She pulled my head back by the hair. 'What did you say?'

I wasn't sure if she hadn't understood the phrase, or if the face full of greens had screwed up my diction, so I rephrased. 'What have I done to make you act like this?'

She put her mouth close to my ear and whispered, 'I know who you are.'

'Who told?'

'My father.'

'Man, he's telling everybody.'

'Just me and Dahy.'

'So let me guess,' I said, wincing from the pressure that was still on my arm, 'unlike your father, you're a prophecy fan and you want me dead?'

'That's right.'

'Then go ahead.'

'My father has forbidden it.'

'Then let me go.'

She let go and walked away. I picked lettuce out of my nose with as much dignity as I could muster. 'Oh yeah,' I called after her, 'well, that tunic makes your bum look big.' It was a stupid thing to say. She didn't look back, but it did make her stop for a second before she continued off.

The afternoon light was disappearing on my second day of training when I received a message to meet with Gerard in his library.

Before I left, Dahy said, 'I have a gift for you.' He handed me a banta stick with copper bark and a pale knob.

'Do you recognise the wood?' he asked.

'I don't, it's too light for oak.'

'It is hazelwood. Light enough to be used for walking, but strong enough for a fight. It was given to me by your grandfather Liam. I want you to have it.'

I looked at the lacquered finish. It almost looked like the skin of a snake.

'Did you know him – my grandfather?'

'Yes, he was a good and wise man.' He chuckled to himself. 'He was also stubborn and careless. For ages I tried to get him to set up a garrison in the Hazellands, but he would not hear of it. "*The House of the Tree of Knowledge is a place of learning, not war,*" he would say. Well, I was right but there is no comfort in that.' He sighed. 'I know he would have wanted you to have the stick. Now go, Conor, Gerard is waiting.'

'Thank you, Master Dahy,' I said, and I bowed my lowest ever bow.

I was surprised to find Fergal and Araf sitting with Gerard in the library. I had not seen Fergal since he had woken me up with a backhand. I had seen Araf around, but as usual we didn't gossip much.

'Sit down, Conor,' Gerard said. I did and almost disappeared into an overstuffed chair. 'It seems that the fates have thrown you and Fergal together. Not only did you meet by chance on the road, but your future paths also seem to be linked. Fergal here would like to meet Deirdre too.'

'Why?' I said, a little shocked.

Gerard replied for him. 'Fergal's motivations are his own, as are yours. I know why both of you seek an audience with Deirdre, and I can assure each of you that the other's reasons are noble. If you wish to tell the other, that is up to you. For now, I need to ask you, Conor – will you accept Fergal as your travelling companion?'

It didn't take long for me to decide. 'As long as he promises not to stab me, or hit me with sticks, or steal my shoes, or sleep with me – then I'm fine.'

Fergal's smile matched my own. He stood up and then, seeing me struggle, helped me out of my chair. We shook on it with both hands and then he slapped me on the back.

'And you have to stop slapping me on the back.'

'OK,' he said, and then he did it again.

'Araf has agreed to accompany you.'

'As our guide?'

'No, Araf does not know the Eastlands. I am having difficulty procuring you the proper guide – but I will. You will leave the day after tomorrow.'

'How will we travel?' I asked.

'I will provide horses,' Gerard said.

'Oh – I can't ride.'

'What!' Fergal and Gerard said in unison.

'It's not my fault. They didn't have horses in… where I grew up.'

'Right,' Gerard said, 'you have a day to learn to ride. Araf, will you teach him?'

Araf nodded.

I looked at Araf. 'In order to teach me, you might actually have to speak, are you prepared for that?'

He gave me one of his hallmark blank stares.

'This calls for a special toast.' Gerard climbed the ladder to the top of his wine rack and found a bottle. He blew the dust off and placed it in a gold bucket. As he went to the cabinet to get glasses, the cork slowly rose out of the bottle by itself. He poured us each a glass of the blood-red wine.

'This is a very special vintage. I pressed these grapes when Essa's mother was pregnant with her. I have saved most of it for her wedding, but I steal a bottle now and again for special occasions.' Gerard raised his glass. 'To your success and a safe journey.'

We drank. Man, was it good. Even if Essa looked like Porky Pig I would have considered marrying her, just so I could have another glass of that wine. As things stood, she wouldn't even talk to me – so I guessed that marriage was a long shot.

That night I dreamt that Sally and Essa had a banta fight. They both kept looking at me – wanting me to root for one or the other. The problem was I couldn't decide who I wanted to win. It finally made both girls so mad, they stopped fighting each other and came at me…

I was shaken awake in the darkness. When my eyes adjusted I saw that it was Essa.

'I was just dreaming about you.'

'Get up,' she said. 'We have to go.'

'We? Go? Where?'

'We leave for the Fililands – now.'

'You are coming with us?'

'I'm your guide.'

'Cool, but I thought we were leaving tomorrow.'

'Change of plans,' Essa said. 'We leave now.'

'Why?'

'Because Cialtie and his Banshee witch are on the way. They will be here for breakfast.'

That popped me wide awake and out of bed. I threw on some clothes. 'Does he know I'm here?'

'I'll go and ask him, shall I?'

'Hey, unnecessary sarcasm. Are you going to be mean to me this entire trip?'

'We'll see.'

I grabbed my sword and hazel stick. 'Seriously, do you have any idea what Cialtie is doing here?'

'I think he is coming to see me,' Essa said.

'Why you?'

'Rumour has it, he is going to ask me to be his bride.'

'Yuck!' I said. 'We gotta get out of here.'

Chapter Twelve
Acorn

Araf and Fergal were waiting for us in the hallway. We followed Essa down a narrow stairway that was concealed behind a tapestry. With every step the smell of horses became stronger. A short passageway led to a bale of hay that we pushed aside, and we found ourselves in the stables.

Gerard and Dahy were almost finished saddling the horses. Let me tell you – the horses in The Land are just huge! I had no idea how I would even get up on one of those guys, let alone ride it. The thought terrified me.

Gerard bid Fergal and Araf goodbye and then gave me a hug so he could whisper in my ear. 'When you see your mother and father, tell them they are welcome here. Take care of yourself, son of Duir, and take care of my daughter.'

'Yes, sir, and thank you.'

Dahy presented me with a knife. 'It is a throwing dagger,' Dahy said. 'The gold tip assures that it hits its target. Only use it as a last resort. Remember, when you throw a weapon, your enemy can pick it up and throw it back. It's bad form to be killed by your own knife.'

That was Dahy's idea of a joke. I smiled, bowed and stashed the knife in my sock.

'OK,' I said, 'how do you get up onto one of these monsters?'

Essa broke off from her goodbye embrace with her father and said, 'You don't know how to ride? I don't believe it!'

'Maybe I should have a T-shirt with *I CAN'T RIDE* printed on it. That way it won't come as a shock to everyone that finds out around here.' Araf pointed to a horse to my left. 'Is this one mine?'

He nodded. I examined the magnificent stallion. He was light grey with a wild white mane. As I craned my head back I wondered if I would actually be able to make it *all* the way up to the saddle.

'Don't you have any ponies? I rode a pony once at a birthday party.'

Araf interlaced his fingers together to give me a step up. I put my foot in his cupped hands and he hoisted me up over his head. I had an inkling that Araf was strong but I didn't realise just how strong. He damn near threw me over the beast without the slightest hint of effort! I arrived on top of my horse and unceremoniously hung onto its neck until I got some semblance of cool.

'Does he have a name?'

'Acorn,' Gerard replied, and smiled at me. '*From a tiny acorn grows a mighty oak.* He belonged to my son. Acorn here wandered back from the Hazellands after it was destroyed. He is the only thing to have made it out of there alive.'

I patted the enormous neck in front of me. 'Well, Acorn, you and me are going to be pals – right?'

Acorn turned his head and gave me a look with a plum-sized black eye that I unmistakably read as – '*We'll see.*'

A servant appeared and informed us that Cialtie's entourage would be arriving at first light – in about half an hour. Gerard and Dahy pushed aside a wall of hay bales, revealing a back door.

'Do you have any advice on riding this thing?'

'Hold on,' Araf said, and started through the door.

Acorn seemed happy to follow the other horses, which was fine with me. I leaned down and whispered in his ear, 'You just follow those guys and we'll be OK.'

He gave me a snort, as if to say, '*Don't tell me my business.*'

Even though the doorway was massive, I still had to duck as I went through. My confidence level was low. I couldn't help thinking what a long drop it was going to be *when* I fell off this monster. The back exit of the stables led almost directly into a path cut through a field of towering grain. We didn't have to hurry – the vegetation hid us completely. Just when I thought this horse riding lark wasn't too bad, the horses broke into a trot. Never in my life have I ever been bounced around so much. I figured another ten minutes of this would ensure that I never had an heir.

'Is riding supposed to be this uncomfortable?' I asked Araf with a jiggling voice that came out higher than normal.

'Stand up in your stirrups every three gaits,' he said.

I did, and what a difference it made. I got into the rhythm of the strides and started feeling like a rider.

We rode silently in single file for about an hour. I was behind Fergal, Essa was in the lead and Araf brought up the rear. The sun was fully up when we cleared the field. We entered a vast open meadow dotted with two-hundred-foot spire-like poplar trees. The land was green and rolling, a vast emerald carpet scattered with massive poplar exclamation marks. Essa gave what I now know is a hand signal and all of the horses broke into a canter – including Acorn. I grabbed the reins for support and Acorn ground to a halt, pitching me over his head. I flew butt over noggin and landed on the grass – still holding the reins. Luckily the grass was as soft as a gymnastics mat and I hurt nothing. It was probably the first time that I learned a lesson in The Land without pain. An upside-down Acorn gave me a look of pity. The company turned around and rode back.

'Don't say anything, Araf,' I said, 'let me guess. If you pull the reins the horse stops, right?'

'Everyone knows that!' Fergal said.

'Including me – now,' I said, slowly standing.

After two tries at remounting Acorn I said, 'Why don't these things come with ladders?'

Araf dismounted and helped me up. Essa warned me this time and we all broke into a canter. Compared to trotting, cantering is a breeze. My back and arms fell into rhythm with Acorn. I was so delighted with myself I let out a '*YEE-HA!*' I think a few trees gave me a dirty look. Fergal wanted to know why I shouted. I told him that it was the kind of thing that cowboys did.

'Are they boys that look like cows or cows that look like boys?' he asked.

'Never mind, just try it – it feels good.'

He let out a pretty good '*YEE-HA!*' for a beginner.

Essa pulled up next to us. 'If you insist on letting the entire land know where you are, I'll be leaving now.'

Fergal and I looked at each other like naughty schoolboys. When she was out of earshot we both let loose with a very quiet '*yee-ha*' in defiance.

The sun was low in the sky by the time Essa decided to stop. 'We'll make camp here,' she said. 'Araf and I will double-check the maps and get some food ready. Fergal, you tend the horses. Conor, go *ask* for firewood.'

Everyone dismounted except me. 'I can't move,' I said.

Fergal laughed and Essa told me to stop acting the fool, but I really couldn't move. I hurt in places I didn't even know I had places. We had ridden *all* day. I was exhausted. After the poplar meadow, all that I really remember of the ride was not stopping for lunch. We begged apples from a particularly unpleasant apple tree (a crab apple maybe) and ate them on horseback. Fergal complained all afternoon. I joined him, but after a while I was so tired, it was painful even to speak. The countryside was a blur after that.

I looked around to find that everyone had left. 'I'm not kidding,' I moaned, 'I really can't get off of this thing.' I flopped forward and dropped my arms around Acorn's neck. 'You wouldn't do me a favour by any chance,' I whispered in his ear, 'you wouldn't mind crouching down so I could roll off?'

It was meant to be a joke but Acorn did just that! He dropped to his front knees, then his back and then laid his belly on the ground. My stirrups almost touched the ground. With a monumental effort, I hoisted my leg over and flopped face first in the grass. I lifted my head and looked at my new best friend. 'Thank you, Acorn. I owe you one.' He stood up and went to find his fellow horses.

My legs were killing me. All of the hairs on the inside of my thighs had been rubbed out of my skin, which was turning the colour of a Caribbean sunset. After taking my trousers down for a look, I didn't have the strength to pull them back on. I flopped on my back and instantly fell into a dreamless sleep. It was in this unseemly position that the rest of the group found me – asleep on my back with my trousers at my ankles. Fergal told me later that he tried to wake me up but I just babbled. I didn't open my eyes until it was dark and the smell of food hit me.

Dinner was beans around a fire. Essa ate, then walked off by herself. Araf handed me a cup of much-needed willow tea. 'If I could get some of this tea back to the Real World,' I said, 'I could make a fortune.'

'The Real World?' Fergal said. 'You're from the Real World?'

Me and my big mouth. 'Yes, I am.'

'So that's why you say so many stupid things.'

'I don't say stupid things.'

'You do,' Fergal said, flashing a smile that seemed to light up the place. 'Is that why you want to see Deirdre, to help you get back?'

'That's part of it. I really can't tell you the rest – sorry.'

'That's OK. Can you tell me about the Real World? What's it like?'

'Some of it is like here, only not as vivid. Compared to The Land, the Real World seems to have a thin veil of grey over everything.'

'Sounds awful.'

'Sometimes it is – but it's my home, or at least was – and no one ever tried to kill me there.'

'I didn't try to kill you!' Fergal protested.

'I didn't mean you.'

'Who else has tried to kill you?'

'It's a long list.'

'Conor,' Araf said, and I jumped. The guy is so quiet, you forget that he is there. 'If you have enemies, your travelling companions should know about it.'

He had a point. 'OK, two people have tried to kill me – Cialtie and Nieve.'

'Cialtie and Nieve,' Araf repeated, 'this is not good. Why do they want to kill you?'

I searched for a lie to keep them happy but couldn't do it – I had to trust these guys. I just hoped they weren't big prophecy fans. 'Because Deirdre is my mother.'

110

For the first time, probably in history, Araf looked startled. 'Who is your father?'

Before I could answer we heard the whinny of horses and a cry for help – it was Essa. I grabbed my stick and leaped to my feet. We found her with her banta stick drawn, standing between the horses and four wild boars. I had never seen a live boar before but I am certain that the ones in the Real World are nowhere near as big as these boys. They had Essa surrounded and looked mean. I was shocked to see Fergal and Araf walk up to them like they were puppies. One turned and charged at Fergal, four hundred pounds of flesh pushing two enormous tusks, hurtling towards him, and he just stood there, like a rabbit caught in headlights. I dived and pushed him out of the way, almost getting clobbered myself.

'What is the matter with you?' I screamed as we both clambered to our feet.

'What's the matter with me? What's the matter with the boar?'

We circled over to Essa.

'I have never seen anything like this,' she said. 'Something is very wrong with these animals.'

'What do you normally do when a boar attacks?' I whispered.

'Boars don't usually attack,' she said. 'This is a very bad sign.'

'Shoo!' Araf said, waving his hands and walking towards the biggest one of them. 'Go home!'

I was a bit jealous that Araf was having a longer conversation with this pig than he had ever had with me. Suddenly the boar charged him. Amazingly Araf stood his ground and with the reflexes of a cat, grabbed the boar's tusks and twisted. The two of them rolled once and came up on their feet. Araf skidded backwards then found footing on a tree root and held fast. I have never seen such a display of strength.

As I marvelled, the boar that had attacked Fergal charged back for a second shot at him. Fergal legged it into the night. I would have helped him but the remaining two animals simultaneously came at Essa and me. Now I understood why Fergal had frozen. Forget horror movies, if you really want a fright that will soil your trousers, then stand in front of a charging boar. It's amazing how fast your mind can work when you are about to be gored. The first thing I hoped was that I was somehow related to the charging swine, then I remembered an old history lesson that mentioned how people in medieval Europe used to hunt boar. They would plant the end of a sharp stick in the ground and wait for the animal to charge. If they got it right, the boar impaled itself – if not, the hunter was the one that got run through.

This animal was almost on me. I dropped to one knee, planted the base of my stick in the ground, aimed the knob of my staff just below the neck and ducked my head. I got lucky. If I hadn't hit directly in the centre of its chest the stick would have glanced off and I would be singing soprano in the boys' choir. Amazingly my aim was true and that sucker was actually launched over my head! Its back hoof clipped me on the forehead as it went over, but other than that I was unharmed. My hazel stick bent but it held and pole-vaulted a very surprised creature sideways into a tree. It ran off, squealing into the night like a frightened piglet.

I didn't have time to gloat – Essa was in trouble. She had lost her stick and was down on her side, and her attacker was preparing for a killer charge. There was no way I was going to cover the distance between us in time to help. I reached into my sock and threw Dahy's dagger just as the boar began to move. I swear that knife swerved with the movement of the animal and stabbed it in the neck – right up to the hilt. It literally stopped it dead.

Essa had been winded by her own staff as she tried to block the first charge, but she hadn't been gored. Araf's opponent just gave up and ran away – smart animal. Fergal returned with a flaming branch from the fire that he had used to frighten his pursuer away.

Essa got slowly to her feet and looked at the dead animal. 'You shouldn't have killed it,' she said.

'Excuse me, didn't you mean to say, "*Thank you, Conor, for saving my life*"?'

'We don't kill animals in The Land without their permission.'

'I didn't see the boar asking you if you wanted to be turned into a pegboard!'

'Nevertheless, you shouldn't have killed it.' She placed her hands on the dead hulk and mumbled a prayer.

'I can't believe this. I thought you might at least be grateful enough to maybe not want me dead.'

'She wants you dead too?' Fergal said. 'What is going on?'

It was moment of truth time.

'My father is Oisin – OK?'

'You are the son of the one-handed prince?' Araf said.

'Yes, I am.'

Araf raised his banta stick and came at me.

Chapter Thirteen
The Hazellands

This was an attack I was not going to survive. I had seen Araf's banta stick prowess and I had seen his strength and agility with the boar – plus I was unarmed. I dropped to my knees and covered my head. I felt the swish of his lead-filled stick as it travelled close to my head, and then I heard a crack and a squeal of a boar behind me. I opened my eyes, without taking my hands off my head, looked around and saw an unconscious boar.

'Good one, Araf!' Fergal yelled. 'I didn't even see him coming.'

'This is a bad sign,' Essa said. 'The Pookas need to be informed of this.'

'Pookas?'

'Pookas are the animal tenders in The Land. They are having a hard time at the moment. Cialtie has stopped their gold allowance completely. They must have abandoned the Eastlands. We should get back to the fire.'

'So, none of you is going to kill me?' I called after them, still on my knees with my arms covering my head.

'Not me,' Fergal said.

'Maybe later,' Essa said.

'How about you, Araf?' I asked, standing.

'I'm just a farmer,' he said. 'I don't kill people.'

After the animal attack Essa decided we should keep a guard. My trouser-less sleep, the boar fight and a near-death experience had left me wide awake. I volunteered to take first watch.

My three companions went out like cheap light bulbs. I was relieved to see that that I wasn't the only one who was tired after a long day of riding. I threw a piece of wood on the fire and softly said, '*Thank you*,' to whichever tree gave it to us. It was the first time in The Land that I had been outside at night and not been unconscious. I studied the stars. It unnerved me to see a night sky so unfamiliar. The air above me was packed with stars that seemed close enough to throw a rock at. There was no moon but the night didn't need one – the starlight cast a shadowless glow on everything that made the forest seem incandescent. Other than Fergal's flopping in his sleep, all was perfectly still.

It was nice to be out of the closet – so to speak. I'm not a very good liar and it felt right to be honest – I liked these people. OK, it would be nice if Fergal talked less and Araf talked more – but those were not big problems. I really liked Fergal. Underneath the laddish exterior I knew he had heart. Araf, on the other hand, was a tough nut to crack. I was beginning to realise that although he was the most taciturn man I had ever met, when he did say something, it was important. I had no problem placing my life in their hands.

Essa was my real dilemma. She was just the most wonderful girl I had ever met, but she was so hostile. If she had been like this when I first met her, I don't think it would have bothered me so much. A beautiful woman who turns out to be a jerk, loses her beauty in my eyes, but Essa and I got along great at first. These days I flinched every time she scratched her nose. I watched the firelight dance on her face. No matter how cold she had been to me lately, I couldn't help thinking how lovely she was. I don't think I fell asleep looking at her but I kind of got hypnotised. I let the fire get low and didn't snap out of it until Essa shot open her eyes.

'What are you looking at?'

'I was just thinking how nice you are – when you're asleep.'

'You have almost let the fire out. Did you close your eyes?'

'No. But I will now. It's your watch.' I put my head down. It stung where the boar hoof had clipped my forehead, and I winced.

Essa picked up a twig, set fire to the end and brought it towards my face for light. 'Let me clean that wound for you, it looks nasty.'

'No thanks,' I said, 'I prefer not to be nursed by people who want me dead.'

I rolled over but sleep wouldn't come. She was trying to be nice and I was mad at myself for being stubborn. I stewed over how I could have dealt with that better. Soon the stillness of the night and the crackle of the fire lulled me. Then I heard it. It might have been a dream but I don't think so – just before I fell asleep I could have sworn I hear Essa whisper, 'Thank you, Conor, for saving me from the boar.'

I awoke to the smell of bacon. *Ah, it was all a dream,* I thought to myself, *I'm back home in my bedroom and Dad is cooking me breakfast,* but instead of a face full of cotton I opened my eyes to a face full of grass. Araf had butchered the boar I had killed and was cooking ham steaks over the fire. Essa was not to be seen and Fergal was still asleep.

'Good morning,' I said, not expecting an answer and not getting one. I stood up and went over to Fergal and shook him on the shoulder to wake him. His Banshee blade popped out of his sleeve and stabbed the air in the exact place where my nose had been seconds before. I jumped back and grabbed my banta stick.

'For crying out loud!' I screamed. 'You almost killed me with that thing.'

'What are you talking about?' Fergal said as he got up. Then he saw his blade was out. He cocked his wrist quickly and it disappeared up his sleeve. 'I did it again, didn't I?'

Araf nodded.

'That's it!' I said. 'From now on I wake you with a stick too.'

Essa returned. 'What is all the noise?'

'You have heard of sleepwalking? Well, Fergal was sleep-stabbing.'

'What?'

'Never mind. Just be careful if you have to wake him up.'

We broke camp. I washed the dried blood off my head wound. It hurt like hell. I should have let Essa do it last night. I climbed into Acorn's saddle unaided. I was quite proud of myself, even if no one seemed to notice. The inside of my legs howled in protest at the prospect of another day on horseback but it didn't hurt as much as I expected.

The landscape was green and rolling, sprinkled with the odd tree here and there. The day was warm and pleasant. The Land was in the height of summer. It made me wonder how spectacular the autumn must be.

Since it seemed we weren't being followed, we rode in pairs and talked freely. Essa had lightened up – a bit. She told me we were not taking the most direct route to the Reedlands, so as to avoid castles and villages.

We would be travelling all day in the Eastlands – the so-called No-rune Lands – and tonight we would camp on the edge of the Hazellands.

'The Hazellands?' I said. 'You mean my mother's home?'

'Yes. The shortest path is through Castle Cull.'

'Castle Cull? You mean the Hall of Knowledge?'

'Yes.'

'Wasn't it destroyed?'

'It was, my father told me to avoid it, but I want to see…'

'Where your brother died.'

Her head snapped around and she had a fierce look in her eyes. 'How do you know that?'

'Your father told me. I'm sorry – it must be awful to lose a brother.'

Her face softened. 'He left to study at Cull when I was very young. He sent me a letter every week telling me all the gossip from the Hall of Knowledge. I so desperately wanted to study there when I grew up. He used to write quite a bit about your mother, he was very fond of her.'

'Does anyone know what happened?'

'No. Your grandfather Finn called a meeting of the Runelords. Ona was going to try to find out who (or what) destroyed Cull, but the night before the runecasting she died in her sleep.'

'My father accused Cialtie of killing Ona.'

'What did Cialtie say?'

'He didn't deny it.'

'The more I hear about this uncle of yours – the less I like him.'

'Well, I certainly took an instant dislike to him.'

'I'll leave it up to you, Conor, should we go to the Hall of Knowledge and see for ourselves?'

'I think we should.'

She smiled. A weak smile, but a smile nonetheless, the first one I had seen on her face since the party.

Fergal yelled, 'Cherries!' and broke into a gallop.

Araf and Essa kicked into a gallop and Acorn followed suit, and I almost fell off his back. Once I got used to the terrifying speed I found that galloping was the smoothest ride of all. Acorn seemed to almost float in the air as I pumped my arms in rhythm to his bouncing head. Ahead, the others had stopped in front of an orchard of cherry trees. Acorn stopped next to them and I nearly went over his head again. (The riding part, I was getting good at – it was the stopping, turning and starting I was having trouble with.) Fergal reached up, picked a fruit and popped it in his mouth.

'You didn't ask permission,' I said.

'You don't have to with cherries,' Fergal mumbled, and then spat out a pip. 'Cherries are the friendliest trees in The Land. They love getting picked. It's like you are doing them a favour.'

As we walked our horses through the grove, the trees lowered their branches to us, and we picked and ate to our hearts' content. Some trees even dropped cherries on me. They were delicious. Araf filled his hat and I stuffed as many in my saddlebag as I could fit. The feeling of welcome among these trees was overwhelming, and when we left I could sense that they wanted us to take even more.

That night around the campfire Fergal told me why he wanted to see Deirdre. 'I want to find out who I am,' he said. 'I was raised by a woman called Breithe – she was Araf's nanny. As you can see I am not an Imp. Breithe knew who my real parents were, she promised to tell me all when I reached Rune-age. She died before she could tell me.'

'How did she die?'

'She went out foraging for mushrooms and ate a poisonous one. A lifetime of mushroom picking – I can't imagine how she could have made such a mistake. She was a good woman.'

'I'm sorry for you both,' I said.

Araf nodded.

'So that is why I want to see Deirdre,' Fergal concluded. 'I hope she can use her magic to tell me who I am and where I came from.'

'I hope so too,' I said.

Essa took the first watch. I was asleep the moment my head hit the ground.

I dreamt I was in a rainstorm but it wasn't raining water, it was raining cherries. I put my arms out to my side and lent my head back and caught cherry after cherry in my mouth. I looked and saw Fergal doing the same. Scores of cherries were pouring into his mouth, and as he tried to chew them the dark red juice poured out of his mouth. I awoke with that image in my eyes.

Essa woke me – it was my watch. She had just closed her eyes when I saw a light approach. It was erratic, like someone running with a candle. As it got closer I saw that no one was holding it; an incredibly bright light just floated in the air and it was coming directly for us. I shook Essa and pointed.

She sat up alert and then laughed. 'Conor, haven't you ever seen a firefly before?'

'Not like that. That's a flying sixty-watt light bulb.'

'I don't know what you are talking about but it's just a firefly. Look.'

She closed her eyes and whispered, '*Lampróg.*' It flew straight to her and lit her face.

'I used to do this when I was a little girl.' The firefly flew into her cupped hands, she whispered to it and it fluttered into her hair and sat there like a magic jewel.

'Good night, Conor.' She put her head down and closed her eyes. The firefly stayed in place and illuminated the side of her face.

'You must have been a lovely little girl,' I said.

She didn't open her eyes but she smiled and said, 'I was.'

The firefly stayed there until her breathing became regular and then flew off, I imagined, to find a proper little girl.

The next morning, we had travelled for less than an hour when we reached the border of the Hazellands. You could actually see it on the ground. One step was green and alive, the next was brown and dead. Acorn was hesitant to cross the line. We travelled in silence and saw nothing alive. I had seen drought-stricken land before, but this was worse – it was as if the life force of the place was gone and nothing had the will to survive.

Araf was in front. He crested a hill, stopped and dismounted. Actually to say he dismounted is being generous, he almost fell out of his saddle. He stared at the landscape ahead of him and dropped to his knees. I crested the hill and saw what he had seen. A huge field as far as the eye could see was blackened with ash and burnt crops.

'Oh my gods,' I heard from behind me. It was Fergal. 'Is that the Field?'

Araf nodded without looking up.

'What is so special about this field?' I asked.

'They studied everything at the Hall,' Fergal explained, 'even farming. This was a special garden where the Imp students would try new things. It was supposed to be beautiful. Araf lost a cousin here.'

I dismounted and put my hand on Araf's shoulder. 'Sorry,' I said. It didn't seem enough but he placed his hand on mine in thanks.

This was the true beginning of the desecration of the Hazellands. Before, everything was just dead; here as I got closer to the Hall, I could see the deliberate destruction. Hazel bushes were torched, and worst of all, we saw an apple tree cut down and left to rot. It made me feel ill. As the top of the Hall started to come into view, Acorn got very jittery. He sidestepped, whinnied and stopped unexpectedly. I got the impression that Acorn had memories of this place and they were not pleasant ones. I toyed with the idea of getting down and walking. I wish I had. Just as I crested a rise and received my first full view of the ruins of the Hall of Knowledge, we startled a flock of ravens. For hours the Hazellands had been completely lifeless, and this explosion of squawking and beating wings was too much for Acorn – he bolted.

I didn't think anything could be scarier than standing in front of a charging boar – I was wrong. Acorn was breaking all known horsey speed limits and I was powerless to stop or even influence the beast.

I was flying past some outbuildings of the Castle when I heard Fergal come up on my left yelling. Boy, we were moving fast. He reached over to grab my reins, but he didn't make it. He never saw what happened – I did. As we galloped between two burnt-out buildings, I saw a thick rope pop up and stretch across our path. It was too low to duck. I only had time to think, *This is going to hurt*. It did.

Chapter Fourteen
Lorcan

I awoke tied to a pillar inside a roofless ruin of a room. This waking up in bondage and pain was getting old real fast. Fergal was tied to the next pillar over. His chin was on his chest and his eyes were closed.

'Fergal,' I said in a loud whisper. He popped his head up.

'Conor! You're awake. Are you OK? What the hell happened?'

'I'm alright, at least as alright as I can be in this godforsaken place. The last thing I remember, we got clotheslined.'

'That explains why I hurt so much.'

'Hey, do you have your Banshee blade?'

'No, they must have taken it.'

'Where are the others?' I asked.

'I haven't seen them.'

'Have you seen anybody?'

'When I came to, some short guy was tying you up. He was a Leprechaun, I think.'

'A Leprechaun? You mean a little guy with a beard and a green suit?' I chuckled to myself and then started laughing.

'I don't think he was wearing green,' Fergal said. That only made me laugh louder. 'Conor, are you OK?'

I thought about this question for a moment, and all of the humour left me. 'No, I am not OK!' I spat. 'I had a perfectly good life. It may not have been exciting or important, but it was a good life. No one hit me, or made me ride horses, or knocked me off horses, or wanted me dead, or made me sleep outside at night or... or... ANYTHING! The only thing I had to do was homework – which I will never complain about again for as long as I live. Which is probably about five more minutes, because everybody wants me DEAD!' I was babbling now. 'HEY, WHY DON'T YOU JUST GET IN HERE AND FINISH ME OFF!' I screamed.

'Quiet, Conor.'

'Why? What difference does it make? It's not like they don't know we are in here – they tied us up, for God's sake. And who are *they* anyway? WHO ARE YOU? GET YOUR BUTTS IN HERE AND UNTIE ME!'

Well, whoever *they* were, it got their attention. A very short man with a beard came into view from behind me. It was disappointing that he didn't have a green outfit and a pointed hat, because if he did he would have been the spitting image of one of Snow White's dwarfs. He was followed by a bulkier guy who had to be an Imp.

'Is this the Leprechaun you told me about?' I asked Fergal.

He nodded yes.

'Hello, Mr Leprechaun,' I said. 'Top of the morning to you. For my first wish I'd like a chocolate sundae with a cherry on...'

'Silence!' the little beardy guy shouted.

'OK,' I said, 'how about I cut to my favourite wish – I'd like: me untied, you boiling in oil and don't forget to leave me that pot of gold.'

The Imp handed Beardy Guy my sword. 'Is this yours?'

'It looks like it's yours now. You know – finders keepers.'

He crouched close and placed the edge of the sword at my throat. 'I'll ask you again.' I could smell his breath and it wasn't pleasant. 'Where did you get this sword?'

I looked him in the eye and said, 'Do it. Cut my throat. Get it over with. I'm tired of being tied up and threatened. Just kill me and then – LEAVE ME ALONE!'

I actually scared him when I shouted. It made him jump up and back off. He turned to Fergal and pointed my sword at him. 'Who are you?'

'I am Fergal of Ur.'

'Ur! Well, what do you know,' he said sarcastically to the bigger guy, 'a fellow Imp.' He put the blade to his throat. 'Start speaking the truth, Banshee, or you won't be able to speak at all.'

'Leave him alone,' I said. I was just about to say it again, when I heard a voice behind me say the same thing.

'Leave him alone!'

I didn't recognise the voice right away because I actually hadn't heard it that much.

'Who are you?' the Leprechaun said. His question was answered by his Imp partner.

'Prince Araf!'

Sure enough it was Old Chatty himself. He strode in, followed by Essa and a horde of confused Imps.

'Untie my companions,' he demanded.

The Imp made a move to do just that but the Leprechaun stopped him.

'Hey, Leprechaun guy,' I said. 'Don't make Araf repeat himself, he's not fond of saying things the first time.'

Araf and Beardy stared at each other for a while. It was a struggle as fierce as any sword fight. At last Beardy gave in and nodded to his Imp, who untied us.

We stood and joined Araf and Essa. I whispered to Fergal, '*Prince* Araf?'

'Yeah, Araf is the heir to the throne of Ur. Didn't he tell you that?'

'He babbles on so, I guess I just missed it.'

I approached the Leprechaun. 'Can I have my sword back, please?'

He reluctantly handed it to me and said, 'I would still like to know who you are and where you got this.'

'The business of my companions,' Araf stated, 'is of no concern to you. What is of concern to *me*, is who you are and why so many of my kinsmen are here.'

The stare-down started again. Finally the Leprechaun said, 'Lord Araf, if I may speak with you alone?'

'Anything you wish to say, you may say in front of my comrades.'

This provoked another staring contest. At this rate we were going to be here all day. 'Very well. May I invite you all to join me in my headquarters for tea?'

Araf nodded.

'You wouldn't have any of that willow stuff, would you?' I asked.

It wasn't until I got outside that I realised where we were – in the ruins of the Hall of Knowledge. The first thing I saw was a lone standing wall with a beautiful yellow and blue stained-glass window in it. The window depicted a woman sitting in the middle of a willowy tree. Amid all of the destruction it was amazing that the glass had survived.

As we walked, Imps and Leprechauns peeked around corners tying to get a glimpse of the strangers. Beardy's headquarters had obviously once been part of the Great Library. Gerard had told me that the Library was a circular room surrounding a courtyard. What was left of it made my blood boil. I don't even like it when someone folds down the corner of a cheap paperback – here, heaped around the room, were towers of partly burnt books and piles of scorched manuscript pieces. The bookshelves that were still intact were blackened with soot. Who could do this to a library?

Essa spoke first. 'You are trying to save some of the manuscripts, I see.'

'That was not our intention,' Beardy said, 'but none of us could stand to see it like this, so I have delegated a handful of people to try to make as much order of the books as they can.'

'What is your intention here?' Araf asked.

Beardy straightened and thought for a moment. I recognised the look. I'm sure I had worn it quite a bit recently – it was the look of someone who was deciding whether to tell the truth or not.

'I am Lorcan.'

'Lorcan the Leprechaun?' I blurted out and laughed. Lorcan and the others gave me a dirty look and I instantly apologised.

'I am Lorcan, I was chief engineer in the mines of Duir. Three years ago I asked Lord Cialtie what he was doing with all of the gold, now that he had stopped the allowance to most of the Runelords. For an answer he imprisoned my wife in his tower and told me that the next time I had the audacity to ask questions, she would die. Over the next two years I smuggled gold out to the Runelords that had been cut off, and planned a rescue of my wife. I had not seen her for months, and when I finally gained access to the tower, she was not there. I learned that my wife had been killed a month before, defending a fellow prisoner. No one had told me.' He paused and then forced himself on. 'I knew that Cialtie would find out I had been there, so I escaped. Ever since I have been organising this secret fighting force. We call ourselves the Army of the Red Hand. Our goal is to dethrone Cialtie.'

'If your army is a secret one,' I said, 'then why are you telling us?'

'Out of respect for Prince Araf I will not lie to you, and also because you will not be allowed to leave here until we have mounted our attack.'

'What?' Araf shouted.

'I am sorry, my lord, this must be,' Lorcan said, as the room filled with scores of armed guards – none of them, I noticed, were Imps.

We drew our weapons but it didn't look good – even if we hacked our way out of this room there was an army outside.

'Put down your weapons,' Lorcan said, 'your detainment will not be long. Our attack begins soon.'

The way I looked at it, putting down weapons was a good idea. If these guys wanted to stuff Cialtie, I wasn't going to get in their way. I lowered my sword and looked at Araf. He reached into his shirt and came up with a wooden whistle. He blew two shrill notes on it that were so high I thought they were going to pierce my eardrums. The effect was instantaneous: at once there was a tremendous commotion outside the room, and every entrance was flooded with confused Imps brandishing weapons. Araf dropped his staff and held his hands up in a calming gesture. I found myself standing in the middle of a room packed full of confused and agitated Imps and Leprechauns all pointing swords. As usual in situations like this, I laughed.

An important-looking Imp pushed through the crowd. 'Prince Araf, what is amiss?'

Araf glanced at Lorcan. 'Nothing is amiss, my kinsman. Master Lorcan and I were talking about the loyalty of the Impmen and I provided a demonstration – well done. Now, with Master Lorcan's leave, you may all go back to your posts – Imps *and* Leprechauns.'

All eyes turned to Lorcan, who kept his gaze firmly fixed on Araf. We were in for another one of their famous stare-downs. As usual Araf won. Lorcan nodded and once again it was just Beardy and us.

Araf stepped up to the Leprechaun – there was so much tension in the air, you could swim in it. Araf spoke first. 'I have no desire to create a mutiny in your ranks, Lorcan. I understand your need for secrecy and I am not unsympathetic to your ultimate goal, but we must not be detained.' Before Lorcan could speak, Araf continued. 'Let me introduce to you a member of my company. This,' he said, pointing to his left, 'is Essa of Muhn.'

Lorcan looked very surprised. He bowed and said, 'Princess.'

Essa barely nodded back. It was a nice moment.

'By your lady's leave,' Araf said to Essa, 'would you show Lorcan what is around your neck?'

Essa pulled out the finger-length crystal that her father had used on me.

'Do you recognise this?' Araf asked.

Surprising Lorcan seemed to be becoming a pastime of ours. 'Is that an Owith glass?' he stammered.

'It is,' Essa answered. 'I believe the queen of the Leprechauns holds the other one.'

'She does. I have seen it.'

'Then you know what it can do?' Araf asked.

'It catches lies.'

'Essa, would you be willing to give Lorcan a demonstration?'

Essa took off the necklace and held it towards Lorcan. 'What is your name?' she asked.

'Lorcan of Duir,' The glass remained clear.

'This time,' Essa said, 'I want you to lie. What is your name?'

'I am – Finn of Duir.' Lorcan said. The crystal instantly went black.

'Why we are here and where we are going,' Araf said, 'we cannot tell you, but with Essa's leave, I propose that you may use the glass to swear us to secrecy. The glass will show if we intend to break our vow.'

Lorcan agreed. We all, in turn, swore to keep secret our knowledge of the Army of the Red Hand and their plan to attack Castle Duir. The glass remained clear. Lorcan returned the necklace and thanked Essa.

I broke the awkward silence. 'Hey, what about that cup of tea you promised?'

By the time dinner was served we were all pals – comrades in arms. Lorcan explained that he really wasn't ready for an invasion but he had to hurry it because of the meeting of the Runelords.

'What meeting?' Araf asked.

'Cialtie has called a meeting of the lords for a Runecasting. We suspect he is going to try to find out where we are hiding. We need to attack soon if we want surprise on our side.'

'Who is performing the Runecasting?' Essa asked.

'Cialtie said it will be Nieve, but according to our sources Nieve has been missing for days. We can't confirm this.'

Essa and I looked at each other but said nothing.

'How long before you attack?' Araf asked.

'I have sent word to all of my reserves to meet here by the end of the week – after that, as soon as we are ready. Some lords are on our side and are trying to delay the meeting.'

'Too long have the Imps and the Impwives watched our crops wither and our children suffer for the want of gold,' Araf said. 'I do not know Cialtie's motives for hoarding so much gold. I only know that I do not trust him. We will leave in the morning. I cannot speak for my companions, but I will try to return to join you before you move out.' He stood and extended his hand. Lorcan took it.

'I stand with my kinsman,' Fergal said.

Essa and I stood. 'I am ruled by my father and do not know his mind on this matter, but I wish you success,' Essa said.

'My future is just too crazy to promise I'll be back in time,' I said, 'but kick a bit of Cialtie butt for me – will ya?'

Araf and Fergal went outside to address the Imp troops. Essa asked Lorcan if we could see the courtyard where the Tree of Knowledge once stood. It wasn't far. The room we were in was adjacent to the courtyard – it was one of the few rooms that had remained whole. The courtyard was strewn with rubble from walls that had been pulled down. The ground was charred like the bottom of a giant campfire – it smelt like an old campfire as well. Essa walked to the middle and scrabbled in the black dust until she found a charred root.

'This was the Tree of Knowledge,' she said in a faraway voice. 'I sat in it once when I was young.'

'You sat in it?' I asked.

'Yes, it was a hazel tree. It didn't have a thick trunk like an oak, it had hundreds of thinner branches coming out of the ground. Over the ages the branches were trained and bent into a living chair. On the day a student left the Hall of Knowledge, he or she would sit in the tree for a leaving ceremony. The student would receive and eat a hazelnut from the tree. It would ensure that the student would never forget what was learned here.'

'Wow, it sounds like a heck of a tree.'

She looked me in the eyes – hers were wet. 'Your grandfather died trying to defend it – so did my brother.'

Her eyelids could hold back the tears no longer. I reached for her and she collapsed in my arms, shaking with sobs. I cried a bit too. Together we mourned a grandfather I had never known and a brother that she would always remember with the emotions of a little girl.

I don't know how long we knelt there. Being brave only postpones the inevitable – sooner or later you have to mourn your dead with all of your being, and that was what Essa was finally doing. When her sobs subsided, I picked up my staff and used it as support to help us both to our feet. The hazel staff slid into the ground like it was sand and then stuck there. Essa stumbled. I let go of the stick and held her with both arms. She leaned on me until we cleared the courtyard, then she stopped, wiped her eyes and put on her brave face before we joined the others. I forgot all about my staff.

Essa was fine the next morning. We exchanged knowing glances at breakfast. After that, nothing was said. We packed our horses. Acorn had gotten used to the place and was his old self again. Lorcan rode with us to the end of the castle's lands. As we said our goodbyes, I remembered that I had left my staff in the courtyard. Lorcan gave me his blackthorn banta and promised to look after my hazel stick until I returned.

Before he rode off, Lorcan said, 'The Reedlands are more treacherous now than ever before.'

'Who said we are going to the Reedlands?' Araf said.

'There is nothing else in the direction you go. It is a bad place. This land may be dead, but that place is foul. The last two scouts I sent there have not returned. Be careful.'

I was looking forward to getting out of the Hazellands. I needed to see something growing again. I promised myself that I would hug the next living plant I saw. It was a promise I did not keep. If I had hugged the first living plant I saw – it probably would have killed me.

Chapter Fifteen
The Reedlands

I could see the border of the Fililands a mile away. The sight of green in the distance made us all quicken our pace. I couldn't wait to be among living, breathing plants again. I fantasised about galloping straight into the forest. Thank God I didn't. As we approached I saw that the woods were sealed off by a tall, dark hedge. Huge blackthorn trees stretched for as far as the eye could see, and these weren't the kind of thorns that gave you inconvenient scratches – one look at the forearm-length, needle-sharp thorns was enough to make me realise we were not getting into the forest from here. I remembered once seeing razor-wire on top of a fence at an airport. It was barbed wire with razorblades stuck in it. It was the nastiest barrier I had ever seen – not any more.

'My gods!' Fergal said. 'Don't tell me we're going in here.'

'That is where we are going,' Essa said, 'but not through there.'

'Is this the Fililands?'

'Yes, Ona sealed it off with the blackthorns after the Fili war.'

'Do we have to go around? Can't we hack our way through?' I said.

'You would be dead before your sword touched them. They can fire those thorns.'

'How about if I asked nicely?'

'Go ahead,' she said, with a knowing smile I didn't like.

I dismounted. I had gotten pretty good at getting on and off Acorn – I wasn't Robin Hood or anything but I didn't look like a giraffe on an escalator any more. As I approached the blackthorns I could hear the wood creaking as they pointed their *very* sharp thorns at me. I instantly felt this was a bad idea. I found one place where I could reach through the thorns and touch a branch. Before I could say a thing a command shot straight into my brain. '*You have until the count of ten to back off and go away!*' the plant told me.

'But my mom is in there.' As soon as I said that I realised how pathetic it sounded.

'*Five.*'

'But…'

'*Three… two…*'

I backed off fast. This bush was not one for negotiation. I looked up and saw my three companions smiling at me. I straightened my shirt and regained a little composure. 'He said that he would let me through but not you guys, so I thought I might as well stay with the group.'

'How nice of you,' Essa said.

We travelled north along the thorn wall. On the other side of the spikes we could hear sounds of life – birds chirping and an occasional running deer. When a breeze came from the east, we were blessed with fresh, plant-cleansed air that was scented with wildflowers. It made me hate this living barbed-wire fence even more.

I fell in next to Fergal, who was quieter than usual. I asked him what was bothering him.

'It's the way Lorcan said *Banshee* – hell, it's the way everyone feels about Banshees, like we're scum.'

'Why is that?'

'Oh, I don't know. I was raised by Imps, remember? I guess it's because people are afraid of us. Banshees are the undertakers in The Land and nobody likes death. More than that it seems they can sense death approach, so every time someone sees a Banshee they think they are going to die.'

'Can you do that?'

'Sometimes I think I can, but I never learned all of that Banshee magic stuff.'

'I can see how that would make you guys a bit spooky.'

'It's also what makes us – them, such good warriors. Banshee armies can sense if an enemy will die, they almost know if they will win a battle before it begins.'

'So Banshees are warriors?'

'That's their primary role, to defend the western shore from invasion.'

'Men of war always make people nervous in peacetime,' I said.

'I guess.'

'Well, I like you, Fergal, no matter what anybody says.'

That brought a smile that seemed to bring him out of his funk. He babbled on for the rest of the afternoon. I almost regretted cheering him up.

We camped that night still in the Hazellands. We were all exhausted. We had been teased all day with the promise of life but were doomed to be stuck in this land of death. Tomorrow we would reach the Ngetal – the Reedlands – no matter how bad it was there, it had to be better than this. We went to sleep without much chat, in the hopes of a better tomorrow.

I dreamt I crested a hill and saw an army of Banshees. When they spotted me they all pointed, as if to say, *You soon will die.* I ran to escape but every place I turned blackthorn trees sprouted and blocked my path. Eventually I was encased by a blackthorn cage, surrounded by screaming Banshees. The huge thorns closed in on me. I awoke with a scream in my throat.

We smelt the Reedlands before we saw them. Just one whiff of the sulphur and decay dashed any hopes of our landscape getting better. Our only consolation was that we were just going to nip the Reedlands. The plan was to enter it just enough to find an opening to the Fililands, but this was not to be. When we got to the border, all we found was swamp. Murky water choked with black vegetation that bubbled with a smell so bad it put rotten eggs to shame. It was like a disease. You could see in places where it had started encroaching upon the Hazellands. There was no way *we* could walk in that stuff, let alone the horses, so we followed the unholy border west in hopes of finding some sort of a path. This meant that inevitably we would have to trek through a large part of this foul place.

After fifteen minutes the swamp gave way to reed-covered bogs. It was still too soft to travel through but it was an improvement – at least it smelt a bit better. Ten minutes later Essa called a stop.

'What is it?' I asked.

'Someone has been here,' she said, in a low voice that made me look over my shoulder.

She pointed to tracks that I could hardly make out. We followed them until they turned into the Reedlands. The footing was dry and solid where the trail led.

'We enter here,' Essa said. 'Be careful – I don't think we will be alone in there.'

The life in the Reedlands made me miss the desolation of the Hazellands. If this was life – it was a corruption of it. Plants of tan and black grew in odd shapes without the symmetry that nature usually provides. The Land had struck me as being so wholesome – this place was the opposite. It was just plain wrong.

Instinctively we travelled as quietly as we could. We didn't want to meet anyone that would choose to live in a place like this, and I didn't like the look of the vegetation – I didn't trust it. A snake slithered quickly across my path. I grabbed on tight to the pommel of my saddle. I don't know much about riding but I had watched a lot of cowboy movies and I knew that horses freak when they see a snake. Surprisingly, Acorn took no notice, but everyone else did.

'What was that?' came a girly cry from Araf that made me laugh.

'What's the matter,' I said, 'haven't you ever seen a snake before?'

'That's impossible,' Essa said, 'there are no snakes in The Land.'

'Well, it looks to me like there are now.'

'I don't like this place,' Fergal said.

I was just about to make some sarcastic quip to Fergal about the obviousness of his statement, but then I saw his face – this place was really stressing him out.

'None of us does, Fergal,' I said. 'We'll be out of here soon.' I hoped that wasn't a lie.

The path here was easier to follow and obviously well used. Fergal took the lead, anxious to have this stretch over with. He was a good three lengths ahead of us when he reached a stretch of the path that was black instead of brown. As soon as his horse's foot touched it, the black surface seemed to lift off the ground. The path had been covered with flies. Fergal was instantly surrounded by a swarm of black insects. He flailed his arms and kicked his horse into a gallop, trying to outrun them.

We sped after him. It was a terrifying sight. Fergal tried to keep his mount in control while swatting uselessly at his own personal black cloud. It must have been maddening. The sound of incessant buzzing from those oversized bugs was loud from behind – where Fergal was it must have been deafening.

The road ahead forked – we needed to go right if we wanted to get to the border of the Fililands, but Fergal in his panic kept going straight. We followed, not daring to shout. Fergal's breakneck speed was finally working – the swarm was diminishing. The flies couldn't keep up. When his vision cleared, Fergal slowed to a halt. I was quite impressed by the fact that during the whole ordeal, he had never shouted out. It didn't make any difference though – they had seen us.

Fergal and the rest of us were in plain view of a major camp of Banshees. A handful of them were standing around a small fire in front of about fifty tents. They were obviously surprised that the four of us would just gallop into view, but their confusion didn't last long. One of them let loose a scream and, not unlike the flies, the camp suddenly came alive. Hundreds of black-haired Banshees poured out of their tents. All of them armed, many with bows.

'I'm not an expert or anything,' I said as calmly as I could, 'but I think we should – get the hell out of here.'

'Good plan,' Fergal said, and we took off like four mice in a cathouse.

Luckily they were on foot, or we would have been dead meat. As it was, they covered a lot of ground for guys that had just gotten out of bed. We pulled ahead of them, but not as much as I would have liked – these guys were quick as well as handy with the old bows and arrows. I have never been shot at with a gun but I think I would prefer it to being the target of an archer. This was the third time this week someone had fired an arrow at me and I knew it was going to produce nightmares. At least with a gun you can't see the bullet come at you – arrows you see all the way until they either hit you or miss. It only takes a second but it's the most frightening second in your life. The other problem is that the relief you feel when one misses you is short-lived, because there are usually more arrows following. After seeing three shafts over my shoulder just narrowly miss me as I galloped at full speed, I turned my attention straight ahead and waited for one to plant itself in my back.

We got to the fork where Fergal had taken the wrong route, and went left. The Banshees were out of bow range and falling behind but we could see that they were not giving up. They let loose an ominous yell when we took the left fork.

Essa slowed down. 'This path seems to be going in the right direction. If we can get into the Fililands, we can lose them in the forest.'

'If?' I said. 'Can we get a bit more positive here?'

'I can't be sure that there is no blackthorn fence bordering the Reedlands,' she said, 'it's just a guess.'

'At the moment it's very important that you are right.'

Our pursuers were out of sight but we could still hear them scream periodically. On either side of the path was a deep, foul-smelling swamp – there was no turning off this road. If the path ended in blackthorns – we were done for. I remembered the Banshees' yell when we took this route and wondered if they knew something that we didn't. We rode in silence, straining our eyes and trying not to let the others see how scared we were.

We rounded a hill and saw it. The path led straight into – a wall of blackthorns.

'This is not a good thing,' I said.

Araf and Essa sped ahead, Fergal and I followed.

'You won't be too bad with that snap spell protecting you,' Fergal said.

'It only works with relatives,' I said, without thinking.

'What?'

Me and my big mouth – ah, what the hell, we'd probably be dead soon anyway. 'My mother told me that my protective spell only works with relatives. So, Fergal, I guess that means you and I are related somehow. I'm sorry I didn't tell you before but I wanted to talk to my parents about it.'

'So you and I are blood relatives?'

'I think so.'

'Like cousins?'

'Maybe.'

'I never had a cousin,' he said.

'Me neither.'

'I'd like it, Conor, if you really were my cousin,' he said, flashing me one of his famous Fergal smiles.

'Me too.'

The closer we got, the worse it looked. These thorns were more menacing that the ones bordering the Hazellands. Araf and Essa had dismounted by the time we caught up.

'This is not a good thing,' I repeated.

'There are only two options,' Araf said. 'We try to make it through the swamp or we stand and fight.'

Fergal got down and went to the edge of the path. It was definitely not a pretty swamp. The water was black, and choked with unhealthy-looking white roots and reeds, pale imitations of real vegetation. Fergal took a rope out of his pack, tied it around his waist and handed the other end to me.

'This is not a good thing,' he said and smiled.

'I'll keep a good hold on this end – cousin.'

He didn't hesitate, he just jumped right in. I thought it was the bravest thing I had ever seen. I had an instant vision of him disappearing under the black ooze and never being seen again, but the water only came up to his waist. The stench that wafted up from the disturbed water almost made me retch – how Fergal didn't lose his lunch I will never know.

'The footing on the bottom seems pretty solid,' he shouted. 'If you can stand the smell I think it might work.'

So my choice was: fight to almost certain death, or go in *there*. It smelt so bad I was still leaning towards *stand and fight* when my mind was made up for me. All of the vines and roots in the water were converging on Fergal.

'Fergal, get out!' I yelled.

I didn't have to ask him twice, I think he could sense that something was wrong. He got to the bank before the vegetation took hold. The vines that had been creeping up on him seemed to realise that he was trying to escape. They wrapped around him with the speed of a striking snake. He was dragged back into the water with such force, I was almost pulled from my saddle. Araf and Essa ran to the edge of the swamp. Fergal went under. I wrapped the rope around the pommel of my saddle and told Acorn to pull. Sometimes Acorn could give me a hard time, but when the chips were down, I had no better friend. Acorn pulled and Fergal broke the surface with his Banshee blade in hand. He hacked and scrambled onto the road, spluttering, sore and stinky – but unharmed. I jumped off Acorn.

'Are you alright?'

He nodded, trying to get back his breath.

'I thought I lost you there,' I said and hugged him. Boy, did he stink.

Araf and Essa started digging a shallow gutter. For a moment I wondered if it was our graves. They ripped buttons off their clothes and threw them into the trench.

'Do either of you have any gold?' Essa asked.

'No,' I said, 'my mother gave me an amulet but I used it.'

'I have some,' Fergal said, getting to his feet.

He took off his shirt and removed the gold wire that held his Banshee blade in place and handed it to Essa. Her eyes lit up.

'Perfect!' she exclaimed, and kissed Fergal on the cheek. From the look on her face you could tell that she instantly regretted it. Other than not dying, getting Fergal into a bath was our top priority.

Essa and Araf stretched the gold wire along the trench along with the gold buttons. Essa dropped to one knee and incanted a spell that caused the gold to glow and then hum. She stood up, sighed and then she and Araf covered the gold over with earth.

'This should take care of the arrows for a time,' she said.

'And then what?' I said, and instantly regretted it. We weren't going to make it through this. 'There has to be a way through these blackthorns,' I said, drawing my sword.

Araf was on me in a second. I am always amazed at how fast that Imp can move. He took the sword out of my hand. 'Don't,' he said, 'you would not last a heartbeat.'

'Well, at least let me talk to them.'

'Go ahead, but it will do no good.'

I've mentioned before, communicating with a tree is a wonderful experience – most trees, that is. A conversation with a blackthorn is like trying to talk your way past a junkyard dog. It's just no good. The spikes bore down on me as I touched a branch.

'*You have to the count of ten before I run you through!*' The voice of the tree exploded in my head.

'*Ten!*'

'You have got to let us in!' I pleaded.

'*Nine!*'

144

'I'll buy you some plant food.'

'*Eight!*'

'We're gonna die out here!'

'*Seven, six…*'

'I have to see Deirdre!'

'*Five, four…*'

'She's my mother!'

For a second I could have sworn the countdown stopped – then…

'*Three, two…*'

I backed off. I didn't want to find out what happened after *One*. I have no doubt that that tree would have enjoyed perforating me.

I turned back to the others, expecting to see them busying themselves with some sort of plan, but they were just standing there.

'The thorns won't let us pass,' I said. 'What do we do now?'

After a long pause, Araf said, 'Surrender.'

'What!'

'We wait behind the arrow shield. When the Banshees come in sight, we drop our weapons and put up our hands.'

'They didn't look like the prisoner-taking type,' I said. 'What if they attack?'

There was another pause. This time no one said anything.

We stood in a line. Our eyes fixed on the rising path before us. I have always hated waiting. Even if it was for something unpleasant like getting a tooth drilled, I prefer to do it and get it over with. That was not the way I felt now. I had a feeling that getting it over with would be the end of me. I wanted these moments to last forever – and they did. Our pursuers were not hurrying to catch us, they knew there was no place for us to go. I thought about my parents: a mother that I had only briefly known, and a father that I was only now truly starting to understand. If only I could see them again. I had so many questions to ask, so much to say.

I think Fergal must have seen my despair. He leaned into me and said, 'If you get killed, can I have your shoes?' And then he flashed me a Fergal smile.

Well, that was it. I tried to keep a straight face but I matched Fergal's smile and then my shoulders shook and before we knew it, Fergal and I were bent over in hysterics. Araf kept his eyes straight but even he was laughing.

Essa was not amused. 'Stop it. We have no time for this,' she said.

'This is exactly what we have time for,' I said, while trying to get my composure back. 'Laughing is as good a way as any to spend your last minutes. How would you prefer to spend yours?'

She looked at me. Our eyes locked and her pupils dilated. At that moment I read her mind and knew the answer to my question. I grabbed her by the shoulders and planted on her the kind of kiss you see in old black and white movies. As usual with women, my mind reading was all wrong. She pushed me back and swung. Not a slap, like in the movies, a left hook that decked me!

I looked up from the ground to see Essa standing over me with her banta stick high in her hand and her eyes raging. 'We are *not* going to die!'

I looked past her and saw the Banshees crest the hill. 'Tell them that.'

Chapter Sixteen
Big Hair

The Banshees approached slowly. They knew they had us cornered but I think they weren't sure if we had any long-range weapons. The four of us stood shoulder to shoulder, watching their approach. The closer they got, the less I liked the look of them – it was a motley crew. I doubted any of them had ever signed the Geneva Convention on prisoners of war – as they got closer, I doubted any of them could sign their name. A wild-haired Banshee in the front raised his hand and they all grumbled to a stop. They were close enough now that they could see us clearly. Araf undid his sword belt and dropped it and his staff to the ground. He held his empty hands out in a peaceful gesture. We all did the same.

The Banshee with big hair seemed to be in charge. He saw our surrender and bowed to us formally. He then turned to his troops and barked something. A group of twenty archers jogged to the front and nocked arrows in their bows. Hair Guy turned to us, smiled, and yelled, 'Fire!'

A wall of arrows came straight at us. I didn't move a muscle. Partly because Essa said we would be safe behind the shield, but mostly because when a couple of dozen arrows are coming at you, there is no place to run.

The afternoon's light highlighted the chief Banshee's hair – it grew straight out of his head, like too much cotton candy. I remembered a pencil I owned when I was a kid. It had a troll doll with hair like that sitting on the top of it. If you rubbed the pencil in between your hands the troll would spin and its hair would shoot straight out. I wished I had a pencil big enough to impale him on. Under that mop of white-streaked black hair I could see the glee in the Banshee's face. All of this and more went through my mind as the flock of arrows came at me. It felt like an eternity before the missiles hit the shield wall. Just two arm lengths in front of my face, the arrows burst into flames. For a second I thought I was going to be engulfed in fire, then the flames instantly dissipated. I shot a look at Essa who was breathing a sigh of relief. It made me think she wasn't quite as confident in her wall as she said.

The joy of not being killed by arrows was short-lived. The Banshee archers put away their bows, drew their swords and casually came for us. There was no need to hurry. They had us. I felt like I was in a scene in a cheap movie and I was some helpless girl in a dark alley surrounded by a vicious gang (I always wondered what those girls were doing wandering in dodgy alleys so late at night), but there was no superhero in a leotard to save us, this was the real deal. These guys were coming to kill us.

I know it's a cliché but my life flashed before my eyes and it annoyed me because it was so dull. The most exciting time of my life had been in the last week – before that, the biggest thrill I had ever had was in a bicycle accident in the sixth grade. I was actually more annoyed than scared. I was annoyed that I wouldn't see my father again. I had a lifetime of my father making no sense and I was finally understanding him. Sally would never know what happened to me and I would never know whatever happened to her. Maybe she hadn't even missed me. And I wanted to see my mother again. Finding a mom after all these years was the most wonderful thing that had ever happened to me – one more hug would have been nice.

Bad-Hair-Day Banshee stopped his troops about twenty-five feet away. He smiled at me and I smiled back.

Fergal leaned in to me and whispered through his teeth, 'If I go, I'm taking him with me.'

'I was just thinking the same thing,' I replied.

Bad-Hair Banshee ordered his troops to split and come at us from the left and the right. At first I thought it was a tactical move, then I realised that they probably thought that our arrow wall would burn them as well. Well, I wasn't going to tell them their mistake, it was better than a frontal attack – not much, but you take what comfort you can get in a situation like this. Araf and Essa squared off to meet the attack from the left, Fergal and I turned to face the right. I looked at Fergal and he was grinning from ear to ear, we both were. We were definitely related.

When Hair Guy pointed behind us, no one looked. We weren't stupid enough to fall for that old trick. So I jumped when I heard, from the rear, my mother's voice shouting my name. She may not have been there for me when I was a little kid but she sure was making up for lost time now. There she was, in all of her animal-skinned splendour, yew wand in her hand, standing next to a V-shaped gap in the blackthorn wall.

The Banshees were almost on us. I grabbed Fergal by the collar and called to the others. As soon as we jumped through, Deirdre raised her wand and invoked something to close the thorns behind us. Seven Banshees dived through the gap before it closed with a sickening scream on the eighth. Araf, as usual, was ready for action. He instantly knocked out the Banshee that went for Deirdre. I didn't have time to thank him because one came for me.

If I close my eyes I can still see his face, I can still picture the stripes embroidered on his tunic and can still see the eyes – young eyes. I can remember everything about him – he was the first man I ever killed. I didn't want to. As soon as the fight began, I knew I was a much better swordsman. After a couple of parries, I saw that he had almost no defensive skill. One counter-strike would have drawn blood, so I tried the Dahy manoeuvre in hopes of knocking him out with my elbow. He parried the feint just as he should have, but when I went in with the elbow I lost my footing and went down. My opponent was not as gracious as me – he came at me with a *coup de grâce*, and I had only one option. From the ground, I beat the point of his sword to the outside and planted my blade in his chest. I will always remember the shock on his face. I'm sure that when he woke up that morning this was not the way he imagined his day would end.

I stood up and saw the second one coming at me and did nothing. I was in such a daze about actually killing someone that I just stared with almost amusement as this screaming Banshee ran at me with an axe cocked over his head. I probably would have just watched him until he split my head open, but that didn't happen. Like it was in a dream, I saw a shadow step in front of me and the flash of a blade. The next thing I knew, I was casually watching the Banshee run past me – minus its upper arms and a head. I turned to look at my saviour and said, 'Thanks, Dad.'

One of Big Hair's troops on the other side was stupid enough to take a swipe at the blackthorns with a sword. The air filled with flying thorns and screams. The Banshees backed off – fast. Araf, Essa, Fergal and I were miraculously unharmed. Four of the seven attackers that had followed us in were dead, three were unconscious. Deirdre used her wand again and the thorns opened enough for Araf to throw the dead and unconscious Banshees through.

I watched all of this as if in a trance. I was a bumbling idiot. It felt as if my mind had left my body and I was floating above it all, watching with an uncaring attachment. Basically my mind snapped – that's it – no more thinking. I had been seconds away from my death and then I had caused the death of another. I reached inside and switched my head to the *OFF* position. I recalled a T-shirt I once saw that read, *Don't bother me, I can't cope.* That was me. I wished I was wearing it.

Mom and Dad seemed to understand, or maybe they were just patronising me. Either way, they spoke to me in calming tones and got me up onto Acorn. Acorn treated me nice too. He nuzzled up to me before I got on – maybe he wasn't being nice, maybe he just wanted to check if I was the same guy. I sure didn't feel like the same guy.

The Fili forest was dense and dark green. My parents rode on either side of me, stopping branches from swiping my face. I don't know how long we travelled like this and I didn't care. I was in La-la land – completely mindless. I have no memories of riding into the Fili village, all I remember was Mother taking me into a hut and putting me to bed. I slept and didn't even dream.

I awoke the next morning with all of my wits intact. I guess that was a good thing but I couldn't help remembering how nice not-thinking had been. That way I didn't have to see the face of the Banshee I killed in my mind's eye and I didn't have to relive the sensation of my sword piercing his chest. I lay in bed wrestling with the memories. *I had no choice*, I said to myself. *He was about to kill me. I didn't want to do it. It wasn't my fault.* I had convinced my head that I had done no wrong, but my conscience would take time to heal and I knew it would always leave a scar.

Mom woke me up. She sat on the edge of my round bed in a round room and pushed the hair back across my forehead. It was like she had been doing it all of my life – I guess in both of our imaginations, she had. 'Are you up for some breakfast?'

'Yes,' I said. 'I'm OK. Sorry about yesterday. I didn't mean to scare you.'

She smiled and held out her hand. 'Come.'

The reason I didn't remember entering the Fili village is probably because I hadn't seen it in the first place. The door of the cottage opened into what first appeared to be an empty wood. When the door closed behind me, I turned and couldn't see a door. I couldn't even find the cottage until I stopped and looked closely. The huts had been built in and among the trees. They were small and round with bark for outside walls. The trees had grown over them, providing roofs that almost made them invisible to a casual glance. I wouldn't be surprised if someone walked straight through these woods without ever even noticing a hut, just a sensation that something was strange. As we walked I got the feeling that we were being watched, but saw no one.

Deirdre touched a tree and surprisingly a door opened in it. 'You'll get used to it,' she said. 'After a while you see everything and wonder how it fooled you in the first place.'

'It's not just camouflage, there is magic working here, too – isn't there?'

'Of course,' she said.

Inside was a long table. Fergal, Araf, Essa, my father and a woman I didn't recognise were already there, having breakfast.

Dad jumped up and put his arm on my shoulder. 'How are you this morning?'

'I'm fine.'

He looked me deep in the eyes, to see if I was telling the truth. I smiled at him. He laughed and gave me a hug.

'What about you?' I asked when he released me. 'Last time we were together you had an arrow sticking out of your chest.'

'Oh yes, I did, didn't I?' He waved his arms around. 'I'm fine now. There is nothing like Fili nursing. The best medical magic in The Land.'

Araf coughed.

'Except maybe Impwife magic,' he said quickly, and winked at me.

'What happened? Nieve was about ready to kill both of you.'

'There is plenty of time for catching up,' Mom said. 'Sit down and have something to eat, and I want you to meet someone.'

My companions stared at me like I was a Martian. 'I'm fine, guys,' I said, 'I just got a little freaked out yesterday.'

'Conor,' Mom said, 'I would like to introduce you to Fand – queen of the Fili.'

I stood and bowed. 'Your highness.'

She smiled. 'Fand will do. We don't have very much protocol in the Fililands.'

I sat. 'You are Maeve's daughter, are you not?'

'I am, but we do not use her name here.'

'Because of what she did?'

'Yes.'

'Those who forget history are doomed to repeat it,' I said, remembering an old quote.

'You sound like your mother,' Fand said.

'I take that as a compliment.'

'You should.'

Breakfast was fruit and dried meats and some sort of tea that woke me right up.

'I imagine you have met my travelling companions,' I said to my parents.

'Essa and I had a lot to talk about,' Mom said. 'I knew her brother well.'

'And Araf's father and I go way back,' Dad said.

'Have you been properly introduced to Cousin Fergal?'

'Cousin Fergal?' Mom looked surprised.

'Haven't you told them yet?'

'No,' Fergal said, 'I was waiting for you.'

'OK then, Mom, you know that protection spell you put on me – the one that only works on relatives?'

'Yes.'

'Well, it worked when Fergal tried to stab me.'

Mom shot an angry glance at Fergal. 'Why were you trying to stab my son?'

'Whoa, Mom! It's alright, it was an accident.'

She looked me in the eyes, then dropped her shoulders and asked Fergal, 'Who are your parents?'

'That's just it. I don't know. I was hoping you could tell me.'

Fergal told Deirdre the story of his upbringing. When he finished, Mom said, 'Well, I don't know of any Banshees in my line. Yours?'

Dad shook his head.

'I'd like to find out myself,' Mom said. 'Perhaps I could perform a Shadowcasting.'

'I'd be interested in seeing that,' said a voice close to my back.

I turned to see Aunt Nieve standing behind me – a knife in her hand.

Chapter Seventeen
The Druid Table

I leaped to my feet and reached for my sword, as did my companions, but none of us had our weapons with us. Fergal cocked his arm a couple of times trying to bring out a nonexistent Banshee blade. I grabbed a fork from the table and brandished it as menacingly as one can with tableware. Essa and Araf were the only sensible ones – when they realised they had no banta sticks, they each ripped a leg off the table. As food and plates crashed to my feet, I slipped on some fruit and fell backwards onto the semi-legless table.

Nieve smiled and took a step forward. Araf, Essa and Fergal came to my defence, standing between me and my evil aunt. Fergal was holding a silver serving tray in front of him as a shield.

Dad and Mom quickly came between us.

'Whoa!' Dad said, putting his hand up in front of him. He was smiling a little. 'Nieve is on our side.'

'What? What do you mean – *our side*? This is the woman who tried to kill me with a spear and she shot you with an arrow, Dad. Remember?'

'It's true,' Mom said, 'Nieve is a friend.'

I stood up, still brandishing my fork. 'The last time we were all together you two were trying to kill each other.'

'Yes,' Mom said, 'but after you escaped, we nursed your father's wound together and then we talked. We hadn't talked since my banishment. We had a lot to say.'

Araf and Essa lowered their table legs but I was unconvinced. I continued to wield my cutlery.

Mom went on. 'I was consumed with the want of revenge. Truemagic could not tell me who had destroyed my home, so I sought out the Fili and the secret of Shadowmagic. That's when I met Fand. Together, we learned that Shadowmagic was not evil – it was like any other power. The evil came from the person who wielded it. She taught me the wisdom of the Fili and it changed me. I have never used Shadowmagic to find out who killed my father and my tutors. The hate would corrupt me and the magic.'

'What does this have to do with her?' I said, pointing my fork at Nieve.

It was Nieve's turn to speak. Her voice was soft. It surprised me. I had never heard it without venom. 'I am an old woman and thought myself wiser than I really was. I was set in my ways. When your mother learned forbidden lore and produced the son of the one-handed prince – I thought it was my duty to stop her. I now see it was wrong to blame Shadowmagic for the Fili war – it was Maeve who was to blame.'

I looked over to Fand. She lowered her eyes.

'What about the *son of the one-handed prince* stuff?' I said.

'Ona's divinations should not be ignored,' Nieve replied, 'but your mother has convinced me that there are other paths than the one I have been travelling.'

'You mean the *kill Conor* path?' I said.

'Yes,' she said, and sounded sincere.

'I was never a big fan of that road.'

Nieve smiled. 'Nor was I, Conor. You will never know how much it pained me.'

'So how come you are coming at me with a knife?'

She glanced down at her hand and looked surprised to see she was actually holding a knife. 'Oh, I was just in the kitchen. I came in to see if I could slice some bread for anyone.'

Dad cracked up at this. 'Are you going to lower your fork, son, or are you going to eat your aunt?'

I looked at the pathetic weapon in my hand and smiled. 'So we start over?'

'I would like that,' Nieve said.

'OK. Hi, I'm Conor – Oisin and Deirdre's kid.' I extended my hand.

'I am very happy to meet you, Conor. I am Nieve, your father's older sister and your aunt.'

She shook my hand and smiled. You know, when Nieve smiles she doesn't look so scary at all. Saying that, I wasn't ready to hug her.

'Can I have my table legs back?' came a quiet voice on the other side of the room. It was Fand.

'Oh gods,' Araf said, 'I am sorry.' Araf lifted the table with one hand and tried to put the leg back – without much success.

'Do not worry, Araf. The Druid Table has been broken before. In years to come I will point out the repairs and tell how the lord of the Imps tore off the leg to protect his friend.'

'The Druid Table?' I said.

'Most of the Fili were killed in the war,' Dad said. 'The few survivors hid in this forest. The rest became mortals and travelled to the Real World. Irish history remembers them as the Druids.'

'I remember you telling me about the Druids when I was young, you told me no one knew where they came from.'

'I lied. I knew.'

'You lied about a lot of things, didn't you, Dad.'

'I did, and I am sorry.'

'So are you finally going to tell me the truth about how you lost your hand?'

'Ah, that's a great story!' Fergal yelped. 'You see, Oisin and Cialtie were having a...'

'You know how my dad lost his hand?'

'Of course, everybody knows that story.'

'Why didn't you tell me?'

'You never asked. I can't believe you haven't heard it. You see, Oisin and Cialtie...'

Araf placed a hand on Fergal's shoulder. 'Perhaps Lord Oisin should tell his own tale.'

'Oh yeah – sorry.'

'You two go for a walk,' Mom said. 'You have much to talk about and we have much to do here, if I am to cast Shadowrunes tonight.'

'Come, son, and I will tell of things I have long wished I could tell.'

Dad and I walked outside in the dark shade of beautiful trees adorned with clusters of red berries.

'What trees are these?' I asked.

'Rowan. The Fililands are the Rowanlands. Maeve used to hold the Luis Rune,' Dad explained. 'The berries are poisonous but the Fili manage to somehow make jam out of it. I think I saw you have some this morning.'

'I did. It was nice.'

'The Fili are a clever people; my father was wrong in punishing them all. My mother asked him to be lenient but he was so appalled by the war – he ruled with his heart and not with his head.'

'Your mother?' I said, suddenly wondering why I had never even thought to ask before.

Dad closed his eyes for a second.

An evil thought entered my mind. 'Did Cialtie kill her too?'

'No, after I was born she went over the water on a sorceress' quest. She never returned. Finn had Ona perform a Runecasting to find her – but to no avail. She must have died.'

'Who was she?'

'My mother – your grandmother – was a sorceress. Her yew wand held the power of the horses. I never knew her. It was said that she raised the finest horses in The Land. Her name was Macha. There is a town in Ireland called Emain Macha.'

'*Emain* means *twin*, doesn't it?'

'That's right. Cullen – or should I say Cu-cullen – named it during one of his tall tale sessions, I believe. He was referring to Cialtie and me.'

'You and Cialtie are twins? I thought he said he was your older brother.'

'He is, but everyone called us twins because there is only a year between us. Immortals don't have very many children – otherwise the place would be overrun. It is very rare for someone to have two children so close together. So we were called *Emain Macha* – Macha's Twins.'

'But Cialtie is the oldest and heir to the throne?'

'Heirs are not decided by nepotism in The Land. Runelords are made at their Runechoosing.'

'I keep hearing about this Runechoosing. What is it?'

'When a young man or woman comes of age they prepare a small disc of oak and place it on a piece of gold. They then carry the oak and gold through the three antechambers of the Hall of Runes. At each doorway a muirbhrúcht is passed.'

'*Muirbhrúcht*? I don't know that word.'

'It literally means *tidal wave* but most people who have performed the Choosing say it's more like a riptide but in the air all around you. What it is, is incredibly difficult, both mentally and physically. A Chooser may give up after the first antechambers; after that stopping means death. The rune becomes hot in your hand after each muirbhrúcht. The gold melts into the oak. When, or if, you pass through the final barrier, you may turn over the piece of oak in your hand. Upon it, engraved in gold, will be a rune. Some runes are major runes – these are for Runelords. Others are minor runes – these are for heirs. Only after a Runelord has left or died may the holders of the minor runes retake their Choosing to see who is to be the Runelord.'

'What rune do you hold?'

Dad held up his stump. 'One cannot choose a rune without a runehand. I have never attempted the Choosing.'

'Cialtie has, hasn't he?'

'Yes. Everyone expected him to choose one of the Duir Runes but he chose a Virgin Rune.'

'A Virgin Rune?'

'Yes, a Virgin Rune is one that has never been chosen before. It had been so long since a new rune appeared that most of us thought it was myth, but then it happened. Cialtie chose Getal – the Reed Rune. A week later, word arrived that the Reedlands had appeared east of the Hazellands. Then we knew that the legends of the Origins were true.'

'Hold on,' I said, 'let me get this straight. Cialtie chose a new rune and poof, some land appeared out of nowhere?'

'Out of the sea,' Dad corrected. 'The Land is an island.'

'Right, so the Reedlands appeared out of the sea – and this never happened before?'

'Not since the beginnings.'

'And when was that?'

Dad smiled at me like I was a kid again. 'That – was before time. Sit down, son, and I'll tell you of our ancestors.'

We had walked to the edge of the forest – before us was Ona's blackthorn wall. Beyond that was the blackened Hazellands. Dad placed his hand on a fallen rowan tree and asked its permission to use it. He sat on the tree and I sat cross-legged at his feet.

'Ériu was the first, she is the mother of The Land and is considered a god among many – especially the Leprechauns. My father believed that she was his great-great-great-grandmother. When she came, The Land was a tiny island. Some think she found the oak trees here – others say she brought an acorn with her. Either way, she was the first lord of Duir. Together with the Leprechauns, she built the first House of Duir and excavated the mines.'

'Where did the Leprechauns come from?'

'Who knows? They believe that Ériu made them. That is why they are so loyal to the House of Duir. Anyway, Ériu was a great sorceress. Your mother believes she may have possessed Shadowmagic, but most of her skills were with Truemagic, powered by the gold in the mines.

'She sent for her sisters: Banbha and Fódla. Together they created the Chamber of Runes. Banbha chose the Iodhadh Rune and created the Yewlands. Fódla chose the Quert Rune, and her Choosing created the Orchardlands.'

'Where did the Imps and the Banshees come from?'

'When a Virgin Land is created by a Choosing, it is said that often it appears with full-grown trees, but sometimes it appears with people. The Imps supposedly appeared with the Orchardlands. Later, an Imp attempted the Choosing and chose the Ur Rune for the first time, creating the Heatherlands (or the Implands as we call them). That would be one of your friend Araf's ancestors.

'The Banshees are different. They believe they were sent for from the Otherworld by Banbha, to protect our shores.'

'Is this all true?'

'I don't know,' he replied. 'When I was young, I thought all this was just myth and legend. When the Reedlands appeared, I started to think again.'

As I sat at his feet and listened to him, I realised that I had not only missed a mother in my life, but also a father who could tell the truth. The years of holding back were lifting off his shoulders. He looked younger as he told me things that he had been aching to tell before. I was just about to hear the story of how he got his hand chopped off (and it was easy to guess who did it), when we heard the pathetic yelp of a wounded animal.

Dad and I ran to the blackthorns. It was a wolf – a big wolf. It was manically trying to dig under the blackthorn wall, but the blackthorns were having none of it. The thorns had wrapped themselves around the wolf's head. There was fresh blood where a thorn had pierced the side of its ear but that wasn't its only wound. A black arrow stuck out of the wolf's hindquarters. The whole of its back end was caked with dried blood. The beast made a sickening yelp as the thorns pressed harder. Dad spoke to the blackthorns and they reluctantly loosened their grip.

Dad called to the wolf and said, 'It is alright, I'll help you.' I was shocked when the wolf looked him straight in the eye like he understood. Then the animal collapsed on the ground and if I hadn't seen it myself, I wouldn't have believed it – he changed into a man.

'Get your mother.'

Mom was already on her way when she met me on the road. The blackthorns had told her.

When we arrived back with Dad, she used her wand to part the thorns and we carried him in.

'What was that?' I asked, still a bit stunned.

'He's a Pooka,' Dad said. 'They can change into animals.'

'Oh, right,' I said.

Fand and another Fili woman arrived and tended his wounds. They gave him water (which woke him up) and a tonic (that put him to sleep) and carried him back to the village.

The story of how Dad became a lefty had to wait.

Later, back at the village when things had calmed down a bit, Araf, Fergal, Essa, Mom, Aunt Nieve, Dad and I had a late lunch. The food was a vegetarian's dream. It made me think I would buy a pair of sandals, listen to folk music and forgo hamburger joints forever. The others had been collecting tree sap all morning in preparation for a Shadowcasting after nightfall, and they were almost ready. Fand popped in and informed us that her Pooka patient hadn't regained consciousness.

Fergal interrupted the chomping. 'So, Conor, what did you think of the story of how Prince Oisin lost his hand?'

'I didn't hear it,' I said. 'We were interrupted by a rabid Pooka.'

'Oisin,' Mother said, 'it is time you told your son the tale.'

'Now?' Dad said.

Deirdre nodded.

Chapter Eighteen
The Race of the Twins of Macha

Dad planted his elbows on the table and wearily rubbed his eyes. It made me realise that these were probably not the most pleasant memories to retell. He pushed away his lunch plate, slapped his palm on the table and began.

'Ona made many predictions,' my father said. 'We all know about the son of the...' He lifted his handless arm and pointed to it. 'But there was another prediction that only my father knew. Ona predicted that, *The first of Finn's sons to perform the Runechoosing would attain the throne.*

'Now, at a very young age, I realised that my brother was a horrid child that would grow up to be an evil man. Finn, like any parent, was slow to see this but by the time my brother reached Rune-age, even my father knew that he did not want Cialtie to hold the throne.

'Cialtie attained Rune-age a year before me, but Father forbade him to take his Choosing until I was of age as well. Finn told him that he would hold a huge pageant to celebrate The Land's first double Choosing. This infuriated my brother. He left the castle and did not return for almost a year.

'After he left, my father revealed to me Ona's prediction and his wish for me to take my Runechoosing first. We concocted a plan. I pretended to take up fishing as a hobby – in fact, I spent most of my time on Loch Duir, not fishing but – practising rowing.

'A fortnight before my birthday, Cialtie returned with a group of Banshees. He clamed that Banshees were not treated well in The Land and that these men and women should stay in the castle to promote understanding among the races. Even then, it looked to me as if they were at least bodyguards – and at worst, the beginning of a private army.

'Father organised a huge celebration, in honour of the two princes of Duir coming of age. The centrepiece of the event was the *Sruth de Emain Macha* – the Race of the Twins of Macha – a boat race across Loch Duir. Cialtie and I would race the length of the lake, starting at the far shore, and the first to place his runehand on the Castle Beach would be the first to Runechoose.

'The Runelords and the people of The Land looked at the race as good fun – innocent sibling rivalry, but my father, Ona and I knew the truth – it was a race for the crown.

'On the morning of the contest, my brother and I left early and rode to the far shore. With each of us there rode a second. I brought Eth, the son of my father's master goldsmith. He was my best friend, the brother that Cialtie was not. Eth knew my brother's treachery as well as I, and his job was to look out for the dirty tricks that we both knew were coming – Cialtie, as usual, was a step ahead of us. He brought with him a Banshee sorceress named Mná – she was beautiful. All the way to the starting point Mná chatted and flirted with Eth, and by the time we reached the farthest shore, Eth was besotted with the Banshee sorceress – as a security guard he was useless.

'Cialtie only spoke to me once during the journey. He rode up next to me and said, "This boat race is not as innocent as it seems, is it, brother?" He is the only man who can make the word *brother* sound like a threat.

'"I don't know what you mean," I replied, as calmly as I could.

'"I think you do. I think this little contest is very important indeed."

'"What makes you say that?"

'"The way you and Father are acting – you are both such bad liars."

'"No one, brother Cialtie, is as good at that as you."

'He smiled, like it was a compliment. "I don't know what you are up to but I am sure that winning this race is very important. Am I right?"

'He looked me in the eyes – I held his stare without wavering.

'"No matter," he said, "even if this is a bit of frivolity, I can see in your eyes that you want to win. That is reason enough to beat you." He laughed that disgusting Cialtie laugh and galloped ahead.'

'There was a pavilion and a small entourage waiting for us at the starting point. After a short breakfast we entered our boats. Mná actually gave Eth a kiss for luck. When their lips parted, he looked like someone had clubbed him over the head. Even I laughed. You see, I was so confident in my rowing superiority that I let my guard down. No one saw Cialtie put the shell under the seat of his boat.

'The sergeant-at-arms dropped a small gold amulet into a tube that set off a spectacular golden flare. The race was on!

'Cialtie was always stronger than me and he seemed to have grown stronger in the time since he had been away, but his rowing technique was awful. I had spent months experimenting with length of stroke and the depth of the oars in the water, and had built up my back muscles – I was by far the better rower. The race was mine, but I didn't want to pull too far ahead. I needed to make it look at least a little close – besides, it was fun. I was a short way ahead of him, effortlessly gliding through the water, watching him strain with sloppy rowing. I was cocky and overconfident – I let him get closer just so he could see that I was hardly even trying.

'I even allowed my mind to wander. I thought about Deirdre. I had first met her at one of Gerard's parties. She made quite an impression on me and I on her.'

Dad flashed Deirdre a smile across the table that she returned.

'I was distressed, like everyone, when I heard that her home had been destroyed, but what really worried me was the news that she had vanished. I persuaded Ona to perform a mini rune reading that hinted to Deirdre's whereabouts in the Fililands. I told everyone I was going on an extended fishing trip and set out to find her.

'The thorns almost killed me before I could finally convince them to give a message to Deirdre. She brought me into the Fililands and... well, we fell in love. I persuaded her to end her self-inflicted exile. I started to row a bit harder knowing she was waiting for me at the Castle Beach.

'When I saw Cialtie put the gold earplugs in, it didn't even ring any alarm bells. I actually slowed down to see what he was doing. It wasn't until he produced the conch shell and pulled the amulet from around his neck that I realised I was in trouble. I rowed away from him with all of my strength – but it was too late. He dropped the amulet into the shell, shouted "*Gream!*" and threw. I dived to block but the shell ricocheted around the bottom of the boat. Before I could get to it – I heard the scream.

'I know now that the spell he dropped in the shell – it was a Banshee pain scream. I thought it was only a legend but Cialtie was always a master of old lore. He has since made many a myth become a reality. Legend has it that in the War of the Others, the Banshees developed a scream that gave the enemy's men – *the pain of childbirth*. I thank the gods for making me a man and I shall forever look on mothers with admiration. Never again do I want to feel such pain. Not even the arrow in my chest compared to the debilitating agony that hit me in that boat. I doubled up, clutching my knees. I was in too much pain even to scream. Cialtie sped ahead.

'Through closed eyes I envisioned how the future would unfold. I saw Cialtie winning the race. I saw my father and Deirdre's disappointment. I saw Cialtie holding the Oak Rune. I saw Cialtie holding the Sword of Duir. I saw Cialtie sitting on the Oak Throne, and I saw Cialtie with a queen by his side – it was Deirdre!

'That was more than I could bear. I let loose a howl and opened my eyes. The shell was lying on the bottom of the boat, right next to my face. With an effort I know I will never be able to duplicate, I took my hands from my knees, grabbed the shell and hurled it with all of my might. I only threw it about a foot but that was enough – as the shell sank, the scream and the pain subsided. When I finally sat up, I saw that I was in the middle of the lake and Cialtie had an impossible lead.

'I retook my oars and began to row but without heart, for Cialtie's lead was too big. Cialtie will win – *Cialtie will be king* – that thought, like a lightning bolt, shot through my body. "No!" I screamed and I pulled at my oars with all of my strength. The pain of my attack racked my body but I pushed it away. I melded my mind and my body into one. With every stroke, I recalled the indecencies my brother had committed – it fuelled my arms and my back with superhuman strength. The front end of my boat rose up with the speed, and the wake behind me looked as if it came from a galleon ship with fifty oarsmen.

'I was spurred on not only by the desire to stop my brother, but by anger. I was angry with myself. It was my own fault that I was in that position. I should never have let Cialtie get so close. I only did it so I could gloat. It was pride that defeated me. I realised how foolish I had been and that pushed me even more. I had been so confident of winning the race that I had even taken the Sword of Duir with me. I had disguised its hilt that morning with leather straps so no one would recognise it. You see, in my mind I was already king. I thought I had won the race before it had even begun – it had cost me dearly.

'Even these thoughts left me as I became a mindless rowing machine. I forgot I was even in a race. *Rowing stops Cialtie, Rowing stops Cialtie*, ran through my mind like a Fili mantra. I didn't even know that I had caught up to my brother until I heard him sneer, "Too little, too late, brother."

'That snapped me out of it. I heard the roar of the watching crowd. I looked to my left and saw the tip of my boat was almost even with Cialtie's stern, but when I looked fully around I saw that my brother was right, we were almost at the Castle Beach and I was a full length behind.

'I have found that important moments in life either happen so fast you don't even remember them, or so slow that each second seems like a lifetime. I remember what happened next as if I was swimming in honey.

'Cialtie's boat grounded first. He jumped into the knee-deep water and began the thirty-second run to the beach. My boat grounded just as he hit the water. There was no way I could beat him. As I have said, the next few seconds seemed like hours, and although it seemed as if I had plenty of time to think through what I did next – in retrospect, I wasn't thinking at all. I remembered that the winner of the race was the brother that first placed his runehand on the Castle Beach. I lowered my runehand on the seat of the boat, drew the Sword of Duir with my left hand and without even a second thought – I cut off my hand. I didn't even wait for the pain to register, I dropped the sword and hurled my severed runehand to the shore. The throw pitched me out of the boat, but before I hit the water I saw my hand sail past Cialtie's astonished face. It landed on the beach, to the silence of a stunned crowd. I had won, my runehand had been the first to touch the Castle shore. *I had won* – that was the last thing that went through my mind as I splashed unconscious into the reddening water.'

Chapter Nineteen
The Castle Beach

'You did it to yourself?' I almost shouted. 'You cut off your own hand?'

'Yes,' Father said.

'But didn't you realise that you couldn't take the Choosing without a right hand, or that you would become the one-handed prince?'

'No.'

The look on my father's face made me realise how insensitive my questions were. Of course he realised these things – now.

'At the moment I raised the sword,' Dad confessed, 'the only thought that went through my mind was winning – or more to the point, beating Cialtie. All thoughts of Runechoosing, or prophecies, or even the pain, were superseded by the desire to win. It was foolish.' I could see in his eyes, he had paid dearly for that impulsive act.

'It was courageous, Lord Oisin,' said a voice. It was Araf. I had almost forgotten that the others were there.

Dad gave him a soft smile. 'Thank you, Araf. You Imps and Leprechauns are a romantic bunch. You have always considered my moment of madness as courageous. It wasn't, it was stupidity.'

'Is that why Lorcan's army is called the Army of the Red Hand?' I blurted, without thinking.

Mom, Dad and Aunt Nieve simultaneously shouted, 'What?' Araf and Essa gave me a very dirty look. I had made a solemn vow to keep Lorcan's army secret.

Fergal tried to change the subject. 'It must have created quite a commotion at the finish line when you threw your hand to shore.'

Dad ignored him and looked directly at me. 'What did you just say?'

'Me?' I squirmed.'I didn't say anything.'

'You did,' Dad said, 'you said something about Lorcan and an army.'

'No, I didn't,' I interrupted. 'I do have a few secrets that I have kept from you, Father. Most of them, like what happened at the party I had in the house when I was sixteen and you were out of town, I keep so I will not get into trouble – others I keep because I swore an oath on the House of Duir. There are things it is not in my power to tell.'

I wanted to tell him all, especially now that he was finally telling me the truth, but I had sworn an oath. Dad looked me deep in the eyes and I saw that he understood.

'You had a party in the house when I was out of town?'

I smiled.

'Seriously,' Fergal said, 'I want to know what happened after you threw your hand to shore – there must have been pandemonium.' He looked like a little boy being told a bedtime story.

'I wouldn't know,' Dad said, 'I was unconscious at the time.'

'I was there,' Mom said. 'I wouldn't say, Fergal, that it caused a commotion, at least not at first. Everyone was stunned into silence. You have to realise that only a handful of us knew how important this race was – most people thought it was harmless family fun. No one could understand what made Oisin do such a desperate thing. Lord Finn and I dived into the lake and carried Oisin to shore. He was bleeding terribly.

Finn tore off a strip of his robe and tied a tourniquet around the wrist, but the bleeding would not stop. I thought he was going to die. I had some tree sap hidden in my satchel, I used it on the wound and incanted a Shadowspell. I heard Ona and Nieve gasp, "Shadowmagic!"

'Lord Finn looked at me and asked if this was really Shadowmagic. I told him it was and saw the conflict in his face. I had just saved his favourite son, but I had also just performed an act that was punishable by death. Since the damage was already done, I picked up Oisin's hand, and using Shadowmagic again, I preserved it in amber sap.

'Finn came close and whispered in my ear, "Do you have a place to go?" I nodded. He said, "Go there and never come back."

'There were tears in his eyes when Lord Finn stepped back and announced to all that I was banished, and my name was to be purged from our minds, and my memory was to be purged from our hearts. That was the last I saw of anyone from The Land, other than Oisin and the Fili, until the Shadowrunes told me to rescue you and your father from Cialtie's dungeon.'

'How could he do that to you?' I said. 'Finn sounds as bad as Cialtie.'

'Do not judge your grandfather harshly,' Mom said, in that motherly tone that made me a bit ashamed of myself. 'He should have had me executed on the spot. I am sure many thought he was wrong to let me live. You must remember how much pain Maeve and her Shadowmagic had caused. It is hard to be a good man and a great king. Your grandfather Finn was a great king.'

'So you came back here?' I said.

'Banishment was not really that much of a hardship for me. I came back here to live among the Fili. I had found peace here. The only hardship was that Oisin was not with me.'

'I didn't find out about all of this for two days,' Dad said. 'After the boat race, Ona gave me a tonic that made me sleep.'

'Who broke the news to you?' I asked.

That question sent a shiver down my father's back. 'When I awoke, I was in bed being nursed by Cialtie.'

'Cialtie! What was he doing there?'

'Oh, I'm sure he put on that sickening Cialtie charm, and convinced the nurse that he should look after his poor brother for a while.' Dad's face hardened. 'When I opened my eyes, my first sight was his glaring countenance.

'"Well, well, little brother, what were you thinking?" Cialtie asked me.

'I was terrified,' Dad admitted. 'I tried to shout but my throat was so dry, I could hardly make a sound.

'"Shhhh, don't exert yourself, little brother, you have been through an ordeal. What I can't figure out is, what were you, Daddy and that witch Ona concocting that made winning that race so important? Or was it that you just hate me so much that beating me was worth losing your hand?"'

Dad's voice faltered. 'All of the realities of what I had done crashed down on me like a wall of stone. I could hardly breathe.

'"Oh my gods," Cialtie said, smiling, "you didn't think about this before, did you? It's just occurring to you," and then he laughed. "Well, let me sum it up for you – without a runehand you can never take the Choosing and without a Choosing you can never be king, and because you are *a one-handed prince*, you can never have an heir. If I didn't know better, I would have thought you did this as a present for me."

'When I finally found a whispering voice, I said, "Where is Father?"

'"Oh, Father dear is off talking to the other lords, trying to explain why he didn't have Deirdre killed."

'I tried to sit up and failed.

'"Oh, I forgot," Cialtie said, "you have been out of it for the last two days. How can I break this to you? Deirdre is gone. You'll never guess – that little vixen is a Shadowwitch."

'I panicked,' Dad said, 'I couldn't breathe.

'"Oh my, little brother, I can see that you already knew. Shame on you. You see, she performed a little Shadowmagic show with your wrist and hand. You should have seen it. It was quite a demonstration. I thought our big sister Nieve was going to pee herself. I expected Daddy to chop her head off right then and there but instead he just banished her. He is as weedy as you."

'I gathered up all of my strength and took a swing at him. I would have connected, too – if there had been a fist attached to my wrist. Cialtie thought this was so funny, he cackled loud enough to alert the nurse. He explained to her that he was overcome with joy, seeing that his brother was going to recover, and danced out of the room.

'Eth arrived just after Cialtie left. He was beside himself with grief. He blamed himself for what happened to me. It wasn't his fault. I am sure he was enchanted by that Banshee witch Mná, but I was tired and angry. I shouted at him. I told him he was weak, that this was all his fault and that I never wanted to see him again. He left the castle that day. I never had the chance to tell him I didn't mean it.

'In one day I had lost my love, my best friend, my hand and had given my crown to the most evil man in The Land. If I had had the strength – I would have killed myself then and there.'

Dad stopped talking, looked down and wiped his eyes. How could I have lived with a man all of my life and never really known him? I stood up and put my arms around him.

Mom picked up the story. 'After Cialtie's Choosing (where he surprisingly chose the Reed Rune), Oisin came to find me here in the Fililands. By then I was very pregnant with you, Conor. Even the Fili were concerned when they saw that I was carrying the child of the one-handed prince. We consulted the Shadowrunes and came up with a plan. Your father and you would give up your immortality, just like the

Fili Druids had done, and then, after a full mortal life, the son of the one-handed prince would die a natural death in the Real World. It was the best we could do for you, Conor. I performed the spell that sent the two of you to the Real World – it was the worst day of my life.'

This lunch was starting to turn into a blubber-fest. I let go of Dad and hugged Mom, and when I could finally speak again I asked, 'Why didn't you come with us?'

'The Shadowrunes forbade it,' she said.

'These Shadowrunes,' I asked, 'are they really as clear as all that? All of the fortune-telling I have seen in my life was always so vague that it could be interpreted as anything.'

Before Mom could answer, a voice startled me from behind. 'Why don't you see for yourself?' It was Fand. She was standing in the doorway – I was surprised to see that it had grown dark outside. 'The Shadowcasting is ready.'

Mom stood. 'Well, let us see if the Shadowrunes can tell us of Master Fergal's lineage.'

Chapter Twenty
The Shadowcasting

We walked among the rowan trees in fading light. It would soon be pitch dark, not that that would bother our escorts – the Fili seemed to be as much a part of these woods as the trees themselves. Fergal walked like a man in a trance. I caught up to him.

'Are you cool about this?' I asked.

Fergal gave me a strange look. 'I'm a little cool, but it's pleasant out.'

'Sorry, that's not what I meant.' I laughed. 'Are you worried about finding out about your parents?'

'Oh, ah no… well, yes… oh, I don't know what I think,' he said, 'I just have to know. All my life I have been fantasising about having parents – I feel like I won't be whole until I find out. Do you understand?'

'If anyone understands, my friend, it's me.' I stopped him, gave him a hug and whispered in his ear. 'No matter what happens, Fergal, I'm there for you.'

'And I for you, Conor,' he replied, and slapped me on the back. I gave him a dirty look for the slap, and he returned it with a twinkling smile.

We arrived in a glade surrounded by a ring of very old rowan trees. Light was provided by glowing pinecones in glass holders. The golden glow showed the seriousness on everyone's faces. It made me want to crack a joke, but I decided against it. Maybe I was growing up a bit, or maybe I was just chicken.

Mom sat cross-legged on the ground next to two large bowls. We all sat around her.

'Before we begin,' she announced, 'we must state our intentions. Shadowmagic, like any power, can be corrupted. Only by keeping our motives pure can sins, like those done in the past, be avoided. This sap,' she said, pointing to a bronze bowl full of the stuff, 'was given freely by trees who knew what it was for. We thank them.'

The Fili in the circle thanked the trees aloud and then so did we. Mom continued.

'Fergal of Ur, come sit by me.'

Fergal stood up, flashed a forced Fergal-ish smile to Araf and me, and sat next to Deirdre.

'Do you, Fergal of Ur, come to this Shadowcasting freely?'

'I do,' Fergal replied.

'Why do you seek this Shadowcasting?'

'I want to know who my parents are.'

'Do you seek this knowledge out of malice or revenge?'

'I just want to know,' Fergal said, his eyes sparkling in the Shadowlight.

'Very well,' she said, 'I shall instruct the runes to tell us of your life as it has affected others. This may be painful to watch and difficult to share. Are you still willing?'

Fergal thought for a bit, then answered with resolve. 'I am.'

'We shall begin.'

Mom waved her hand and the pinecone lights dimmed. She took a pebble-sized dollop of sap and rubbed it between her palms. She spoke in a language I didn't understand – Ogham, the oldest tongue – the language of the trees. She pressed her ball of sap between her hands and spoke the Ogham word, '*Beith.*'

Mom looked to me for recognition. When she saw none she translated. '*Beith* – birch.'

She opened her hand, revealing a glowing amber disc, and when she turned it over it was engraved with a rune – the Birch Rune. She carefully placed it on the ground between her and Fergal. She rolled and pressed another bit of sap between her palms.

'*Luis* – rowan.'

A second glowing rune was placed next to the birch one. The next word she spoke I did recognise.

'*Cull* – hazel.'

The Hazel Rune, my mother's rune. The real one was destroyed – here was its shadow. Mom made a point of showing it to me before she placed it with the rest. She continued to produce runes for a long time.

'*Fearn* – alder.

Saille – willow.

Nuin – hawthorn.

Duir – oak.

Tinne – holly.

Quert – apple.

Muhn – vine.

Ur – heather.

Nion – ash.

Gort – ivy.

Getal – reed.

Straif – blackthorn.

Ruis – elder.

Ailm – silver fir.

181

Onn – gorse.
Eadth – poplar.
Iodhadh – yew.'

Each rune was placed in a specific order. When she was finished, I couldn't help thinking how it reminded me of an old chemistry class. There were empty spaces for runes not yet discovered, just like in the Periodic Table of Elements.

She rubbed one last ball of sap between her palms and told Fergal to extend his hands. In Ogham and then in the common tongue, she said, 'Fergal of Ur, this is your last chance to back away. Is it your wish to go on?'

Fergal instantly said, 'Yes.' I would have been disappointed with him if he hadn't, especially when I could see in my mother's face how much effort it had taken for her to make all of the Shadowrunes.

She placed the ball of sap into Fergal's palm and then pressed his hands together. 'The rune you make, Fergal, will be blank. Only a Choosing in the Hall of Choosing can give you your proper rune, but your Shadowrune will complete the casting.'

Fergal opened his hands like a book. Deirdre took his rune and placed it in the centre of the pattern – then it began.

The runes began to glow and then to flame. Not a candlelight flame, but a soft, almost invisible flame like the fire on a gas stove. The flames rolled along the ground between the runes. In some cases the runes repelled the fire, other runes absorbed the flames. After a few minutes, it was clear to see that some runes were joined with others by fire. Mom picked up the flaming runes and rearranged them, so that the runes joined by fire were together. The fire obviously did not burn – this was Shadowfire, not the real thing. When she had finished, Mom had five Shadow-bonfires before her. She sat cross-legged in front of them, her face fixed in concentration, her hands, still burning with Shadowfire, outstretched at her sides. Fergal sat opposite her, unmoving. They were both bathed in the same amber glow. Looking at them, I couldn't help thinking how different they were from each other – opposites, in fact. Still, these two opposites were locked eye to eye, both bent on the same goal. It sent a chill down my spine.

Mom waved a hand over a group of flaming runes and its fire increased as the others subsided. The flames grew higher until forms appeared. I began to make out a face and was surprised when I realised it was mine! The vision cleared and I found myself looking into a fiery 3-D movie of Fergal's life. Around the edge the apparition was a golden blur, but at the heart it was crystal clear. The images ran fast and made no sound, but I heard what was happening in my... soul. Like a conversation with a tree – it surpassed language. It was pure understanding. We watched the whole story of Fergal and my meeting: the shoe theft, the comedy of him knocking me out, the terror of the boar attacks and the courage of our stand against the Banshees in the Reedlands. More than just seeing, I was understanding Fergal, from Fergal's point of view. I had already decided that he was a good man – not perfect, but worthy of my trust. Now the Shadowmagic confirmed it. Fergal was a true free spirit. I saw that living for him was a joy, and that malice was a waste of his time. I realised then that I loved him – how could I not?

The images of Fergal and me dimmed as Mom brought up the fire in another set of runes. Visions formed before us of a young (and very cute) Fergal practising sword and banta stick fighting with Araf. Fergal did OK with his swordplay, but never even came close to winning the stick fights.

Another collection of runes showed Fergal turning down a kiss from a pretty young Imp girl. Not because he didn't like her, but because he didn't want her to get teased for kissing a Banshee. It nearly broke my heart.

Another runefire showed Fergal with his nanny – Breithe. Blissful images of walks in the woods, baths, kisses and being tucked into bed made my heart ache. Fergal may not have known his real parents, but he had the kind of motherly love that I always dreamt about.

Finally, Deirdre calmed all of the fires except one. This was it, this was the runefire that had the answer. The other fires sputtered and went out as the last group of runes roared with an amber inferno a third higher than the rest. We all leaned in, trying to make sense of the forms. As the vision cleared we saw Breithe! She was washing her hands in a tent. Could that be it? Was Breithe Fergal's mother? No, Breithe walked to a bed where a heavily pregnant woman screamed in labour. Wild, jet-black hair with a white streak covered her face – she was a Banshee – this was Fergal's mother. It was the moment of his birth. Breithe was the midwife, but who was the mother?

The contractions stopped. The Banshee mother fell back into the bed, her face still obscured. Breithe said, 'It's almost over, Mná dear,' and pushed the hair away from the mother's face. Mná! Dad had just mentioned that name – she was Cialtie's Banshee sorceress. The one who had bewitched Eth and had made the screaming shell for Cialtie in the race. That's when the realisation shot through my mind like a lightning bolt – if his mother is Mná, then his father must be… then he walked into the vision, Fergal's father – Cialtie.

A gasp went through the group. Why didn't I see this coming? Mná looked up and saw that Cialtie had entered. She pushed her hair back in an attempt to look better and smiled at him. 'Is it done?' she asked.

Cialtie smiled broadly. 'It is done.'

'Now you are king?'

'Soon.'

Mná smiled. 'And I shall be your queen.'

Cialtie's smile vanished. 'I don't think so.'

Mná sat up, confused.

'You don't think I could have a Banshee for a queen, do you?' Cialtie said *Banshee* like it was a profanity. 'What would people say?'

Mná went to attack him but was struck by another set of contractions. She fell back onto the bed, screaming. Breithe came up behind Cialtie and told him that he should leave and not upset the girl. Cialtie answered her with a backhanded punch that sent her across the tent, unconscious on the floor.

'You have been very helpful,' Cialtie said to Mná, 'but I'm afraid your usefulness has run out.'

I don't know if Mná was screaming from the pain of labour or because she saw the sword – either way, the screaming stopped abruptly when Cialtie chopped her head off.

Fergal freaked. He screamed, 'No!' and tried to stand.

Mom reached through the fire and grabbed him by the collar. 'It is dangerous to leave before we are done.' Her voice meant business.

'Please,' Fergal cried. His face was soaked with tears. 'Don't make me watch this.'

'I don't want to see any more either, Fergal, but we must. The Shadowmagic would crush us if we broke the casting. We are almost finished.'

I wasn't sure if I was allowed or not, but I had to go to him. I got up and sat next to Fergal and put my arm around him. Araf did the same on the other side and Essa held him from behind. Sobs racked Fergal as, together, we watched to the end.

In the vision we saw Cialtie pick up an oil lamp and walk to the entrance of the tent, then without emotion he smashed the lamp on the ground. He turned and exited, leaving the tent aflame. Breithe came to before the flames reached her. I wish I had met her – she must have been a remarkable woman. When she saw what had happened to Mná, she allowed herself only a second of horror – then she pulled a knife from her sock, jumped on the bed to avoid the flames, and went to work. Breithe performed a Caesarean section. She made a careful incision in Mná's midriff and gently removed Fergal from his dead mother's body. Just as swiftly, she tied off the umbilical cord, cut through the side of the tent and escaped into the night – leaving the evidence of Fergal's birth to burn behind her.

'It is done,' Deirdre said, her shoulders slumping with exhaustion.

Fergal collapsed, shaking, on Araf's lap. He was beyond weeping, he was, as the Irish say, *keening*. A soft, constant wail came from his throat. There was nothing to say. What could I say? I remembered a friend who was adopted who had hired a detective to find her real mother. She told me that all of her life she had dreamt that her real parents were some sort of aristocracy and she was really a princess. She told me how much it hurt when she found that her mother was just a poor, uneducated woman who had tried to forget her. I saw how much pain that caused her; I couldn't imagine what Fergal was going through.

Fand left to prepare a sleeping draught. We got Fergal to his feet and by the time we arrived at our room he was amazingly calm. Araf and I offered to help him get ready for bed, but he shooed us away. He said he wanted to just lie and think, and he promised he would take the sleeping draught in a little while.

Outside, a voice came out of the dark. 'How is he?' It was Essa.

'Who knows? I'm freaked out after seeing that stuff,' I said. 'Fergal won't get over this in a hurry.'

Essa nodded. 'I too won't be able to sleep. Would you like to walk for a bit?'

'Go on,' Araf said, 'I will keep watch here until Fergal sleeps.'

The night had gotten so dark, walking was actually dangerous. The first thing I did was trip over a small boulder.

'Are you alright?' Essa said, with a tone that sounded like real concern.

'Ow, I hurt my leg, but hey, I only need it for walking.'

'Let me have a look,' she said as she crouched down.

'How are you going to look? If there was any light around here I wouldn't have smashed into the damn rock.'

Essa turned her palms face up in front of her and closed her eyes and whispered, '*Lampróg.*'

A light twinkled in the distance and came at us, and as it got closer I actually had to shield my eyes. It was one of those nuclear-powered fireflies. Another came from behind me. They landed on Essa's fingers as she looked at my bruised shin. 'It's only a little bump, you baby.'

'Hey, you're the one that's making the big deal out of it. I just said *I hurt my leg*. You're the one who went all Florence Nightingale on me.'

'Florence who?'

'Never mind, why don't we just sit here for a while.'

She sat opposite me, cross-legged. A firefly landed on each knee, she whispered to them and they dimmed.

'Can you teach me the firefly trick, or is it a chick thing?'

'I don't know what a *chick thing* is but you have to be a bit of a sorcerer to do it. Since Deirdre is your mother, I think you could be taught.'

She smiled at me, her face bathed in firefly light. She was beautiful and I desperately wanted to kiss her, but the last time I kissed her – she decked me.

Like she was reading my mind, she said, 'I'm sorry I hit you back there in the Reedlands.'

'Don't worry about it. It was a learning experience. Next time I'm in a life-or-death situation with a beautiful woman – I'll ask before I kiss her.'

'I didn't hit you because of the kiss. I hit you because you sounded like you were giving up.'

'So you liked the kiss then?'

'I didn't say that,' she said, smiling a Mona Lisa-like smile that I couldn't quite read.

I returned her smile with a swashbuckling grin. 'Let me put it this way – if I were to kiss you now, would you punch my lights out again?'

'I'm not sure, that is just the chance you will have to take.'

I looked deep into her eyes. I had to make sure I was reading this right. The girl packed a serious punch and I had had enough concussions for a week – hell, for a lifetime. I held her gaze and her eyes gave it away. She wasn't looking for a fight. I was sure of it. At least, I think I was. If I got this wrong, I decided I was going to become a monk.

I leaned in and so did she. There is nothing like a first kiss. When I was a kid I remembered complaining about how slow the first kiss scenes in the movies were – now I know that that's exactly what they are like. Seconds take forever and the anticipation is exquisite.

So what was that first kiss with Essa like? I didn't find out. Araf came bounding up to us, shouting our names in the dark. We were both on our feet in a second.

'Araf, what is it?'

'Fergal's gone,' he said, 'and he has taken your sword.'

Chapter Twenty-One
Aunt Nieve

'Where could he have gone?' Essa asked.

Araf shrugged.

'I know where he's gone,' I said. 'He's going to kill Cialtie.'

'That's madness!' Essa said.

'I don't think Fergal is thinking all that straight at the moment.'

'I'll head south,' Araf said. 'He might try to get out the way we came in. May I borrow a firefly?'

Essa mumbled. One of her fireflies danced into Araf's hand and he was off.

'I'll talk to the Fili and see if they can help,' Essa said, and ran off, leaving me alone and in pitch darkness.

'Hey!' I shouted into the black. I couldn't see a thing and I had no idea where I was, so I did something I had always wished I could do. I shouted – 'MOM!'

Deirdre was there within the minute. 'Are you alright?'

'I'm lost and can't see a damn thing.'

Deirdre spoke quickly to a nearby tree and picked up a pinecone. She smeared it with a bit of sap and ignited it. When she handed it to me I was half expecting to be burnt, but the Shadowfire felt of nothing.

'Fergal is missing and he took my sword. I think he is trying to get to Castle Duir.'

'Oh my gods! He will never get past the blackthorns.'

'Will they hurt him?'

'They will kill him if he tries to cut through.'

'You have got to stop them.'

Mom whipped out her wand and touched it to the ground. A small plant pushed through the grass. Mom touched it with a finger. After what seemed like an eternity, she stood.

'He's this way,' she said, pointing west.

'Is he OK?'

'I don't know. He is contained. We had better hurry.'

We found him in the same area where Dad and I found the Pooka. Unlike the Pooka, Fergal wasn't on the other side of the blackthorns, but then again he wasn't on this side either. He was *in* the thorn wall. He had tried to climb the thorns at the same time that Deirdre had spoken to them. Instead of stabbing him, the thorns encircled him. He was off the ground and trussed up like a smoked ham in an Italian supermarket. It must have hurt like hell. The only thing he could move was his head. And let me tell you – he was not happy about it. He was beyond words, thrashing his head, cursing and ranting with sounds that were before language, like a high-pitched mad dog. His mouth was foaming to match.

Mom took some sap out of her satchel and spoke to a nearby tree, then threw the sap into the air. The top of the tree exploded into flame and light – Shadowfire.

'Fand will be here in a few minutes,' she said.

'Can you let him out?'

'I think we should wait till he calms down. Fand will have something.'

'Can I climb up to him without the thorns perforating me?'

Mom placed her hands on the thorn wall and said, 'Go ahead.'

The spikes turned away from me as I climbed. Fergal was still raving when I reached his eye level. He noticed me and his head whipped in my direction – there was murder in his eyes. Mom was right – if we had let him go, I think he would have attacked us. His mind had snapped.

Fand and some other Fili appeared out of the darkness. They had run without any lights – amazing. Upon seeing Fergal, Fand put away the vial she was holding and took out some greenish sap. She lifted the cuff of Fergal's trousers and rubbed the stuff on his skin. Fergal snarled at her but then started to relax. Mom released him enough for me to get a hold of his shirt and lower him down to the throng of waiting Fili hands. Fergal winced but didn't fight. I jumped down, and the blackthorns creaked back to their original position. Fand sat Fergal up. She was just about to give him something that would knock him out when he opened his eyes and saw me.

'Conor?' he said. The mad dog that had taken over his face was gone. He was Fergal again, without the smile.

'I'm here, Fergal.'

'He's my father,' he said. His voiced quivered and his eyes welled with tears.

'Yes,' I said. What else could I say? *It's OK, Fergal, don't worry about it?* That would be a lie. One thing this was not – was OK.

'Oh, Conor.' He sounded like he was five years old. 'He killed my mother.'

I put my arms around him. His head shook on my shoulder with silent sobs, his warm tears fell down my neck. I don't know how long we stayed like this but when I looked up, everyone else was there: Essa, Araf and my father. Dad leaned down and stroked Fergal's hair.

'Nephew,' he said. Fergal looked up, confused. Dad smiled at him. 'That's right, I am your uncle.' He wiped some of the tears from Fergal's cheek. 'Listen to me, Fergal, I know what it is like to lose all and I know despair, but I promise you – it will get a little better every day. I know you feel as if you can't go on, but it will be better tomorrow and the next day. The pain will never go, but it will get easier. You can do it. You are a son of Duir.'

I saw hope enter Fergal's eyes. I loved and admired my father at that moment more than I ever had.

Then Fergal's eyes went dark again. 'What about Cialtie?' he hissed.

'He will be dealt with soon,' Dad said, 'but we must not seek revenge. Revenge is an evil motive that corrupts the soul.' Dad grabbed Fergal under his arm and helped him to his feet. He looked his nephew in the eyes, and then looked at me. 'We shall seek justice.'

Fergal wanted to walk back to the village but Fand wouldn't hear of it. He didn't fight. He drank what she gave him and the Fili carried him unconscious on a stretcher. I was a bit jealous – I could have used a lift myself.

I didn't fall asleep as fast as I thought I would. One reason was the lump I was sleeping on – I had stashed the Lawnmower under my mattress. I didn't think Fergal would run off, but if he did, I didn't want to lose my sword again. The other reason I didn't drop off was because I was afraid to. This was my first undrugged night in the Fililands, I could sense the power in the place and I had a feeling the dreams here were going to be intense – I was right.

This dream was big. It was a full-blown battle. I watched from the ramparts as Castle Duir was under attack from an army made up of not just Leprechauns and Imps but all manner of beings. The odd thing was that the soldiers around me weren't even looking at the invading army. At first I thought they couldn't see them, but then I realised that they just didn't see this attack as a threat. They knew something I did not.

Cialtie showed up with a big red button, like you would see in a crappy movie about a nuclear war. He smiled as he pressed it. I tried to stop him but like all good nightmares, I was moving in slow motion. I reached the edge of the wall in time to see a golden shockwave hit the first group of attackers. To my horror I knew them all: first was my mother and then my father, followed by everyone I had ever known, even Sally was there looking at her watch wondering why I was late for the movie. I saw the flesh being torn from their bones. I was forced to watch the pain and horror of every person I had known and loved, die – die slowly. The guards on the tower didn't even notice what was happening. Cialtie walked away, whistling. The guards only noticed me when I tried to attack my uncle. They grabbed me and threw me over the wall. I awoke screaming on the floor.

Dad was the only person up in the breakfast room. He looked me in the eyes and said, 'Dreams?'

'Yeah,' I replied, 'intense.'

'Me too. When I left The Land I missed the dreams terribly, but I forgot what the nightmares were like.'

We swapped dreams. His was much more vague than mine but we suspected they were both similar. Dad thought we should talk to Nieve about it.

'How can you trust her?' I asked. 'She tried to kill me – twice!'

'That's one of the reasons I know I *can* trust her.'

'Huh?'

'Look, Nieve is my sister and I love her. I know it caused her much pain to try to kill you, but she did it for the good of The Land. She places duty above all else.'

'So why isn't she stabbing me in the back as we speak?'

'Your mother and I have a plan, and the Shadowrunes have told us it might work.'

'I thought Aunt Nieve didn't believe in this Shadowmagic stuff.'

'She's coming around.'

'So, Pop, what's the plan?'

'Cialtie is using my hand, that's how he got the Duir Rune.'

'What, you think he carried your hand through the Choosing?'

'More probably he got someone else to do it, but yes, he practically admitted it when we were in the dungeon, remember?'

It took me a second to think back that far. 'I do.'

'Well, that proves my hand is still working, and your mother thinks she can reattach it.' He flashed a cheeky grin worthy of Fergal's uncle.

'You're joking.'

'No, she definitely thinks it can be done and so does Nieve. There are just a few difficulties.'

'Like what?'

'We have to break into Castle Duir, find my old hand and perform an unauthorised Choosing ceremony in the Hall of Runes.'

'That doesn't sound easy.'

'It is not.'

'How are you going to do it?'

'That I haven't figured out yet, but we have time.'

'Can we take Cialtie out at the same time?'

'Getting in and out of the castle and reattaching my hand will be hard enough without adding assassination to the plan. One thing at a time, Conor. If I get my hand back, the Runelords will follow me. Then we deal with my brother.' He looked away, trying to contain his hate. Despite what he said to Fergal, revenge was an emotion he was struggling with too.

Fand came to the door and said, 'Our Pooka guest is awake.'

'Will he live?' Dad asked.

'No,' Fand replied. I could feel the compassion and pain in her voice. 'He has asked to see Deirdre.'

'Deirdre?' Dad said in surprise.

'Yes, she is on her way.'

She led us to the room of healing. The Pooka we had brought through the blackthorn wall was propped up in bed. The last time I had seen him he had been covered with blood – the Fili had cleaned him up but he looked bad. His skin had no colour and his lips were blue. Fand was right, he wasn't going to last very long. Mom arrived right behind us.

'Do you recognise him?' Dad asked.

'No. Poor thing.'

Mom went to the Pooka's side and held his hand. What life there was left in him sparkled in his eyes when he saw her. 'Are you Deirdre the Shadowwitch?' he said in a high, pathetic voice.

I thought for a second that Mom was going to be insulted by that question, but she simply replied, 'I am.'

'I was sent by Lorcan.' I could hardly hear him. He was using every ounce of his strength to speak, maybe even his last ounce of strength. 'We need your help.'

His voice became so faint that Mom had to lean in and turn her ear to his mouth. From the expression on her face I could tell it wasn't good news. She took a tiny piece of gold out of her pocket and placed it in the Pooka's mouth. He instantly changed into a wolf again. Mom stepped back – so did I, and I was on the other side of the room. He let loose a mournful howl and died – then changed back into a man.

'What did he say?' Dad asked.

Mom covered the Pooka with a sheet, and faced us. 'He said Cialtie is going to kill us all.'

Chapter Twenty-Two
The Army of the Red Hand

'Before he died,' Deirdre began, 'the Pooka told me that Cialtie had the power to destroy all of The Land.' We were back in the breakfast room. Everyone was there except Fergal, who was still asleep.

'Do you believe him?' Essa asked.

'I do. He also said that Lorcan needed my help, immediately. But I don't know where Lorcan is or how I can help.'

Araf, Essa and I looked at each other, but Dad looked at me with one of those Dad looks. I was going to have to break my solemn vow. I opened my mouth and waited for the lightning bolt to hit me. 'Lorcan has an army of Leprechauns and Imps,' I said, with resignation in my voice. 'They call themselves the Army of the Red Hand and they're in the Hazellands. They are planning to attack Cialtie. Just don't tell Lorcan the Leprechaun I told you. I don't want that guy mad at me, he's mean when he's angry.'

'I don't think he will mind you telling,' Dad said, holding up his handless arm, 'after all, he named his army after me.' Dad stood and put on his serious face. 'It has begun. I knew it would, I had just not expected it to be so soon. I fear we are going to war with Castle Duir. Deirdre and I shall leave to join Lorcan's army immediately. This fight is ours and I will not force anyone to come. If you choose to go home, I will not think any less of you.'

Fand was first to speak. 'Neither I nor the Fili will go into battle with you. The memory of the last battle of Castle Duir is still with us. However, I support you. Remember, the freedom of the Fililands is yours. There is always refuge here for you.'

Dad bowed low – the bow of a king to a queen.

'I am with you,' Araf said, standing. 'This battle is not only yours. I would have joined my fellow Imps even if you had not returned.'

'I am with you, and so is my father,' Essa said as she got to her feet.

'You can speak for Gerard?' Mom asked.

'I can. At this moment he is making his way to meet with Lorcan.'

'How do you know this?' Mom asked, her eyes narrowing a bit.

Essa reached in her satchel and produced a sheet of gold framed in dark wood. It looked like an old school slate to me. Everyone else gasped in awe.

'Is that an *Emain* slate?' Araf asked with awe in his voice.

'It is. My father has its twin.'

'What's so special about this?' I said, picking it up and casually looking at it.

My father snatched the slate from my hand and gave me a look like I had just scribbled on the wall with a crayon.

'That is probably the most expensive item you have ever held. I imagine it took a roomful of gold to set the spell onto this slate.' Dad placed it gingerly back in front of Essa.

'Sooorry. What does it do?'

'Whatever is written on this slate appears on its twin slate, no matter where it is.'

'Cool, like magic email.'

Everyone as usual looked confused. Dad rolled his eyes but nodded yes.

'Gerard seems to have all of the cool stuff,' I said. 'Your dad is like a Tir-na-Nogian James Bond.'

'Who?' Essa said.

That was one of the many times I wished I was back in the Real World, just so people would get my jokes.

'Essa, would you send a message to your father for me?' Dad asked.

Essa nodded yes.

Dad turned to his sister. 'Nieve – sister, are you with us?'

Nieve was looking down at the table. When she looked up I could swear she was close to tears. 'I remember you both as babies. I played with you and Cialtie when you were infants. Now you want me to choose between brothers and go to war with my home.' She paused. 'The decision is difficult but I have made difficult decisions before. Choosing to attack you, Conor, was the hardest, and now it seems it may not have been the right thing to do.' She stared at her hands for a moment and then slapped them on the table. 'I can no longer blindly follow the prophecies of the past. I must be guided by my heart and mind. Cialtie must be stopped.' She stood. 'I am with you, Lord Oisin.'

Dad's eyes were shining when he bowed to her.

'Well,' I said, 'I think I'm just gonna stay here and work on my tan.'

Everyone looked at me, completely stunned.

'Hey, I'm kidding, for crying out loud. Of course I am in. Mom, Pop, I'm sticking with you.'

'Thank you all,' Dad said. 'May the gods be with us. We leave at dusk.'

'Great,' came a voice from the doorway. It was Fergal. 'Where are we going?'

We waited until it was pitch black before we left the Fililands. The arrow that we found in the Pooka was a Banshee arrow and we didn't want to tangle with those guys again. The only light came from the tiniest sliver of a moon. Sorley, our Fili guide, led the way. I swear the Fili can see in the dark. The horses had ribbons in their tails that Fand said were visible in the dark only to horses' eyes. It must have worked. Acorn was perfectly happy to follow behind Essa's horse.

We didn't stop until the sun came up. I was beginning to realise that here in The Land I was capable of feats of stamina that would have been impossible back in the Real World. Still, I welcomed the break. It was the first time I had a chance to talk to Fergal since our journey began. Mom, Dad and I had all spoken with him before we left, and we were surprised at how sane he seemed. We all agreed it was probably an act and that deep down he was a seething mess. There was talk of leaving him with the Fili but Dad said he had as much right to see this through as the rest of us. Fergal promised he would do as he was told. By the time we left, his smile was almost convincing.

He was sitting on a rock eating a packed lunch the Fili had made for us.

'How you doing, cuz?' I said.

'I wish people would stop asking me that.'

'It's a rule – when someone freaks out like you did yesterday, you have to ask him how he is. So how are you?'

'I'm alright.'

I looked at him.

'I really am,' he said. 'OK, when I start thinking about it I feel myself tensing up and going crazy, but then I take a few deep breaths and clear my mind, like the Imps taught me to do, then I can go on.'

'I was worried about you. I thought you were going to do something stupid.'

'Me?' he said, flashing me a Fergal smile. 'I never do anything stupid, except when I wake up and stab people – but you don't even have to worry about that – look.' He pointed to his Banshee blade in a scabbard on his belt. 'I tried to get some more gold wire so I could replace my blade in my sleeve, but the Fili don't do that kind of magic. I hate having my sword at my waist but at least I won't kill you next time you wake me up.'

We didn't rest long. Dad wanted to make the Hall of Knowledge before dark. We quickened our pace. Acorn was a star. I could sense he didn't like being back in the Hazellands but he trudged on like a trooper. At one point he let loose a whinny when I started to fall asleep in the saddle. The hours on horseback, the sun, the fresh air and Acorn's rhythm lulled me into a bit of a hypnotised state.

Late in the day, we entered the outskirts of the Hall of Knowledge's grounds. Sorley, our guide, was in the lead when we reached a small hill. He turned when he reached the top of the rise. I think he meant to shout a warning, but all he managed was a grunt as he fell from his saddle. He had an arrow sticking out of his chest. That woke me up.

It was Big Hair and about ten other Banshees. It must have been a scouting party. We had practically stepped on them. I think we surprised them just as much as they did us, but that didn't stop them from instantly going on the offensive. I tried to turn Acorn to get some space between us and the screaming attackers, but as I tried I saw something fly through the air, and Acorn fell over – hard. I got my foot out of the stirrup in time and hit the ground rolling.

'You hurt my horse!' I screamed. 'You son of a…' The first Banshee came at me and I ducked and rolled. When I got to my feet he came at me, holding his sword like a baseball bat. His whole left side was wide open. It was so obvious I thought that maybe it was a trick, so I decided to parry the blade instead of attacking his weak spot. I was right – the handle of the Banshee's sword had a dagger sticking out of it. If I had attacked on his left, he would have stabbed me. Instead, I planted my back foot and put all of my weight behind my sword. He was so shocked that I had not gone for his weak side that he was completely unprepared for the impact. The Lawnmower pushed his blade back so hard, that *his own sword* sliced his neck right up to the bone! That's the problem with tricky sword manoeuvres, the first time they don't work – they can kill you.

I didn't have time to marvel at the fact that I had just semi-decapitated a guy with a parry, there was a lot more fighting going on. I looked around – everyone seemed to be doing OK. I almost felt sorry for the guys who were attacking Nieve and Deirdre. I saw one Banshee take a swing at Nieve and bounce off her like he had hit a stone wall. Araf and Essa were using sticks against swords, but the way they used sticks meant that the swords weren't doing very well. Dad was in a fight with two men. I was about to go and help him when I saw the Banshee with the big hair coming up behind Fergal.

'Hey, you!' I shouted as I ran to intercept. 'Yeah, you with the bad perm!' He probably didn't know what a perm was but he understood the tone and knew it wasn't a compliment.

He turned. The smirk on his face meant he recognised me. Well, I remembered him too. This guy didn't make the mistake the last guy made. No mad advances, no tricks, he just pointed his sword and walked towards me. Up till now, the Banshees I had fought hadn't impressed me. Big Hair was the exception – his swordsmanship was good. The two of us cut and parried half a dozen times, trying to size each other up. I was very impressed with his speed. His thrusts were so fast that I had trouble seeing them coming. This was a problem. Dad had taught me to cut and parry until my opponent tired, but I had a feeling his speed would get me before he flagged. I looked for a flaw in his technique and I found it. His attacks were fast but he hesitated a microsecond afterwards to see if he connected. On his next attack I shouted, 'Ouch!' even though he missed me. When he looked, I came at him with a quick jab to his shoulder. He saw it coming and twisted out of the way, but lost his footing and went down. I had no moral qualms about attacking this guy on the ground but I didn't get the chance. He rolled backwards and was on his feet in a flash. I was going to have to work for this one.

And then he did it – the oldest trick in the book. His left hand slid down to the butt of his sword pommel. I thought maybe he had a dagger stashed in there, but when his hand came away seemingly empty, I thought nothing of it. That was a big mistake. He closed the distance between us, brought his sword up, as if to attack – and threw something in my eyes with his left hand. I found out later it was sand that had been soaked in lime juice. It felt like he had thrown pins in my eyes. I was completely blinded. I tried to open them, so I could defend myself, but my eyelids would not obey. I was as good as a dead man. I swung my sword wildly in front of me, while back-pedalling; amazingly the attack failed to come. The bastard was toying with me. I calmed myself and listened. Maybe if I could hear where he was I could get in a lucky stab that might catch him off guard.

I listened – nothing. Then I heard a soft footstep to my left. I didn't move. I didn't want him to know I could hear him. He was trying to come up from behind me. It was terrifying. I knew I had to wait until he was in striking distance, but I also knew I could get a blade between my ribs at any second. I waited for one more footfall and I made my move. I spun and sliced into the space I was sure he occupied. My sword hit steel, was parried up and then something hit my hand and I lost my grip. My sword went flying. I was blind and disarmed. I might as well have been naked too. I toyed with the idea of running but I knew that would do no good.

The last time I thought I was going to die, my life flashed before my eyes. I always have hated reruns on TV, so this time I just raised my arms and said, 'Do your worst.'

Chapter Twenty-Three
The Return of the Hazellands

'I never do my worst,' said a familiar voice. 'I always do my best.' I knew that voice. It definitely was not Big Hair. 'Master Dahy?' I asked into the darkness.

'You were doing well until you let him throw sand in your eyes,' Dahy said.

'Where is the Banshee?'

'He is quite dead,' Dahy stated. 'I hated to interfere – but I lost my temper when he used sand. I threw a knife into his neck.'

'Thanks,' I said. My knees started to buckle as relief washed over me. I sat down hard. 'How are the others?'

'They are all fine, don't worry. Let us take a look at those eyes.'

He left me and came back with a water skin to rinse out my peepers. They stung like crazy but I was relieved to find that I could see again. I was afraid the Banshee had blinded me for life.

By the time I could use my sore eyes properly, all of the fighting was finished. The ground was littered with dead Banshees. Mom and Nieve were tending Sorley, and no one else seemed to be harmed. I was relieved to see Acorn on his feet. Essa was examining his front legs.

'Is Acorn OK?'

'I don't think anything is broken,' she said. 'He was tripped by some sort of rock and rope weapon. You should not ride him for a while.'

'You've got the rest of the week off, old friend,' I said as I stroked his nose.

He snorted a reply, as if to say, *'Don't worry about me.'* What a great horse.

A shout came from Dahy. 'Deirdre, I think you should look at this!'

Something in his voice made us all gather around. In his hand he held a leather cord with a small gold amulet hanging from it.

'I found this around the neck of that Banshee with all the hair. It looks like the one that your father used to wear.'

He held it up and showed it to my mother. She gasped and placed her hand over her mouth. Her eyes instantly watered up. 'I made that for him when I was a little girl,' Mom said.

A voice behind me spoke with so much venom that I didn't recognise it. 'Now we know who destroyed the Hall of Knowledge.'

I turned – it was Essa. You could almost feel the heat from the fire in her eyes.

I always wondered what it would be like to be a celebrity walking into a movie première and having hundreds of people pushing, just to get a glimpse of me. Now I know – it's quite nice. Gerard and Dahy had arrived the night before and had told Lorcan all about us. The news that the one-handed prince, Oisin of the Red Hand, was about to arrive at the camp apparently sent the whole place buzzing. Imps and Leprechauns lined our route and saluted as we passed – even me. Luckily Imps and Leprechauns don't believe in prophecies much.

Lorcan and Gerard were waiting for us outside of Lorcan's headquarters in the ruins of the Hall of Knowledge. Lorcan obviously wanted to greet the returning prince of Duir with pomp and ceremony, but Gerard spoiled that idea. As soon as we came into view, Gerard started laughing that infectious laugh of his. Essa broke ranks and ran into her father's arms. Lorcan was about to salute my father when Gerard stepped forward and took Dad by the shoulders.

'My gods, Oisin, what has the Real World done to you?' Gerard's voice was without his usual mirth.

'It has made me older, Lord Gerard,' Dad said.

Gerard smiled. 'Has it made you wiser?'

'That is what we are here to find out.'

Gerard nodded in agreement, then gave Dad a big hug. 'Welcome home, Oisin.'

Lorcan tried once more to introduce himself but Gerard thwarted him again. He grabbed Fergal and me by the neck and then gave us a hug that almost banged our heads together. 'Well, well, Deirdre, these two young things found you after all.'

'They did indeed,' Mom answered, 'and I am very glad that they found you too. Thank you for looking after them – Lord Gerard.'

Gerard laughed. 'Ah, they are good boys,' he said as he tightened his uncomfortable hug. 'Give them a hundred years and they will make good men.'

We rubbed our sore necks as he approached Mom. 'Deirdre, you have been too long away. Why did you never contact me?'

'I did not want to get you into trouble,' Mom answered.

'From now on, let me be the judge of the trouble I get into,' Gerard said. He took Mom's face in his huge hands and kissed her on the forehead.

'Speaking of trouble, I think we should get a drink and make some plans.' Gerard grabbed Mom and Dad by the arms and whisked them into the Hall. Everyone followed except Lorcan, who was still standing to attention. I seemed to be the only person who noticed how uncomfortable he was.

'Would you like me to introduce you to my dad?' I asked him after everyone else had gone.

'Yes I would, Prince Conor,' he replied very stiffly.

Well, well, I thought, *it's* Prince Conor *now.*

'Should I tell him that you knocked me out and tied me up?'

'I would appreciate it if you did not,' he replied.

I let him stew for a bit and then smiled. 'Come on, Lorcan, we have a war to plan.'

Inside the headquarters it was pandemonium. Gerard was laughing and dishing out drinks and generally being the life of the party that he is famous for.

'Excuse me,' I said, but Gerard took no notice. I looked over to Essa, who gave me a *He's always like this* look. She tapped him on the shoulder and I whispered in his ear. He settled down after that.

'Lord Oisin, Lady Deirdre,' I said in my most regal of voices, 'I present to you Lorcan the Leprechaun' – Lorcan obviously didn't like the title but I couldn't resist it – 'Commander of the Army of the Red Hand.'

'I remember your father, Lorcan,' Dad said. 'Where is he?'

'Dead, my lord. Soon after you left, most of the senior engineers died in a mining accident. Now many of us are suspicious about the cause.'

'I am sorry for the trouble my family has caused you,' Dad said, bowing his head.

'Your family had caused me no harm, my lord, the source of my – *our* – trouble is Cialtie,' Lorcan went on. 'I am sorry to interrupt your reunions and I know you must be weary after your travels, but we have little time.'

Lorcan walked up to a large round table in the middle of the room. Everyone circled around it. From a satchel around his waist Lorcan produced a medallion and threw it on the table. It was about the size of a beer mat, made of silver and crafted into the shape of a tree. The branches of the tree flowed into the roots, making a continuous circle. It was beautiful and very stylised. 'This is a template for an amulet,' Lorcan said.

'What?' came the instant response from almost everyone around the table. This seemingly innocuous statement made Mom and Nieve snap their heads around and drop their mouths wide open. It was as if Lorcan had just said, '*I eat babies for breakfast.*'

'Cialtie is making this out of *gold*?' Mom asked.

'He has done it already.'

'How do you know?' Dad asked.

'We have spies in the castle,' Lorcan said. 'Cialtie has set up a secret gold smithy in the east wing.'

'We must stop him before he uses it,' Nieve said.

'I am afraid it is too late. He already has.'

'Where?' Dad demanded. 'When?'

Lorcan turned to a soldier and said, 'Ask Master Brone to join us.'

The soldier nodded and left.

'Excuse me,' I interrupted, 'sorry for being a little thick, but I'm new around here. What's so bad about making this thing out of gold?'

Nieve answered me. 'Most of the magic in The Land is fuelled by gold. Most gold is used to make amulets, like the *rothlú* amulet you once wore around your neck. The most important rule when designing an amulet is to make sure the power has a place to go. An amulet must always have a point for the spell to exit from.'

'What if it doesn't? What if it's a circle like this one?'

'Then it explodes.'

'Did you notice,' my father said, 'that you hardly ever see gold finger rings in The Land?'

I hadn't, but when I looked around the room I saw that everyone there was wearing at least one ring but all were made of silver.

'There are very few goldsmiths that can make a ring that won't blow your hand off,' Dad said.

Nieve nodded in agreement. 'An amulet in a circle will explode – an amulet like that one, where all of the power is channelled back to the centre, is...' she searched for a word.

'A bomb,' Dad said.

'Not just a bomb,' Mom said, 'there is no way of knowing how much energy it will build up before it explodes.'

'You mean it's like a magic nuke?'

Nobody knew what that meant except Dad. 'That's about right.'

How bad?' I asked. 'Could it take out a village?'

'It can,' came a weak voice at the door, 'and it has.'

I have seen people who were depressed and down on their luck, but I had never seen a truly broken man before. The man who entered the room was in bad shape.

'This is Brone from the village of More,' Lorcan said.

'I know Brone,' my father said. 'You run the Riverside Inn – I have fished there.'

Brone perked up a bit when he saw Oisin but then the weight of his news pushed back on his shoulders and he looked down. 'It's gone, Lord Oisin, all gone.'

'What is gone, Brone?' Dad asked gently. 'The inn?'

'Everything, my lord.' I didn't think he was going to say anything more, but then he gathered what little strength he had and went on. 'A week ago I was upriver fishing when I heard an awful sound, and then a wave came that threw me out of my boat. A wave came upriver! I never heard of such a thing. My boat was damaged, so I had to walk back to the village, but when I did – it was gone. At first I thought I was lost but I was not – I was home. Not one stone was left on top of another. Everything – everyone, gone.' Brone could speak no more. A soldier caught him before he could fall and led him out of the room.

Dad looked to Lorcan for confirmation. Lorcan nodded *yes*.

'Why would he do this? Why destroy a village as peaceful as More?' Dad said as he sat heavily into a chair.

'I think it was a simply a test,' Lorcan said.

'A test for what?' Dad said, smashing his hand on the table. He looked at Lorcan with daggers in his eyes and then composed himself.

'For this.' Lorcan unrolled a sheet of paper on the table. It was obviously printed plans of Castle Duir, as seen from above. Around the castle was a thick circle in red ink with thinner lines circling under the castle and then back into the outside circle. It was obvious even to me what it was.

'You are saying that Cialtie is going to circle the whole castle with a circular amulet?' Dad asked.

'We think he is almost finished,' Lorcan said.

'That is why he was hoarding all of the gold,' Gerard said, understanding. 'Can you imagine how much gold it must have taken?'

'I saw this in a Shadowcasting, but I didn't know what it was,' Mom said in a faraway voice. 'How could I know? How could I imagine anyone would do such a thing?'

'Let me get this straight,' I said. 'If Cialtie sets this off, he kills any army attacking the castle – right?'

'If Cialtie sets this off,' Nieve replied, 'it could destroy all of The Land and everything in it.'

Chapter Twenty-Four
The Evil Eye

'Is there any chance of getting another boarburger?' I asked the Imp that was serving food. He replied with the customary blank look I seemed to get from everyone around here when I tossed in a Real World reference.

I was delighted to sink my teeth into some meat. The Fili food was amazing but I was tired of nuts and berries. The Imps had barbecued a couple of dozen boars. They were so good it made me think that McDonald's should have McBoar on the menu. Araf, Fergal and I were chowing down, while most of the others were having high-powered meetings: Essa was off with Nieve, and Mom and Dad were with Gerard. After my second burger I spotted Essa walking among the ruins and excused myself.

I found her standing alone, staring at the stained-glass window of the woman sitting in the hazel tree. She saw me and quickly turned away, wiping her eyes.

'Hey, are you OK?' I said.

'Yes,' she said, putting on a brave face, 'it's just this place. How would you say it? – *It freaks me out.*'

I laughed, and so did she, but it was a bit strained.

'Are you sure that's all?' I asked.

She looked away and didn't answer.

I took her hand in mine and said, 'It will be alright.'

She turned and looked at me, but I still couldn't read her expression. 'So you have become an oracle, have you?'

'I have talents you can't even begin to imagine,' I said, flashing a smile that I learned from Fergal.

And then the strangest thing happened. She threw herself into my arms and kissed me – hard. It wasn't a tender kiss. It wasn't even passionate – it was almost desperate. Then she turned and started to run off, saying, 'I can't do this.'

I grabbed her arm before she could go. When was I going to learn never to grab Essa when she wanted to leave? She did her customary anti-attack manoeuvre – which meant I ended up on the ground, with her holding my arm behind my back in an extremely unnatural position.

'Ow, ow, ow,' was about all I could say.

'We have a battle to prepare for,' she said, letting me go, and stormed off.

'Hey!' I shouted after her. 'You kissed me, remember?'

I sat there, rubbing my arm, and thought about Sally. She may not be as beautiful as Essa, but at least she was less painful.

'Girl trouble?' It was Dad, with a smile on his face, the first smile I had seen him wear since he heard about what Cialtie was doing.

'Are all the women in The Land that fiery?' I asked.

'The good ones are,' he said and helped me up. 'I'm just about to meet with Lorcan. I think you should be with us.'

214

Lorcan and his generals were standing around the table, looking at the map of Castle Duir. They all came to attention when Father and I entered the room.

'Lorcan, your army is not large enough to breach Castle Duir.'

'It must be, my lord, we have to attack before Cialtie completes his circle of gold.'

'How do you know it is not finished already?'

'We must assume it is not. If it is finished – all is lost.'

'We must assume that the circle *is* complete, but all is not lost. Cialtie thinks his weapon is a secret and therefore has not bothered to guard it sufficiently. Deirdre says that the perimeter of the castle is only patrolled by a single troop of Banshees.'

'That is so.'

'I assume you have some goldsmiths in your ranks.'

'Half of my army are Leprechauns, my Lord, they know how to work gold.'

'Give me ten of your most trusted goldsmiths. Cialtie's ultimate defence may prove to be his downfall. Can your army be ready to march at dawn?'

'It can, my lord.'

'Can you make Castle Duir in two and a half days?'

'We can.'

'Good. Deirdre, Nieve, Conor, Fergal, Essa, Araf and myself shall try to gain entrance to the castle on the morning of the third day. If all goes well, my brother will open Castle Duir for you.'

'And if all doesn't go well?' I said, and instantly regretted it.

'Then,' Dad said with a sigh, 'there won't be anyone left to worry about it.'

215

That night Gerard opened several barrels of his finest wine.

'Remember when Cialtie came to visit me a little while back?' Gerard said as he tapped another barrel. 'Well, he came in person to complain about the quality of the wine I was sending him.'

'What a jerk,' I said.

'No,' Gerard said, 'he was right to complain. I have been sending him swill for years. This is the good stuff, but I can't let him have it. It shall go to people who deserve it.'

All of the army got at least a cup. It wasn't a celebration, it was more like a ceremony – something solemn.

That night I had another dream. Dad's right hand was on fire. I tried to run to him but I couldn't move. I was forced to watch him burn as I was frozen solid.

Lorcan woke me at dawn. 'Good morning, Lorcan the Leprechaun,' I said, rubbing the sleep out of my eyes.

'I would appreciate it if you stopped calling me that.'

'Sorry, General, what can I do for you?'

'Why did you not tell me you were a prince of oak and hazel?'

'Well, everyone I ever told tried to kill me. Now that I think of it, you tried to kill me without even knowing.'

'I am sorry for that.'

'No probs, you were just doing your job. Speaking of jobs, shouldn't you be leading an army into battle?'

'My army awaits but I must show you something before we leave.'

I dressed quickly and followed him into the ruins of the Hall of Knowledge.

'You left something behind last time you were here.'

'Oh yeah, my banta stick, I almost forgot.'

'Do you remember where you left it?'

I tried to think back that far. Days in The Land seem like lifetimes. 'I think I left it in there.'

We rounded the corner into the courtyard and I saw it. The hazelwood banta stick that Dahy had given me, and had once belonged to my grandfather Liam – Runelord of the Hazellands. It was exactly where I had left it.

'You cannot take it back.'

'Why not?'

'Take a closer look.'

I had stuck it into the ground in almost the exact place where Essa had found the roots of the Tree of Knowledge. I drew closer and had a good look. Three green shoots with tender leaves had sprouted from the sides of my stick. My grandfather's hazel staff had taken root.

'It looks as if a hazel will once again bloom in the Hall,' Lorcan said behind me. 'A new Tree of Knowledge perhaps?'

I touched it. It was too young to speak, but I could feel the life in it.

Lorcan placed his hand on my shoulder. 'This is a good omen. Good luck, son of hazel and oak. When we next meet, it shall be in your father's house.'

'I'll buy you a beer.'

He smiled and left me alone with the young hazel. 'This is for you,' I said aloud to a grandfather I had never known.

It was strange being on horseback without Acorn beneath me. Lorcan had lent me a mare named Cloud. She was smaller than Acorn and lived up to her name by giving a softer ride, but I refused to get too friendly. It felt like I was having an affair with another horse.

I was relieved to find that our route wouldn't be taking us through the Yewlands – I didn't want to go through that again. Apparently, the only reason we went that way the first time was to make sure no one was following us. I can understand that. There is no way I would take a walk among the yews again, unless my life depended on it. Even then I would have to think about it.

There were nineteen of us in our party. On horseback were: Mom, Dad, Nieve, Essa, Fergal, Araf, me and ten Leprechaun goldsmiths. Gerard and Dahy rode in the front of a wagon pulled by a pair of magnificent workhorses. I thought the horses I had seen here before were big, but these things were colossal! They might as well have been elephants for the size of them. Gerard's wagon was packed with about three dozen massive barrels of wine, but they pulled them as if they were hauling feather pillows.

We kept a leisurely pace. We wanted to arrive at the castle only half a day before Lorcan's army, so we didn't have to press too hard. Nieve and Deirdre spent the first day gabbing on horseback like long-lost sisters. Essa and Fergal were both in introspective moods. I understood it with Fergal but I couldn't figure out what was bothering Essa. The Leprechauns were a bit in awe of us, so they pretty much kept to themselves. I rode abreast with Araf – and you know how chatty he is. Actually, I wasn't in the chattiest of moods myself. I know this sounds crazy (after all I had been through), but for the first time since I had been here – I was nervous. When I first heard Ona's prophecy, I wondered – *How could I possibly destroy the whole land?* – but now it occurred to me, that that might be exactly what I was doing. Cialtie had a weapon that could trash everything, and we were on our way to provoke him. Maybe I was playing right into destiny's hand.

That night around the fire, I put that point to Dad.

'I remember when I was working at the university,' Dad said, 'I used to laugh at the science professors who were so sure that everything could be explained. They were all buffoons except for one of them. His name was Tobias, he was Italian.'

'I remember him. He taught physics, didn't he?'

'That's right. Even though his entire life was dedicated to provable facts, he believed in *the Evil Eye.*'

'The what?'

'*The Evil Eye* – some Italians think that a person with special power can harm you with just a look. Tobias even wore a gold necklace to protect him from it.'

'That sounds like one of Mom's amulets.'

'Exactly. I asked him once how a man of science could be so superstitious and he told me about quantum physics. Apparently there are things going on in the tiniest of matter that just cannot be explained. He told me about an experiment where a scientist made an atom spin in some laboratory and it made another one spin in the opposite direction ten miles away. He couldn't explain it – no one could. He said if the smartest people in the world can't explain something like that – then he was keeping the necklace on. I liked him, he had an open mind.

'One day, he explained the Chaos Theory to me by holding up a piece of paper. He asked, "What would happen if I let go?" I told him that the paper would flutter to the ground, but then he asked me – "*Where will it hit the ground?*" He let the paper go and it landed not far from his feet. He said he could explain mathematically how the air and gravity reacted with the paper and why the paper landed where it did –

"*but,*" he said, "*no one could ever predict where the paper would land before it was dropped.*"

'That is the essence of the Chaos Theory. We know things *will* happen but until they do, we cannot tell *how* they will happen. I am sure Ona was right – she always was – but we don't know the how, or the when. Just because we have a glimpse of the future does not mean we should run and hide. We must do what must be done. Cialtie must be stopped and I must get my hand and fix the damage my brother has done.'

I looked at the man I had spent my entire life with, and realised just how much I had underestimated him. I remembered a Mark Twain quote: he said something like – '*I left my family at fifteen because my parents were so stupid. When I arrived back home two years later, I was amazed how much they had learned in that time.*'

'I haven't said it in a long time, Dad, but I love you.'

'And I you, son.' He kissed me on the cheek. 'Get some sleep, we have a long day tomorrow.'

We spent the next day riding fields dotted with poplar trees – the Eadthlands. I think the poplars are my favourite trees in The Land. They are solitary, straight and unimaginably high, like huge green rocket ships. I leaned back to try to see the top of one as we rode by and almost fell out of my saddle. I wanted to stop and speak to one of them but Mom said they are not very good conversationalists – their thoughts are too much in the clouds. Apparently the Fili used to converse with them about philosophy, but only if they would climb to the top. If I was to climb that high, the tree had better say something pretty important. I would be angry if I risked life and limb to get to the summit and the only thing the poplar said was, '*I can see your house from here.*'

The other nice thing about the Eadthlands is that the trees are so far apart. It gives you a chance to notice all of the other plants and animals that populate The Land. Rabbits the size of puppies came out of their burrows to watch us go past. I saw a fox with a coat so red and lush I wanted to hug it. The wildflowers were in full bloom. Fields were covered with colours that you just don't get in the Real World. There were reds, yellows and purples the like of which I had only ever seen in a tropical fish tank, and then colours I didn't even have a name for.

Essa rode up beside me and said, 'Stop it.'

'What are you talking about?'

'Stop looking at The Land like you are never going to see it again.'

'That's not what I am doing,' I protested, but she had fallen back already. The thing is, she was right – that is exactly what I was doing. I think everyone was. Even Gerard was quiet. To give you an idea of how nervous we all were, Araf came abreast of me and started a conversation without me even saying anything to him!

'I went to Castle Duir with my father once, when I was a boy,' he said without prompting. I almost fell out of my saddle with shock. 'I remember sneaking off and exploring the castle and getting terribly lost. I ended up in the library. I had never seen so many books before, but being a child, what interested me the most were the weapons. There was a beautiful oak banta stick on the wall. I was climbing on a desk to have a closer look at it when Lord Finn – your grandfather – came in. I must have startled him – he shouted, "What are you doing here?" I was terrified and ran out of the room. He gave chase and caught me at the end of the corridor. I kicked and screamed as he picked me up by my shoulders and held me at arm's length. Then he laughed, that wonderful laugh that your family seems to own, and he gave me a smile – now that I think of it, it was a smile just like the one Fergal has.

'I stopped kicking and Finn said, "You must be young Prince Araf." I only managed a nod. Then he said, "Come with me. I want to show you something." I followed your grandfather down, deep into the castle until we came to a chamber lit with a hundred candles. He told me that the Leprechauns make the candles with wax mixed with gold dust and that they burn for years. Did you know that?'

'No,' I said, smiling. This was an introspective and loquacious Araf that I had never seen before. I liked it.

'I will never forget what he told me. He said, "This is the Chamber of Runes; some day you will undergo the Rite of Choosing here. I suspect, my young Imp, that you will eventually choose the Major Rune of Ur. When you do, you will be a Runelord. Most people think us lucky to become Runelords and they are right – but it is also a responsibility. We do not choose the runes – the runes choose us. To hold a Major Rune means that you give up part of your life to The Land, or even all of your life if The Land demands it."

'When I left, Finn gave me that oak banta stick. It's in my room in Ur Keep. I wish I had it with me now.'

'It will still be there when you return home,' I said.

'I hope so, Conor, but if we fail, and tomorrow we are no more, then at least I know I have done my duty.'

Believe it or not, Araf chattered on for the rest of the day. He talked about his home, banta fighting and the joys of farming. It worked for both of us – Araf talked and talked to allay his nerves, and I concentrated on what he was saying and didn't have time to think about my possible impending doom.

I spoke to Fergal only once in the day. When I pulled up next to him he said, 'If you ask me how I am, I'm going to punch you.'

'How are you?'

He did punch me, on the arm. It made me sad that Fergal and I had just met. We should have grown up together. His punch was like a punch between brothers, not hard enough to do any damage but hard enough that it hurt.

I rubbed my arm and laughed. 'Any time you want to talk, cuz, I'm right here.'

Long before dark, Dad called a halt and made an announcement. 'This is as close to the castle I want to get in daylight. We will leave well before dawn tomorrow. Tonight we can camp at Glen Duir.'

Glen Duir was at the beginning of the Oaklands, and a more picturesque spot is hard to imagine. We camped near a stream nestled in rolling hills. I was helping set up camp when my father tapped me on the shoulder. 'There is a tree I want you to meet,' he said.

Chapter Twenty-Five
Mother Oak

Dad mentioned Mother Oak once when I was a boy. He caught me carving my name in a tree and was furious. He took my knife from me and said, 'If you had done that to Mother Oak you would be dead now. I would have killed you myself.' It sounded like he meant it too. He was so mad I didn't have the nerve to ask him what he was talking about. Now I know.

We walked upstream for about ten minutes. The way my father said, *Mother Oak*, I was expecting something magnificent. When he stopped at an unremarkable tree and beamed, 'Here she is,' I was a bit disappointed. Mother Oak was pretty much a normal-looking tree. I'm sure I have seen bigger oaks in parks at home. The difference came when you touched her.

Dad went first. He wrapped his arms around her trunk like some hippy tree hugger. I swear the tree hugged him back. A huge canopy of branches covered him over to the point where I couldn't see him any more. When the leaves retreated, he had a goofy look on his face, like a kid who just got offered an ice-cream cone. 'Say hello to Mother Oak,' he said.

I placed my hands on the knurled bark and it hit me like a wave. A feeling of goodness and love swept over me, and into me, and through me, the likes of which I had never known. I am sure I was wearing the same stupid grin that I saw on Dad's face a moment ago.

'*Oh my, my, my*,' came a voice in my head that was as gentle as it was obviously wise. It felt as if I had instantly found the grandmother that I had never known. I hugged her in earnest as she swept her leafy arms over me. Tears involuntarily poured from my eyes. '*There, there,*' she said soothingly, '*oh my, you have had a difficult time lately, haven't you, my child?*'

I had, I realised. In the last week, my life had been turned completely upside-down and I had dealt with it by being brave, but now, in the face of such compassion, all of the fears and the weariness that I had been hiding in every bone, came to the surface. My knees buckled and I wept openly.

I was in such a state I didn't realise what was happening. She caught me and carried me up into her branches and held me like a child that won't go to sleep. I finally got a grip on myself and noticed I was about ten feet off the ground and let loose a little shriek.

Mother Oak laughed. '*Don't worry, I have you, I won't let you fall. Now let me get a look at you. Climb up a little higher.*'

I hadn't climbed a tree in years and realised then just how much I wanted to. Mother Oak placed branches in my path for me to grab, and boosted my footholds.

'*Oh, my dear, I think that is far enough.*'

A tangle of branches congealed behind me and I sat in them. I felt like a newborn baby being admired at arm's length.

'*Oh yes, you definitely are Oisin's seed. There is so much oak in you but also something else – let me guess – hazel. Am I right?*'

'Yes, ma'am,' I said out loud. I still hadn't gotten used to talking to trees without speaking.

She seemed tickled that I called her *ma'am*. I felt her smile. '*Oak and hazel*,' she mused. '*Strength and suppleness, brawn and brain – what a good combination, no wonder Oisin is so proud.*'

I had a question on my mind since I first touched her and I finally found my voice. 'Are you the first tree?'

'*Oh my, what a question. I can't remember that far back, I'm an old woman, you know. I have been here a long time. I imagine all of your fathers and most of your mothers have climbed in my branches. I know I have watched over the children of Duir since the beginning. But am I the oldest? Who can tell?*' She chuckled to herself. '*I feel like the oldest sometimes. Picking up a big strapping boy like you was harder than it used to be.*'

'I'm sorry.'

'*Don't be. It is a pleasure to meet you, young Conor. I don't like to say it, but not all in your family have such a good heart. It pleases me down to my roots to meet a child of oak as fine as you.*'

I stood up and hugged her – I couldn't help myself.

'*Will you come and visit me again?*'

'If I can,' I said, thinking about the dangers that lay ahead.

'*Oh, my poor dear, your trials are not over, are they?*'

'No.'

'*Do not you worry. Remember you are oak and hazel, you will know when to be strong and when to bend.*'

Then she hugged me, a hug of wood and leaves that was softer than any I have ever had from flesh and blood. '*Will you be alright climbing down by yourself? I have had enough bending for a day. I'm an old woman, you know.*'

Dad was asleep when I reached the ground. When I woke him he looked at me and said, 'Well?'

I couldn't even begin to put my feelings into words, so I just said, 'That's a heck of a tree.'

Dad roared with laughter at that. 'That she is, son. That she is.'

On the way back to camp several of our horses galloped past us. 'Where are they going?' I asked.

'Deirdre is sending them home, we don't need them any more.'

Back at the camp Mom was whispering in Cloud's ear. She finished and Cloud galloped off. 'You can talk to horses?' I said, amazed.

She started to answer and then remembered she had a small gold disc on her tongue. She took it out and said, 'One of my tutors was a Pooka.' Then that little shadow of sadness passed in front of her face for a second. The same look she always gets when she is remembering her youth at the Hall of Knowledge.

'You know, Mom,' I said and then paused – I didn't know how to continue. I wanted to tell her how glad I was to have found her and how wonderful and brave and beautiful I thought she was. I wanted to tell her that I loved her. 'I just…'

'I know, son, me too,' she said and then held me. She was right, we didn't have to speak.

Dahy whipped up a roast rabbit dinner. He only cooked about five of them but they were so big they fed us all. We ate pretty much in silence. After dinner, Dad announced that he and Dahy would finalise the plan tonight. He told us to get some sleep and he would fill us in at breakfast. At the mention of sleep I instantly realised just how tired I was. Two days of riding and the outpouring of emotion with Mother

Oak had drained me so much, I hardly had the strength to unfurl my blanket.

At about the same time I put my head down, Fergal came over. He sat next to me, cross-legged. He looked like he wanted to talk but he didn't say anything.

'How you doing?' I said, hoping he wouldn't hit me.

He gave me a weak smile. 'Conor, I want to tell you something.'

I let loose a big sigh and said, 'Fergal, I don't think I can take another emotional scene today. I already had one with my mother and my father and even one with a tree. Look, cousin. I'm glad I met you and I love you too, but we are not going to die tomorrow. Why don't you get some sleep?'

'Yeah, I guess you're right, Conor. Good night,' he said and left.

As soon as my head hit the ground I remembered what I had said to him earlier, about *always being there, if he wanted to talk*. Damn, I can be a jerk sometimes. There was no way I could just go to sleep now, so I dragged myself off the ground and went looking for him. I couldn't find him. He told someone in the camp that he was going for a walk. There was no way I was going to find him in the dark, so I went back to my blanket. When I got there Essa was lying on it.

'I think you will find that that is my blanket,' I said.

'I know,' she said, 'lie with me.'

'Essa,' I said in a whisper, 'your father is just over there.'

'Oh, shut up and lie down, Conor, I just need someone to hold.'

I lay down next to her and she placed her head on my chest. We didn't speak. Her hair tickled my nose but I didn't mind. It was what she needed and to tell the truth, it was what I needed too. Just before I fell asleep I had a scary thought. I imagined Sally standing over us with her arms crossed, saying, 'And just what is going on here?'

229

That night I had another vivid dream but this one was not about The Land, it was about the Real World. I saw buses and hamburger joints, sweet shops, TV sets, traffic lights, shopping malls, and Sally was everywhere. I didn't see these things in a bad light. I missed them. This was my home – or at least it used to be my home. *Is The Land my home now?* I asked myself. *Do I fit in here? Do I fit in there?* The Real World was all I had known and I loved it. Had I lost it? I didn't want to.

Essa wasn't there when Gerard woke me – thank the gods. I didn't want to have to explain that. It was long before dawn. He handed me a cup of tea that made every cell in my body stand at attention. 'Come and get something to eat, Oisin wants to talk to us.'

There was a big cauldron of porridge on the fire. It was stodgy but it did the trick. I was glad to see Fergal there – he looked OK.

Dad stood up and put on his leadership face. 'The Leprechauns have left already. They are going to try to sabotage the Golden Circle from the outside. The map shows us that there are interconnecting gold lines buried in the courtyard. Essa, Araf and Fergal, it is your job to sever them where they meet by the central well. Deirdre and Nieve, you go to the Chamber of Runes and prepare for my Choosing. Conor, you are with me, we have to find my hand.'

'Where is it?'

'Cialtie has taken Finn's bedroom. It must be in there. Any questions?'

'Yeah,' I said. 'How are we going to get into the castle?'

'You are going to be delivered personally,' said Gerard, 'by the finest winemaker in The Land.'

Chapter Twenty-Six
Born Ready

Never in my entire life have I ever been so uncomfortable. When Gerard told me that he was going to smuggle us into the castle in empty wine barrels, I thought we would hop in just before we got there. Oh no, Dad insisted that we hide in them for the entire three-hour journey to Castle Duir. He wanted to make sure we were not spotted en route. Which was fair enough, but three hours! The porridge I ate for breakfast was sitting in my stomach like a rock. I had a scary moment when I thought I was going to see it again. I cursed Dahy for cooking it and then I cursed him again for devising a plan that put me in here and allowed him (along with Gerard) to sit comfortably up front. Every bump jarred me like an ice cube in a cocktail shaker, and with every one of those bumps I knocked my head into the side of the barrel. At one point we went over a rock that was so big I hit my head on the lid, and howled. Fergal was in the barrel next to me. 'Shut up,' he said, 'I'm trying to get some sleep.'

'Sleep!' I shouted over. 'How can you sleep when your head is being bounced around like a pinball?'

'What's a pinball?'

'Never mind.'

'Put the blanket next to your head,' he said, 'then it's not so bad.'

'I don't have a blanket.'

'You are travelling three hours in a barrel and you didn't bring a cushion? I thought you were smart. Didn't you say you went to a place of learning in the Real World?'

'They didn't have any courses on how to sneak into castles,' I said.

'Doesn't sound like a very good school to me. Now will you please keep the groaning down.'

I suffered in silence. I actually started wishing the cart would drive over a huge boulder that would knock me out. Another concussion would have been a small price to pay, if it made the journey quicker.

Gerard had no trouble getting in to the castle. A delivery of the Vinelands' finest was a cause for celebration.

Cialtie met the wagon himself. 'Lord Gerard,' he said. The second I heard that voice all of the hairs stood up on the back of my neck and I stopped breathing. I was instantly terrified, but at the same time I had to overcome the urge to pop out like a deranged jack-in-the-box and chop his head off. 'I hope this shipment,' Cialtie continued, 'is better than the vinegar you sent me last time.'

'I am so sorry, Lord Cialtie, that you found my last batch not to your liking,' Gerard oozed. 'I assure you this is the finest of vintages.'

'I should hope so,' Cialtie said.

I had plenty of reasons for hating my uncle, but the disrespectful way he talked to Gerard made me want to throttle him – after I decapitated him.

'Your daughter is not with you.'

'No, my lord.'

'Why not? You know I wanted to meet her.'

'It is a very busy time in the fermentation cycle. I needed her to supervise the winemaking in my absence. I'm sure she is up to her neck in a barrel of wine as we speak.'

I had to put my hand over my mouth to stop from laughing out loud. You had to love this guy.

'Lord Cialtie,' Gerard said, putting on a serious tone, 'may I ask you why you have an entire army on patrol? Is there something amiss that I should know about?'

'What are you talking about? I have no army on patrol.'

'Oh my,' Gerard said in a fey aristocratic tone that was definitely not him. It made me smile. 'Then I think you should know that there is one on the way.'

'What? How do you know this?'

'Oh, I have a very good Elvish spyglass, they use gold in the optics you know. I saw them yesterday. I'm surprised you haven't noticed. I'd say they were only half a day away.'

Gerard hadn't turned traitor – this was part of the plan. Lorcan and Dad figured that if Cialtie thought he was under attack from the outside, he wouldn't be guarding the inside all that well. It seemed to work.

Cialtie instantly sprang into action, shouting orders. 'Put the wall fortifications on alert,' he yelled, 'and send out a scouting party to find out what he is talking about. Gerard and Dahy, come with me.'

'Of course, my lord, if I can be of any help, but I would ask if Master Dahy could supervise the stowing of the wine. It is a delicate vintage and I wouldn't want to see it bruised.'

'Very well. You two help him,' Cialtie grumbled.

I heard them leave and then the wagon began to move. We travelled a way over cobbled streets. I had a childish urge to sing just so I could hear my voice vibrate. We stopped for the opening of large doors and then turned left. I could tell by the sound that we were inside.

'Close those doors, you idiots! You are letting the cool air out,' I heard Dahy bark – then I heard two bangs, two short grunts, followed by the unmistakable sound of bodies hitting the ground.

Fresh air! The things you take for granted. I stood up, breathing deeply and stretching, while everyone else went to work.

Dahy crawled under the wagon and brought out the weapons. Araf and Fergal went about stealing the two guards' uniforms. The shocking bit was when Mom, Nieve and Essa started tarting themselves up. They unbuttoned their shirts and pushed up their cleavages. Essa and Mom put on skirts with revealing slits in them while Nieve started ripping one in hers.

Essa caught me staring. 'What are you looking at?' she snapped.

'What are you doing?'

'We are blending in,' Mom said, giving me a practice provocative smile. 'Women of, how shall I say, dubious virtue are common in Castle Duir these days.'

'Well,' I said to Essa, 'you look – great.'

She didn't return the compliment with a provocative look. It was more like an evil eye.

'Conor,' Dad said, 'stop gawping at the women and help Dahy and me stow the barrels.'

Dad was being his thorough self. They might not miss the guards, but if someone saw that the wine was still on the wagon, they might know something was up. I promised myself that I would have a word with Gerard about putting his wine in smaller barrels. Man, they were heavy.

When we were finished, Dahy said, 'I will stable the horse and then rejoin Gerard. Good luck.' We hid behind the door as he left.

Mom gave the naked guards a dose of Shadowmagic that would ensure they slept the rest of the day, and then Dad lined us up for an inspection. People like the women, Dad and me were commonplace in the castle, so we wouldn't raise too much suspicion. Fergal looked just like the Banshee guard he had stolen the uniform from, but Araf was a problem. Imps were not very welcome in the castle and the guard uniform could not disguise the mop of sandy hair on his head – he stood out like a sore thumb. That's when Mom pulled out the wig.

To call it a wig was to do an injustice to every hairpiece that was ever made. It was supposed to simulate Banshee hair but in reality it looked like a skunk that had been dead on the freeway for a week. Araf put it on and I lost it. I don't think I ever saw anything so funny in my life. I was laughing so hard that Dad actually slapped me.

'I'm sorry,' I said, struggling to get my composure back, 'I get like this when I'm nervous.'

'Don't,' Dad said in that voice that meant business. A voice I know only too well.

I shot a glance over to Fergal for support, expecting to see his cheesy grin, but he wasn't even smiling. That kind of sobered me up.

'You three have the most difficult job of all,' Dad said to Essa, Araf and Fergal. 'Those gold lines must be severed.'

'We will not fail, my lord,' Araf said. I felt my stomach churn. This was it. They were my friends and they were heading straight into danger. Fergal didn't look at me but Essa and I locked eyes before she left. She smiled but it was a strange little smile. It seemed to mean something, but as usual I couldn't figure out what. They walked out the door like they owned the place. Essa, dressed as a loose woman, arm in arm between two soldiers. Essa even tried a provocative swish of her skirt, but to be honest, she wasn't very good at it. Then it was just family.

Mom gave Dad a passionate embrace. Nieve offered me her hand. 'Come on,' I said, 'you're my aunt for crying out loud.' I gave her a hug that she didn't return very well.

Mom gave me a kiss on the cheek. 'You look after your father.'

'I will. I'll see you in a little while in the Chamber.'

They sashayed out the door and then it was just Dad and me – like old times.

'Are you ready, son?'

'Born ready, Dad.'

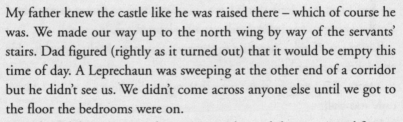

My father knew the castle like he was raised there – which of course he was. We made our way up to the north wing by way of the servants' stairs. Dad figured (rightly as it turned out) that it would be empty this time of day. A Leprechaun was sweeping at the other end of a corridor but he didn't see us. We didn't come across anyone else until we got to the floor the bedrooms were on.

Dad stuck his nose into the main corridor and then motioned for me to follow. At the end of the corridor was a T junction with a grand oak door. There was nobody around.

'That's Cialtie's bedroom,' he whispered.

We tiptoed towards it. I wasn't as worried about the sound of my feet as much as I was worried about the sound of my pounding heart. We were about halfway there when a soldier came up from the corridor on the left. Cialtie had a guard posted at his door! If the soldier had been looking our way, he would have seen us. There was an open door next to us – we both ducked into it.

That's when I heard the scream.

Chapter Twenty-Seven

Aein

The scream came from a slight Leprechaun chambermaid. We scared the hell out of her. Dad tackled her onto the bed and covered her mouth. She looked up with wild eyes. Then Dad called her by name. 'Aein, shhh, I won't hurt you. It's me, Oisin.' He showed her his missing hand. Her eyes widened more, which I didn't think was possible.

A voice came from the corridor. 'What's going on in there?'

Dad rolled off the maid, hitting the floor on the far side of the bed. I ducked behind the door, my banta stick ready.

The guard stepped into the doorway. The maid quickly sat up in the bed. 'What's all this noise?' the guard asked.

She shot a quick glance to me behind the door. I didn't know what she was going to do. If she raised the alarm, we were done for. I'm surprised I didn't pass out – I wasn't breathing.

'I, I,' she stammered, 'I saw a mouse.'

I could see the guard through the space in the doorjamb. He let out an exasperated sigh and said, 'Stupid cow.'

'No! Don't go,' she said.

Oh no, I thought, as every muscle in my body tightened to breaking point, *she is going to give us away.*

'No, please come and look.'

'I have got better things to do than catch mice.'

She shot a knowing glance to me and nodded slowly once. 'Please, I think this mouse has *two* heads.'

I smiled at her then. She was on our side. She knew I couldn't get a clear swing at the guard from where I was – she was luring him into the room. I was impressed by her fast thinking. If I was the guard, there was no way I would have missed a chance to see a two-headed mouse.

The guard stepped into the room. I adjusted the grip on my banta stick and clocked him good, square in the temple. I felt the solidness of the contact clear down to my toes. He did a little comedy pirouette and crumpled to the floor. I leaned over him and said, 'That will teach you for calling her a *stupid cow.*'

I closed the door. Dad popped up from behind the bed. 'Thank you, Aein,' he said.

The maid threw her arms around Dad and pressed the side of her face into his chest. 'Oh, Prince Oisin, it really is you.'

Dad stroked her hair.

She stepped back and wiped her eyes. 'Are you going to fight your brother?'

'I'm afraid I am.'

The sweetness vanished out of her – all of a sudden she looked like she was made of granite. 'Good,' she said, almost spitting. 'How can I help?'

Dad's smile covered his face. At that moment he looked a lot like Fergal. 'Do you know where Cialtie keeps my hand?'

'In his room, in that fancy box of his.'

'Of course,' Dad said. He kissed her quickly on the forehead and turned to leave.

'But,' she said, 'he keeps his chamber door locked.' That stopped us both in our tracks, and then we heard a jingle behind us. We turned to see Aein holding a fob of keys in her hand and smiling. 'But I have a key.'

Cialtie's chambers were decorated with dead things. The walls were covered with mounted animal heads and on every surface there were stuffed birds and beasts. I hate this kind of stuff in the Real World – in The Land, it was a sacrilege beyond measure.

The box was in a small alcove. It was a beautiful thing. It must have been made of wood from every tree in The Land, an intricate patchwork, lovingly made from timber of every hue. Dad put it on a table and stared at it. There was a strip of cherry-coloured wood running along the top. Dad slid it to the left about an inch and then moved a darker strip of wood down. He stepped back and sighed.

'What's the problem?' I asked.

'It's a puzzle box. Some Elf lord gave it to Cialtie when we were kids. You have to perform about thirty of these little moves, in the right order, to unlock it.'

'Can you do it?'

'I did it a couple of times, but that was a long time ago. This is going to take hours.'

I picked up my banta stick and came down hard on the lid of the box. It shattered into about twenty pieces. 'My way is quicker.'

'I wish you hadn't done that,' Dad said.

'Why?'

'What happens if Cialtie comes back here and finds his favourite box has turned to kindling?'

'Oh, I hadn't thought of that.'

Dad gave me that Dad look. 'Obviously.'

With his lone hand he gently pushed aside the splintered wood – he was shaking a bit. Underneath was a packet wrapped in a red velvet cloth. He unwrapped it and – there it was. Something I never thought I would see – Dad's right hand. It almost glowed from the yellow Shadowmagic that encased it, like those dragonflies trapped in amber. He picked it up and stared at it. It was a very strange moment. I tried to imagine what I would be thinking, the first time I saw the back of my own hand in twenty years, and I couldn't.

'Is this going to work?' I asked.

'Deirdre thinks so,' Dad said, dreamily.

'Well, that's good enough for me. Come on, let's get out of here.'

We reassembled Cialtie's box as best we could. It looked OK, as long as you didn't touch it – or sneeze.

❖

We had to get all the way to the other side of the castle in order to get down to the Chamber of Runes. Aein offered to scout ahead for us. Dad told her it was too dangerous, but she insisted. Who says you can't get good help these days? Whenever we came to a corner we couldn't see around, Aein got down on her hands and knees with a scrubbing brush and crawled around the corner pretending she was cleaning. Once we had to wait a couple of minutes for a guard to pass. Another time, the way was too well guarded, so we ended up on the walkway that overlooked the courtyard. It was more exposed than we liked but it was our only choice. It actually wasn't a bad route. There was a lot of activity above us, with the soldiers fortifying the ramparts, but this level was empty.

It also allowed us to get a look at how Essa, Araf and Fergal were doing. They looked OK. Araf had his back to the well. He was hiding it, but if you looked close you could see he was holding a length of rope that was hanging into the well. Fergal was standing guard, so we assumed that Essa was down the well cutting the gold cables. The strange thing was, even though Araf was wearing that ridiculous wig, Fergal was the one that looked out of place. As a Banshee his appearance was perfect, but his body language was so rigid I could feel the tension all the way to where we were.

We came to the south wing and entered a corridor. This part of the castle was old, real old. You could sense it. The end of the corridor sloped around to the left. Aein got down on her hands and knees again and did her cleaning routine. She was gone for what seemed to be an eternity, then appeared back, still on her hands and knees.

'There is a guard in front of the door to the Chamber,' she whispered.

'What did he look like?' Dad asked.

'He is standing at attention.'

'Go up to him and ask him if he wants a glass of water.'

This obviously scared her, but she did it. She came back looking a bit confused. 'He completely ignored me.'

Dad smiled, walked around the corner and right up to the guard. I thought I was going to have a heart attack. What was he doing? I followed. I mean, what else was I going to do? Dad strolled up to the guard and snapped his fingers in front of his face. The guard didn't even blink. He just stared straight ahead, like he was in a trance – which he was.

'One of Nieve's specials,' Dad said. 'She practised it on me once when I was younger; it's not very pleasant.'

Aein wouldn't go down to the Chamber of Runes. It wasn't that her bravery was faltering, it was just that it was not her place. She offered to guard the door and warn us if anyone approached but Dad said that wouldn't help. 'Can you do one more thing?'

'Anything, Prince Oisin.'

'Make sure there are no Leprechauns in the east wing. It might get dangerous today.'

'Leprechauns don't go there if they can help it but there might be some servants. I will only warn the ones I can trust.'

'Don't stay there too long yourself.'

'May the gods protect you, Prince Oisin.' Aein hugged Dad quickly and left.

Dad opened the door.

The Chamber of Runes was a long way down. The spiral staircase was lit by huge candles every couple of steps. I remembered what Araf said about them being able to burn for years. I was glad they were there, otherwise we would have broken our necks. There were no windows, but I suspected after a little while that we were well underground.

Halfway down was a landing and an unconscious guard – so far, so good. I knew we were getting close to the Chamber by the glow. It got so bright I half expected to walk into a television studio. Mom and Nieve had heard our approach – they were standing at the bottom landing, posed, each holding some magical weapon: Nieve's made of gold and Mom's of amber sap. They lowered them when they saw us.

'Hi, girls, did you miss us?' I said.

Mom flew into Dad's arms. Nieve asked, 'Did you get it?'

'No problem,' I said. 'Dad's got one hand on his wrist, and another hand in his pocket.'

Nieve gave me a dirty look. It's amazing how quickly the women I meet learn that expression.

The Chamber wasn't as big as I expected, but it was sure well lit. Araf said there were a hundred candles down here – it was more like a thousand. The walls looked as if they had been there forever, seen it all. It made me want to ask them questions. It gave a new meaning to *talking to a wall.* The chamber had no furnishings except for a stone table. At the opposite end of the room was an archway made of oak, like a proscenium in an old theatre. Beyond that were two more just like it, and at the far end was another stone table exactly like the one in this part of the room. I walked towards the archway.

'Don't go near that!' Nieve warned.

'Why not?'

'That's the First Muirbhrúcht. Trust me, you do not want to cross that by accident.'

I couldn't see anything but I stepped back. I could tell by her voice that she was not kidding.

Dad unwrapped the hand and held it in place. Mom produced a wide golden bangle and opened the clasp. The gold bracelet was a clamp and she used it to secure Dad's hand to his wrist. Dad held his amber hand up to his face. He turned it, staring at the front and back. He had that faraway look in his eyes, like he had in Cialtie's bedroom. It took my breath away. I had always known this man as a one-handed wonder – now I was looking at him whole – the way I had seen him in my dreams.

Mom placed a piece of gold on his amber palm and then a square of oak, a blank rune. He turned to the archways – he was finally going to take his Choosing, something that he had been preparing for all of his life but had thought was denied to him forever.

He took a deep breath and said, 'I'm ready.'

'I'm going with you,' Mom said.

Dad, who was out of practice with his right hand, was so shocked he dropped the gold and the rune. 'You most certainly are not!'

It was Mom's turn to be shocked and she shot back with the same indignation, 'Yes I am!'

Oh my, I thought, *I'm witnessing my first parental argument.* I wondered if I should go upstairs and hide in my bedroom.

'Deirdre,' Dad said, softening his tone a bit, 'you can't take a Choosing, it will disrupt your sorcery.'

'I'm not taking a standard Choosing, I'm going to choose a Shadowrune.' She placed a glob of tree sap in her palm and placed a disc of dark amber over it.

I hadn't seen Dad that shocked since – well, never. I was shocked too. Dad had explained to me how gold was the fuel that powered the creation of a rune – Mom was going to attempt it using tree sap powered by Shadowmagic. I was sure no one had tried that before. Even with my limited understanding of all this stuff, the suggestion terrified me.

'That is the craziest idea I have ever heard,' Dad said.

'It should work, Oisin,' Mom said. 'You and the Duir clan have had the monopoly on magic forever. You think that your gold is the only power there is, but you are wrong, I have proved it. And you might need help in there. What I'm doing may be unknown, but no one has ever tried to do what you are doing, either.' Mom looked fierce. I made a mental note to get into as few arguments with her as possible.

'Nieve,' Dad pleaded, 'help me on this.'

'Deirdre and I have discussed it,' Nieve said. 'I think this has a good chance of working – possibly more of a chance than even you have.'

I heard the words *good chance* and *possibly*, and I didn't like it. I had an awful thought that instead of having only one parent, I was soon to be an orphan.

Mom picked up the gold and the blank rune and replaced them in Dad's hand. Dad attempted one last pleading look, but Mom was not for turning. A look of acceptance washed over his face, and they turned to the archway.

'Wooh, hold on,' I said, as I ran in front of them. 'I, I love you both.'

'You don't have to tell me that, Conor,' Dad said, 'I know.'

244

'And I, my son,' Mom said, 'will never grow tired of hearing it.'

I didn't want to touch them and break their concentration. I said, 'Good luck,' and got out of the way.

'May the gods be with you,' Nieve called.

Then together, as if they had been rehearsing it all of their lives, they took a step towards the archway.

Chapter Twenty-Eight
The Choosing

'They have entered the First Muirbhrúcht,' Nieve said. I couldn't see anything before but I sure could now. A wall of light sprang to life as Mom and Dad hit it. It was like a force field in a science fiction movie, the air filled with tiny particles that glowed every colour of the rainbow and some colours that rainbows hadn't even thought of yet. Mom's black hair flew up and wildly floated about, as if she was underwater and caught in a riptide. It was beautiful and terrifying.

Their progress was painfully slow. It was obvious that this was not easy. At one point, Dad turned his head enough so I could see his face. He looked like he was screaming but I couldn't hear anything. In fact the Chamber was eerily silent. Nieve told me that no sound could penetrate the barriers.

'The first barrier is the easiest,' she explained. 'A Chooser can abandon an attempt and come back after the First Muirbhrúcht and survive – after that, there is no turning back.'

It didn't look easy. I could tell that Mom and Dad were using every ounce of strength they had in order to push forward, but even so I've seen hour hands on a clock move faster. We watched in silence. All the muscles in my body tensed up in sympathy. I looked on helplessly for what seemed like an eternity, and then the wall of light subsided – they made it through and I found myself breathing again. Neither of them turned around or even paused. I could see Dad's leg shake as he put his weight on it, like a weightlifter who had just overexerted himself. He was having a tough time of this.

'Do you think they are going to make it?' I asked.

'I do not know,' Nieve said. 'I *do* know that both of them would rather die than fail.'

The second barrier was a lot brighter than the first.

'The Second Muirbhrúcht is the hardest,' Nieve stated calmly.

Mom and Dad pushed on. I ached to see their faces, to get a sense of how they were doing, but was also glad I couldn't. I don't think I could have stood it.

'Conor, place the Sword of Duir on the table.'

Nieve's request came so out of the blue. I said, 'Huh?'

'The Sword of Duir,' Nieve explained, 'always sits on the stone table when a child of Duir is chosen.'

She said it in such a matter-of-fact voice that I just did as I was told – I figured she knew what she was doing. I placed the sword on the table and turned my attention back to Mom and Dad. I didn't think it was possible but they were moving even slower than the last time.

'Do you have any other weapons?'

'What?' I said, distractedly, not even looking at her. 'Oh, just a knife that Dahy gave me.'

'One of Dahy's throwing blades? Can I see it?'

Oh, for heaven's sake, I thought, *my parents are a second away from killing themselves and you want to admire cutlery*, but then I thought, *OK, if this is how she is dealing with the pressure, who am I to complain?*

It didn't even occur to me what she was really doing. She was disarming me.

I reached down in my sock and handed her my knife without even looking. She took the knife and with the reflexes of a cat came up behind me. Her left hand grabbed me by the side of the neck and her right hand brought the blade to my throat. I was so stunned I didn't react right away, but when I did I realised I couldn't move. My neck was killing me. Nieve was wearing a ring with some sort of needle in it, a gold needle, I rightly assumed – I was completely paralysed. I tried to pull away but nothing was moving. I was rigid as a flagpole. I attempted to speak and was surprised that I could.

'What are you doing?'

'Don't try to move, Conor.'

I tried anyway, but the only things that seemed to be working were my eyeballs. I looked down and saw that my own knife was about an inch from my throat. 'Nieve,' I repeated, 'what are you doing?'

'My duty,' she said.

'Hey, I thought we dealt with this already. Dad gets his hand back and I'm no longer one-handed junior.'

'If Oisin succeeds, I will let you go.'

'If he doesn't?' I asked. She didn't answer, but I guess it was a stupid question.

I continued to watch Mom and Dad – I had no choice, it was the way I was facing. The Second Muirbhrúcht was putting on a spectacular display. It was so beautiful and terrifying that I almost forgot I was paralysed and had a murderous relative holding a knife to my throat – almost. I relaxed for a second when I remembered Mom's protection spell, but then I remembered that it only works once – Nieve had tried to kill me already. I had an infantile urge to call out to my parents but they couldn't help me, or even hear me, and I wouldn't have wanted to break their concentration anyway.

We were so engrossed in the fireworks that we didn't hear the footsteps coming down the steps until the last second. Nieve spun me around on one of my tent-pole legs, like a comedian dancing with a department store mannequin. She took the knife from my throat and cocked her hand back in readiness to throw. It was Essa. When Nieve saw who it was, I felt her relax and replace the knife to my throat.

Essa stood still and took in the situation. Her expression turned serious but it wasn't the look of shock that I had expected. 'How is it going?' she said.

'How is it going?' I shouted. 'What do you mean, "*How is it going*"? She is trying to kill me! That's how it's going!'

Essa lowered her eyes in guilt.

'They are almost through the Second Muirbhrúcht,' Nieve replied, calmly.

'You knew about this, didn't you?' I spat at Essa. 'You're part of this!'

'Conor,' she said in a compassionate voice that I had never heard come out of her before, 'if this works, you have nothing to worry about.'

'What if it doesn't work, eh? Maybe you'll allow me to worry about that!'

'Conor…'

'Don't *Conor* me. I'm not surprised that my dear old aunt would pull something like this. She has been trying to kill me ever since we met – but you! I thought we… Aw, never mind.'

'Nieve,' I said, trying to turn around, which of course failed, 'if this doesn't work, I want *her* to be the one that sticks the knife into my neck. I don't want someone who loves me doing it!'

Oh boy, I may have been paralysed but I sure got her in the solar plexus with that one. Essa instantly placed her hand over her mouth and then turned her back on me. Right away, I regretted saying it – but I was mad. And what was I supposed to do? Apologise to a girl who was trying to kill me? She finally looked at me again – her face was wet with tears. I don't think I have ever seen a more miserable countenance. Then her eyes widened in sudden alarm. She looked around the chamber and said, 'Where is Fergal?'

'What do you mean, "*Where is Fergal*"?' I said. 'I thought he was with you!'

'Araf sent him down here to tell you that I had found the gold lines and would be done soon.'

'You let Fergal wander around the castle alone! How long ago was that?'

'Ages ago,' she said. Panic took over her face. 'It took longer than I thought to cut the gold lines, and then I wasted time before I discovered that the guard upstairs was petrified.'

'Oh my God,' I said, as the realisation dawned on me, 'I know where he is. He's going to kill Cialtie.'

'Oh my gods,' Essa said, 'oh my gods.'

I was about to tell her to get out there and look for him, when the whole chamber started to rumble. Nieve spun me back around.

'They have entered the Final Muirbhrúcht,' she said.

The overall colour of the third barrier wasn't as bright as the second's, but Mom and Dad's right hands looked like they were spouting out the entire contents of a fireworks factory. The rumble got louder and the floor vibrated beneath our feet. That's why we didn't hear him approach.

Chapter Twenty-Nine
The Truth, a Second Time

'You lied to me!' Fergal shouted as he appeared in the Chamber in a rage. He flew at me with murder in his eyes – it shocked the hell out of me. I instinctively wanted to run, except that I couldn't. For a split second I had a moment of hope in thinking that Nieve would be startled enough to take that damn needle out of my neck, but she was her usual cool self. She didn't even take the knife from my throat. Essa stopped Fergal before he throttled me. She had to use all of her strength.

His arms were flailing and spit was flying out of his mouth. 'You lied to me. You and that witch mother of yours!'

'Fergal, what are you talking about?' I said.

'You're not from the Real World,' he shouted, with so much vehemence that I could feel the force of his breath. '*You* killed my mother. You and that lying family of yours!'

The rumble in the Chamber increased, as if in sympathy with his mood. To say I was baffled doesn't even come close. It was like having a cuddly cocker spaniel that all of a sudden turned into a killer.

'Fergal, what are you talking about? Who told you that?'

'I did,' Cialtie said as he stepped into the chamber. He was flanked by four guards holding crossbows. 'Son,' he said in that dripping voice of his, 'come over here.'

Fergal did as he was told and Cialtie actually put his arm around his shoulders. I wanted to throw up.

'Oh, Fergal,' I said as I put the pieces of this puzzle together, 'you don't believe *him?*'

'Of course he believes me,' Cialtie said as he smiled down at Fergal. 'Sons should always trust their fathers.'

I tried to speak but nothing came out. The guards looked pretty edgy and their crossbows were aimed at our heads, but I hardly even noticed.

'Sister Nieve, I must say I'm surprised to see you with a knife to my young nephew's throat and it looks like you've paralysed him as well. If I didn't know you any better I would think you were on my side.'

Nieve didn't move a muscle.

'Oh, and you must be Princess Essa of Muhn,' Cialtie said, addressing Essa who had backed up next to us. 'I have been longing to meet you. You are even more beautiful than I had heard.'

Essa didn't say anything, she just pulled her banta stick out of her belt and assumed an *en garde* position.

'Ooh, feisty. I like a girl with spirit.'

I wanted to kill him but judging from the sound that came out of Essa's throat, it seemed like I would have to get in line.

The rumble in the chamber abruptly stopped. Cialtie looked past us.

'Well, well, my son told me what Oisin was attempting. I could hardly believe it, but what do you know, it looks like he did it.'

Nieve spun herself around and me with her. Mom and Dad were at the far end of the archways. The pyrotechnics had stopped. I could see them clearly. They were standing on either side of the stone table. Both were looking at Dad's right hand. The gold bangle that had been on

Dad's wrist was gone, presumably used up to fuel the magic that made possible the reattachment – because reattached it was! I followed the line of Dad's right arm down and I'll be damned, there was a hand on the end. I gasped as Dad opened his fingers. It worked! In his palm was a rune. He tilted his wrist down and it fell to the table. Mom did the same, and an amber-glowing rune dropped on the stone surface next to Dad's. They were ecstatic, but their ecstasy was short-lived. They looked to us and their faces filled with horror. I felt so sorry for them. Dad ran towards us but the Third Muirbhrúcht sparked to life and threw him back, like a tennis ball off a racket. I heard Cialtie laugh at that.

Then I felt the needle leave my neck. Nieve whispered in my ear, 'Don't move.' I felt the sensation returning to my body. It took all of my will not to stretch at the relief but I pretended to stay frozen. Nieve turned back around and I spun with her, Dahy's knife still at my throat.

'They will take ages getting out of there,' Cialtie sighed. 'Oh, what a shame, all of that effort and I'm just going to have to cut it off again. I wonder if I can convince Deirdre to preserve it a second time before I kill her.'

'You said you weren't going to kill anybody,' Fergal said.

'Oh my, my,' Cialtie said. 'Fergal, was it? You are as gullible as your mother. She actually thought I was going to make her a queen. Can you imagine – a Banshee queen? You know, I was shocked when I learned that you survived after I lopped her head off, but now that I know you, I'm astonished you have had the wits to live this long.'

There it was – the truth. It was awful watching Fergal learn it the first time – this time it nearly killed me. The realisation of it hit him in waves, like a baby standing hip-deep in the ocean. I could almost read his mind: first came the pain of reliving his mother's murder, next came the shame of being so easily duped, and then came the horror at the realisation that he had betrayed his friends. He wasn't broken, it was more like he was shattered.

Cialtie pushed him and he crashed into me. 'I think you should stand over there with your friends.'

Fergal crumpled to the floor. He hugged my legs and made a noise that I had never heard from a person before, and never wanted to hear again. Tears poured out of his clenched eyelids, and his mouth hung open, saliva spilling out of it. 'I'm sorry,' he whimpered. 'I'm so sorry.'

'Pathetic,' Cialtie said.

Never in my life had I wanted so badly to do two things at once. I wanted to put my arms around my poor cousin and tell him it was OK, and at the same time I wanted to tear Cialtie limb from limb – with my bare hands. I didn't do either. I don't know how I did it, but I stood perfectly still. Cialtie thought I couldn't move. It was the only advantage that we had.

'You know, I suspected you were here, even before my sprog showed up and spilled the beans,' Cialtie said. 'You know what gave you away? It was that rinky-dink army. I've seen bigger circuses. I thought to myself, *What could that tiny gaggle of stumpy people do, other than disturb my sleep?* And then I realised it must be a diversion. Oh well, I'm glad they are here. I'll enjoy seeing them all dead.'

As if I hadn't had enough shocks for a day, Cialtie reached into his pocket and removed a crystal vial that was filled with gold. It wasn't the vial that shocked me, it was what was attached to the top of it – a red button. It was the only Real World-looking thing that I had ever seen in The Land, other than my clothes. I almost craned my neck to get a better look, but I managed to remain perfectly still.

'Ah, nephew, I see you recognise this. I wondered if you would. I had a dream a little while back, it was a good one. You had it too, didn't you? I thought you must have, because in it was the strangest little device that was completely foreign to me. I liked it so much, I had my goldsmiths whip one up. Now all I have to do is push this little red thing and that pesky army will pester me no more.'

'Cialtie,' Nieve said, 'don't do it, you will destroy everything.'

'Oh, sister, I'm disappointed in you. I thought you clever in the ways of magic. I won't destroy *everything* – we will be fine. All of the rest of The Land will be wiped clean, but I never really liked them anyway. Everyone and everything I need is right here inside my Golden Circle. Trust me, The Land will be a better place when I rebuild it in my own image.'

He had his thumb on the button. I didn't know what to do. Even if I surprised him, by being able to move, he was still too far away. I wouldn't be able to stop him from pressing it.

'I'm waiting,' Cialtie said. 'Is this not someone's cue to tell me I'm mad?' He looked around. 'Disappointing.'

That's when Araf burst into the room and all hell broke loose.

Chapter Thirty
A Time to Bend

Araf didn't know what was going on. He instinctively went for one of the armed guards first, not my uncle. Cialtie had time to press the button – and he did. The entire chamber lurched to the sound of a huge explosion. Burning candles toppled all over the place and everyone lost their footing.

It worked! Not from Cialtie's point of view, but from ours. The explosion meant that the Leprechaun goldsmiths had done their jobs. Mom had explained to me, that if the Golden Circle went off the way Cialtie wanted it to, we wouldn't hear anything in the castle – but if the Leprechaun goldsmiths succeeded in crafting spikes in a section of the Golden Circle, the explosion would blow out the whole east wall of the castle. It did, and that's what Lorcan's army was waiting for.

All of the guards let loose their crossbow bolts. Two of them were way off the mark, one from a soldier that fell down from the explosion, the other from the guy that Araf had just clocked with his banta stick. Two bolts unfortunately were right on the mark. One came directly at Essa's chest. With skill that must have made Araf and Dahy proud, she actually deflected the bolt with her banta stick – then she performed one of her head-over-heel manoeuvres. That was the last thing her attacker saw.

The other bolt flew straight at my chin. I think The Land has given me two special gifts: one is dreams and the other is the way time seems to slow down in a crisis. I actually saw the bolt spring off the bowstring. I had time to remember what Mother Oak had said to me, '*You are oak and hazel, you will know when to be strong and when to bend.*' It was time to bend. With flexibility that a Russian gymnast couldn't duplicate, I arched my back and watched the bolt sail past my face. Nieve wasn't so lucky. It got her in the shoulder, but not before she could flick my knife at the archer. Her throw was wide of the mark but due to the extraordinary properties of Dahy's golden tip, it honed back on its target like a guided missile. The heartbeat it took for all this to happen was the guard's last. I didn't stop bending, I went right over like an upside-down U. How I stayed on my feet, I will never know. I kept going until I planted my hand on the stone tabletop – right next to the Sword of Duir. In that upside-down world I grabbed the Lawnmower and reversed the process.

When I straightened up, I saw a scene that has haunted my thoughts ever since. Fergal was on his feet. His face was contorted with rage and he was charging Cialtie. As he stepped forward, he cocked his wrist in the gesture that I recognised as the sequence that released his Banshee blade, but the sword wasn't in his sleeve – it was on his belt. He never did get to replace the gold wire.

Cialtie recognised the gesture, too – because he had a Banshee blade of his own. He mirrored Fergal's wrist movements, with the difference that when he did it, a shiny silver sword appeared in his hand.

I screamed, 'No!' and flew at the sword in hopes of deflecting it. I was too late. My slow-motion gift became a curse. I saw the tip of the blade touch Fergal's chest, I saw the threads on the fabric of his shirt part and break, I saw every single millimetre of that cursed weapon enter my cousin's chest and not stop until it reached his heart. My swing was late, Cialtie was too fast. My blade came down a foot behind where I needed it to be. I sliced into Cialtie's right wrist and took his hand clean off. He screamed in pain as blood shot around the room.

Fergal looked down in shock. What he saw was Cialtie's sword sticking out of his chest with his father's hand still wrapped around the pommel. Then he did that most Fergalish thing – he laughed. He pointed to the handle of the sword and said, 'Will you look at that.' He wore a typical Fergal, ear-to-ear grin on his face, as he fell over backwards. Just then Dad burst through the First Muirbhrúcht.

With a force of will that was unprecedented, Dad had pushed back through the three barriers in record time. He came out roaring and, as if he had never missed it, he drew his sword with his right hand and flew at his brother. Dad didn't even see what happened next, but I did. Cialtie saw him coming. With his remaining hand, he quickly reached to his neck, grabbed an amulet and shouted, '*Rothlú!*' Dad connected with nothing but air. He would have smashed into the far wall, if Araf hadn't caught him.

Fergal was still conscious. I dropped down next to him, just as Mom popped through the Muirbhrúcht. She quickly joined me. I pried Cialtie's hand off the pommel and threw it across the room. When I started to remove the sword Mom stopped me. She placed her hands on both sides of Fergal's head and closed her eyes. When she opened them they were filled with tears. She shook her head *no*. It felt like *my* heart was the one that had a sword in it.

'Hey, cousin,' Fergal said, 'why the long face? We've laughed through worse times than this.' The tears came so hard I had to squeeze my eyelids to clear my vision. When I opened them, he was gone. He still had a little smile in the corners of his mouth.

It wasn't me. It was Fergal. Fergal was the one. He was *the son of the one-handed prince.* Fergal was the one who had to be sacrificed in order to save The Land. Oh, Fergal. At that moment I couldn't imagine anything that was worth that price.

Chapter Thirty-One
A Decision

The ensuing battle didn't amount to much. At the moment Cialtie's ring misfired, most of his crack troops were standing on the ramparts of the eastern wall watching Lorcan's army approach. They were killed in the blast. The battalion that had been sent to meet Lorcan legged it back to the castle when they saw the explosion. The Imps and Leprechauns charged after them. During a fierce battle in the courtyard, Dahy killed their captain with a knife throw reportedly from fifty yards away. Without any commanders Cialtie's army surrendered. Maybe their Banshee sixth sense informed them that they had lost.

At sunset most of the mopping up was done. Lorcan ordered all of his troops to muster in the courtyard. Aein gathered the servants there too. Many of them she had saved by telling them to evacuate the east wing. Dad and I climbed to the upper walkway.

At the top of the stairs, he said, 'I'm afraid I'm going to have to ask for the Lawnmower back.'

I handed it to him and together we walked to the edge of the railing. In his right hand he held aloft the Major Rune of Duir, and in the other hand the Sword of Duir. The roar that went out was deafening. After several tries Dad silenced the throng and put his arm around my shoulder.

'People of The Land,' he shouted, 'this is my son of whom I am exceedingly proud – I give you – Conor of Duir!'

The crowd just went crazy. I used to want to be a rock superstar but after that experience, I'll take being the son of the two-handed prince any day.

The week that followed was mad. Reconstruction of the eastern wall started immediately. News of Dad capturing the throne and regaining his hand spread even faster than if they had television around here. Dignitaries poured in every day to meet with Pop.

Mom and Nieve spent most of their time tending to the wounded. Dad would wheel me out periodically to meet Lord Whoosit or Lady What's-her-Name but other than that I really didn't have much to do.

There was a nice moment when Dad sent for me to meet the king of the Brownies and his two sons. I entered from the rear of the throne room, nipped up next to Dad and without looking bowed just like Pop taught me to. When I straightened up I saw a very potbellied Brownie flanked by two open-mouthed youths.

'Frank, Jesse, how the hell are you?'

A look of terror crossed Frank's face as I walked towards him. He pulled his head back from his father's peripheral vision and shook his head. The desperado boys had obviously not told their father about their little walkabout.

'You know my sons?' the Brownie king asked.

I walked up close and looked each of them square in the eyes from about six inches away. I was close enough to see the sweat form on their brows – it was fun.

I backed off. 'I'm sorry, your highness, I don't see very well since my ordeal in the battle, I am mistaken.'

As they left, Jesse glanced back smiling and slipped me a little wave.

'What was that about?' Dad asked.

'I'll tell you later,' I said.

I left the throne room and sent a message to Dahy to have the two Brownie boys' luggage searched by the porters before they left. I found out later they both had a couple of choice souvenirs in their bags.

I got tired of everybody gaping and bowing to me everywhere I went, so I spent most of my time sitting in my room trying to piece Cialtie's wooden box back together and thinking of Fergal. So when I heard that Lorcan was returning to the Hazellands to clear out his old headquarters, I jumped at the chance to go.

I overslept on the morning we were supposed to leave. I still hadn't gotten used to the luxury of sleeping in clean sheets and in a soft bed. I ran down to the courtyard to see a stern-looking Lorcan and his guard all mounted and waiting for me. I ran into the stables to get Cloud (Acorn was still on the disabled list) – and imagine my delight when I saw Mom saddling up.

'Are you coming?'

'Nieve can handle what is left of the wounded, and more importantly, I have not spent enough time with my son.'

'Cool,' I said.

'Yes, it is pleasant out.'

Araf came in and chose a horse.

'Are you coming too?' I asked.

'Yes,' he replied, with one word more than usual.

Lorcan set a swift pace. I think he was trying to punish me for being late. Cloud seemed to be obeying not only my commands but my thoughts. I'm not sure if it was because she was responding to the glorious morning or I was becoming a pretty good equestrian. I'd like to think it was the latter. I didn't imagine it was possible but the place seemed even more alive than before. The air was crisp and clear and the colours of the landscape were more vivid than ever. It was as if Tir na Nog itself knew that the proper order had once again come to The Land.

We camped that night out in the open on the edge of the Eadthlands. Lorcan's guards sang songs and passed around some sort of Leprechaun brew that made me feel shorter. Mom told tales of the Fili and Shadowmagic. You could see how delighted she was that these things were, by the order of the new king, no longer forbidden. The only one who seemed not to be enjoying himself was Araf. I went over to where he was sitting.

'You seem awfully quiet tonight,' I said, 'and when you seem quiet that's saying something.'

'Quiet, yes. That's the problem,' he said, staring into his mug of Leprechaun-shine. 'I often would pray that Fergal would just stop babbling so I could have a chance to think. I never imagined how painful silence could be.'

'Yeah, I miss him too.'

We sat for a while in painful silence before I said, 'You know, I can babble on good as anyone.'

And I did. I told him all about the Real World and my life with Dad. How we lived in Ireland and then England before we came to Scranton, Pennsylvania. I explained: TV and shopping malls, soccer and baseball, hamburger joints and airplanes.

When I had finished he said, 'You have devices that toast bread with a touch of a button and machines that fly? It surely must be a magical place.'

I laughed – then thought – maybe he was right.

I spent the next day riding abreast with Mom. She told me about the history of the Hall of Knowledge, her childhood in the Hazellands and stories of my grandparents. By the time we were ready to camp for our second night, she had just about reached the part where she discovered her home destroyed. The rest of our party sensed the seriousness of our conversation and left us alone.

'It must have been horrible for you,' I said. 'I can't even imagine what it must have been like.'

'To be honest, son, I was so consumed by rage, I do not truly remember much. I knew the Fili were the only ones that could help me with my revenge. As it transpired, they did not help me with revenge – only my rage.'

'Now that you know it was the Banshees from the Reedlands, do you think Cialtie had anything to do with it?'

'I would be lying if I said that thought did not cross my mind. We know he is capable of terrible things, but he has done one thing for which I am truly grateful. He brought you back to me.'

The next day we rode parallel to the blackthorn wall. The thorns pointed at us in respect to Mom as we passed – a creaky vegetable Mexican wave. When we reached the scorched border of the Hazellands, Mom stopped, dismounted and stared into her former home. She looked lost. I dismounted and stood beside her.

'Are you OK, Mom?'

'I have been back here twice,' she said. Her voice betrayed the slightest of trembles. 'The last time was with you. We had pressing business then and I performed a Fili concentration trick on myself so as not to think about it. The time before that was when I found it destroyed.'

'If you want to go back I will ride with you.'

She turned and smiled at me – a pained smile, the same expression I had seen recently in the mirror when I thought of Fergal stealing my shoes.

'Thank you, son, but no. I have delayed this too long. But first there is something I must do. Lorcan!' she called to guards who had been waiting a respectful distance away. 'Bear witness to this.'

Mom stood with her back to the thorns. Lorcan and his men dismounted and stood to attention around her in a semicircle.

Mom drew her yew wand and spoke. 'By order of Oison, Chooser of the Rune of Duir, I forthwith lift the banishment of the Fili and once again grant all of the peoples of The Land the freedom of the Fililands.'

She touched her wand to the blackthorn wall, incanted and stood back. Nothing happened at first – but then began that spooky creaking sound, the sound that usually means the plant is about to kill you. This time the thorns parted, leaving a huge archway large enough for at least four horsemen to ride abreast.

Although they were standing to attention, Lorcan and his men strained their necks to get the first glimpse of the Fililand in a generation – and a generation is a long time around here. The ominous rowan forest was lush and shadowy – the exact opposite of where we were standing. It took a moment for our eyes to adjust to the dark, green leaf-filtered light. A gasp went though the crowd as Fand appeared. Like some TV magician's optical illusion, she seemed to appear right out of a tree trunk. Behind her, dozens of other Fili seemed to fade in from nothing.

Fand stopped at the edge of the archway. She looked at Mom and me and said in that soft voice of hers, 'I have never been outside of the Fililands.'

'Well then,' I said. 'I think it's about time.'

Fand stepped blinking into the sunlight.

Mom turned to me and said, 'Prince Conor...'

'Prince Conor what?'

'As the senior representative of the House of Duir, announce the queen.'

'Oh,' I said, clearing my voice. 'Ladies and gentlemen and Imps and Leprechauns and whoever else – I give you Her Excellent Royal Highness the Queen of the spookiest folks I have ever met – Fand of the Fili. She's a great cook too.'

Lorcan and his men saluted and then cheered. Mom looked at me and shook her head.

'I guess I have to work on this princely stuff.'

'Yes, you do,' Mom said with that disapproving look I cultivate.

Mom and Fand embraced. The soldiers broke ranks to shake hands and feel their first Fili.

We all mounted up. Fand rode with Mom, more for emotional support than for Fand's benefit. A group of Fili jogged along beside us like presidential bodyguards.

The small contingent that Lorcan had left behind had been busy. The stones that had made up the ruined Hall of Knowledge had been stacked as if in preparation for rebuilding. Mom went to work immediately. She helped organise all of the documents that had been found, and insisted, for some reason, that every piece of parchment, no matter how small, should be saved.

That night after dinner I found Fand and Mom in Lorcan's old headquarters, engrossed with Shadowmagic.

'I hate to bother you, Fand, but can I borrow my mother for a little while?'

'Of course, Conor.'

When Mom looked at my face she asked, 'What is it, Conor?'

'Come with me, I have a surprise for you.'

I led her out of the room past the wall with the stained-glass window and stopped her before we entered the courtyard.

'Dahy gave me a hazelwood banta stick that had belonged to Liam.'

'I remember Father giving that to him. And he gave it to you? That was nice of him.'

'Yes, it was. The first time I was here I left it behind in the courtyard. I'd like you to see it.'

We turned the corner together. I was shocked at how much it had grown. The last time I had seen it, my staff had sprouted tiny green shoots – now it sported full leaves and had grown almost a foot. Mom dropped to her knees and placed her hand on what once was my weapon. She removed her hands and beamed at me – tears sparkled in her eyes.

'Lorcan thinks it may be a new Tree of Knowledge,' I said.

'He is correct – it is. It is a miracle.' She hugged me. 'You, my son, are a miracle.'

'Aw shucks, Ma – it was nothing.'

If not for the nagging feeling that something was missing, that I knew was the absence of Fergal, the following few days were the happiest I spent in The Land. I helped the Imps and Leprechauns shift rock, organised papers with Mom and even did a little gardening with Araf.

The night before we left to return to Castle Duir I asked Mom if she was going to reopen the Hall of Knowledge.

'That is not a task for me,' she said. 'This is no longer my home. My home was destroyed. That is a job for another. You, perhaps?'

'Mom, I'm eighteen years old.'

'Some think youth has a certain kind of wisdom.' Her eyes twinkled and I didn't like it.

'No thanks. One Professor O'Neil in this family is quite enough.'

I was loath to leave this place. Not just because I enjoyed it so much, but because I knew I was now forced to make a decision. During most of the ride back I wrestled with comparisons between the Real World and The Land. When we reached Glen Duir I let everyone ride ahead except for Araf, who insisted on remaining as my royal bodyguard.

'*Oh my, my,*' Mother Oak said to me as she swept me into her limbs. '*You have a difficult decision to make.*'

'Yes,' I said, 'and I don't know what to do.'

'*My poor dear, I can feel the conflict inside you. A choice between the heart and the brain – is it not? Most say one should go with the heart but I have touched many a brain that has regretted that decision.*'

'What should I do?'

'*Oh dear, do not ask me. My advice would be to grow bark and sprout leaves. There is nothing I would love more than to calm your mind but that decision, I am afraid, my son, is yours.*'

I hugged Mother Oak and dreamily mounted Cloud, but I didn't go anywhere. I sat there thinking, long enough to try even Araf's patience.

Finally he asked, 'What do you want to do now?'

'I think,' I said, making up my mind on the spot, 'I want to buy a new pair of sneakers.'

Chapter Thirty-Two
Goodbyes

We buried Fergal in the family plot, next to his great-grandfather's memorial. Gerard and Dahy sang a lament. There wasn't a dry eye in the house.

When it was finished, I was left alone except for about ten Imps. They lifted a massive flat rock across two upright stones that stood on either side of the grave. It was just like the *dolmens* that the ancient Irish chieftains were buried under. That was my idea. I threw a pebble on top for good luck and said goodbye. On the way back to the castle I got a stone in one of my sandals. It hurt but it made me laugh. I had an image of the ghost of my cousin slipping it in there, for a joke. I had buried Fergal in my Nikes.

Gerard and Dahy were standing next to me when I stood up.

'I don't think my dagger will work in the Real World,' Dahy said, 'but it might come in handy anyway.'

'I won't need it,' I said, 'I've got an even better weapon.' I cocked my wrist and Fergal's Banshee blade, newly equipped with a gold wire, dribbled out of my arm and then I missed it. It hung from my sleeve like a child's mitten. 'I still haven't got the hang of it yet.'

Gerard laughed that hearty laugh of his. 'There is always a beer waiting for you in the House of Muhn, Conor.' He gave me a bear-hug that lifted my feet off the ground. When I got my breath back, he asked, 'Have you spoken to Essa?'

'No,' I said, a little ashamed.

'Speak to her at least.'

I spotted Lorcan outside the castle before I went in. He was supervising the rebuilding of the east wall that had been destroyed by Cialtie's Golden Circle. He had traded in his sword for a straight edge and a hammer. He was an engineer again and looked happy. He climbed down from the scaffolding when he saw me approach.

'I'm sorry I missed the burial, but I need to get this done before the winter sets in,' he said.

'That's OK, I don't even think Fergal would have minded.'

'He was a good man, Conor. I'm sorry.'

'Thanks,' I said.

I shook his hand. As I walked into the castle I shouted, 'Goodbye Lorcan the Leprechaun!'

'Do not call me that!'

I smiled. One of his workers, who must have been listening, yelled, 'Look, it's Lorcan the Leprechaun!' Lorcan shook his fist at him but he didn't look that mad. He wasn't a general any more and that suited him just fine.

Araf was in the courtyard planting flowers.

'I'm leaving today,' I said. I can't thank you enough for all you did for me. I'll miss you.'

He nodded and said, 'Goodbye.'

That's all he said. I think I would have been disappointed if he said more.

I hesitated before I knocked on Essa's door. This was going to be difficult. She stood up like a nervous schoolgirl when I came in, and brushed down her dress. She looked fantastic.

'You're leaving today?' she asked.

'Yes.'

'I wish you wouldn't.'

'It's not because of you,' I said. But if I was honest with myself, a lot of it was. I couldn't get over what she had done to me in the Chamber. I just didn't think I could trust her again. 'So I guess this is goodbye.'

She threw herself into my arms. I could feel her warm tears fall down my neck.

'Oh, Conor, I am sorry. I am so sorry about everything.'

'I know,' I said, stroking her hair. 'I know.'

Then we kissed. Not counting that attack kiss in the Hall of Knowledge, or the movie kiss in the Reedlands, this was our first real kiss. It almost made me want to stay.

Mom, Nieve and Dad were waiting for me in the Room of Spells. Mom explained that it was the most magically charged place in the castle and she could get me back to the Real World from there.

Nieve's arm was in a sling. I know it was mean of me, but I hoped it hurt like hell.

'I was wrong,' Nieve said. 'I will never again try to force the hand of fate.'

'Well, I'd certainly be a happier guy if you quit the prophecy-fulfilling business.'

'I'm sorry you are leaving, I'd like to be a proper aunt to you.'

'Well – maybe I'll put you back on my Christmas card list, if you promise to behave.'

'What is a Christmas card?' she asked, as another joke bit the dust. Then she kissed me on the cheek. 'That is what I really wanted to do when I first saw you,' she said, and left me alone with my parents.

Mom was wearing her new rune around her neck. It appeared to be made of amber but it was almost insubstantial. It looked like if you tried to touch it, your hand would pass right through. Engraved in it was a marking that I didn't recognise – no one did.

'Have you figured out what your rune means?'

'No. When things calm down around here, Oisin and I will organise an expedition to see if there is any new land.'

'If it is your land, then I know it will be wonderful.'

Mom hugged me even harder than Essa. 'I only just got you back.'

These women, who were so strong in battle, were killing me with just their tears. 'I know, Mom,' I said, 'but I...'

She pushed back and wiped her eyes. 'No, no, you don't have to explain. You have to make your own way.' She wasn't the first mother to have to say that. 'Here, I have a present for you.' She picked up a velvet bag and took out two *Emain* slates and handed me one. 'Write to me.'

I looked down at the wood-framed sheet of gold. 'Will it work?'

She smiled – my mother *is* the most beautiful woman in The Land – in any land.

'It is worth a try,' she said.

I embraced her again – I thought my heart was going to break.

My father stood in front of me – all of him, right hand included. That was going to take some getting used to. He looked ten years younger, a picture of vitality in his royal clothes, standing in his castle. For the first time I can remember, he looked like he belonged somewhere.

'You know, you look great, Pop.'

'Deirdre here thinks I have my immortality back. We'll see.'

'What about Cialtie?' I asked.

'We'll find him, and if not, I'm sure he will find us.'

'Maybe he didn't survive.'

'Maybe, but if I know my brother, he probably did.' He put on his concerned father look. 'There is nothing back there for you,' he said. 'This is your home.'

'I think I have to find that out for myself.'

Boy, had things changed, he didn't even try arguing with me. His face softened and he said, 'I guess you're right.'

'Dad, I want to thank you, not just for the recent stuff but for everything.'

'If I had to do it all over again, I wouldn't change a thing. I'm proud of you, son.'

And then we did something that I never thought would happen. We shook hands.

I woke up on the floor of my living room. I was back. I was back in the Real World and it amazed me how fast Real World concerns flooded into my brain. Believe it or not, it was the first time I wondered, *Just what in the heck am I going to tell Sally – or anybody, for that matter?* I pushed those problems aside for a minute and stood up.

The room was completely trashed. The tables and chairs were mostly smashed. There was a horrible odour, which I soon discovered came from a pile of horse dung behind an overturned sofa. I surveyed the disaster area and almost said out loud, 'There's no place like home,' but there wasn't anyone around to hear it, and nobody ever gets my jokes anyway.

THE END